PENGUIN BOOKS

THE BEST

Peter Passell writes about economics (and other matters that come to mind) for *The New York Times*.

T H E B E S T
. . . .

The BEST

PETER PASSELL

PENGUIN BOOKS

PENGUIN BOOKS
Published by the Penguin Group
Viking Penguin Inc., 40 West 23rd Street,
New York, New York 10010, U.S.A.
Penguin Books Ltd, 27 Wrights Lane,
London W8 5TZ, England
Penguin Books Australia Ltd, Ringwood,
Victoria, Australia
Penguin Books Canada Ltd, 2801 John Street,
Markham, Ontario, Canada L3R 1B4
Penguin Books (N.Z.) Ltd, 182–190 Wairau Road,
Auckland 10, New Zealand

Penguin Books Ltd, Registered Offices:
Harmondsworth, Middlesex, England

First published in the United States of America by
Viking Penguin Inc. 1987
Published in Penguin Books 1988

LIBRARY OF CONGRESS CATALOGING IN PUBLICATION DATA
Passell, Peter.
The best.
1. Consumer education.   2. Curiosities and
wonders.   I. Title.
TX335.P35   1988   641.73   88–12516
ISBN 0 14 00.9420 2 (pbk.)

Printed in the United States of America by
R. R. Donnelley & Sons Company, Harrisonburg, Virginia
Set in Perpetua
Designed by Ann Gold

FOR LENNIE
. . . .

ACKNOWLEDGMENTS

· ·

With my thanks to Joan Peters, Frank Rose, Penny Stallings, Sharon Avery, Amy Berkower, Sandra Berg, Tracy Brown, Herman Chernoff, Kathy Cox, Mabel Crossmon, Warren Crossmon, Andrew Dalsimer, Michael Deneny, Nancy Elcock, Nancy Evans, Richard Eyster, John Freiden, Charles Gerson, Howard Goldberg, Peter Hamburger, Jean Hewitt, Bob Israel, Robert Kabcenell, Tom Kempner, Myer Kutz, Richard Mooney, Honor Moore, Harriet Norris, Linda O'Brien, Tony Pappas, Nick Passell, Bette Peters, Dan Peters, Beth Rashbaum, Gloria Rosenstein, Sandy Ratkowsky, Jack Rosenthal, Holly Russell, Barry Secunda, Caryn Schulz, Meri Spaeth, Roger Starr, Marcia Storch, Judith Thurman, John Wallace, Dan Weiss, Jeffrey Weiss, and Seymour Wishman.

Just who is Peter Passell, and where does he get off pontificating about the best painkillers, sports cars, and chocolate chip cookies?

According to one story, Passell was a taste panelist for *Consumer Reports,* known for his work on instant coffee and bottled salad dressings. By this account, something went badly wrong last year during a grueling series of breakfast cereal tests. Passell became agitated when fellow panelists took issue with his preference for Fruit & Fibre Tropical Fruit over the chewier Harvest Medley, and stalked out of the conference muttering about sugar shock. He was finally eased out of the job, it is said, after alienating his co-workers with the theory that Cap'n Crunch was responsible for the decline in average SAT scores.

Another story places Passell on the staff of "Late Night with David Letterman," in charge of auditioning candidates for the "stupid pet tricks" segment. He was reportedly nipped by a bull terrier trained to crush beer cans by sitting on them. The bite apparently did little damage, but in the ensuing confusion Passell is said to have tripped over an armadillo that doubled as a doorstop. According to the story, Passell wrote *The Best* to pass the time during his long hospitalization.

The truth is less colorful. Passell is a mild-mannered editorial writer for *The New York Times,* with a weakness for Hawaiian-style potato chips, weird electronic watches, and those little bottles of designer shampoo they give away in expensive hotels. Known to intimates as Mr. Fact, he has one of those obsessive minds that recall the flavor of sorbet served between courses at Le Grand Ve-four back in 1974,* but can't remember the name of the plumber. Passell hopes *The Best* will be taken seriously—but not too seriously. If you disagree with his choices, let him know. Mr. Fact welcomes good arguments over such important issues as the best peanut butter.

*pear

THE BEST
. . . .

Northwest Airlines "Executive Class" (Courtesy of Northwest Airlines)
. . . .

Airline Business Class

· ·

*F*irst class on a good international airline is all leather and smiles and Taittinger '79—"Dynasty" without conflict or commercials. Unfortunately, imitating the lifestyles of the rich and famous at 37,000 feet has become outrageously expensive, a luxury beyond the means of almost everybody who doesn't import addicting substances for a living.

Coach class, on the other hand, is the new steerage, a swamp of tipsy tourists, sleepless infants and overhead bins bursting with cartons of Drambuie and Chanel No. 5. If the queue for the stopped-up lavatory doesn't get to you, one whiff of the mystery meat will. Hence the popularity of the middle cabin, where airlines fight for the loyalty of travellers who have neither the stamina to scrunch nor the expense account to stretch.

Both Qantas and British Caledonian claim to have invented business class back in 1978. But it really came into its own on the North Atlantic, where tour groups have made the back of the bus particularly unbearable and competition has given travellers a choice among airlines. Today virtually every international carrier offers a business class, and at a price just above the nondiscounted coach fare.

The rock-bottom minimum amenities consist of a separate (possibly less crowded and certainly less noisy) cabin, a choice of meals, free drinks and headsets, expedited check-in, and priority boarding and baggage handling. Almost all airlines provide an extra baggage allowance, advance seat selection, separate lavatories, plus miscellaneous freebies like sewing kits, shaving lotion, and cabin socks. But that doesn't mean all business classes are created equal.

The Seat

British Airways and TWA got a jump on the competition with chairs almost as wide as first class. Pan Am fought back with a redesigned seat with a footrest. The contest is now virtually a draw.

The Space

Everybody wants direct access to the aisle, and many want to be within sight of a window. At last count, Aer Lingus, Air Canada, American, BA, CAAC, Canadian Pacific, Lan-Chile, Pan Am, TWA, and UTA have all switched to six-abreast seating. Some airlines even guarantee four abreast, usually by converting the upper deck of a 747 to a cozy business cabin for nonsmokers. Included in this category are Aerolineas Argentinas, Air New Zealand, Alitalia, All Nippon, Avianca, China Airlines, Egyptair, KLM, Korean, Northwest, Olympic, Royal Air Maroc, Singapore, and Thai International.

Limited density is nice; room to lean back or stretch out is even nicer. The best single measure here is "pitch," the number of inches allotted for each row of seats. Thirty-six inches is average on the Atlantic; 38 inches on the longer-haul Pacific routes. Alia Royal Jordanian, Olympic, and China Airlines come through with 42 inches. Thai International offers a luxurious 45 inches.

Door-to-Door Service

Most carriers now hand out free tickets for scheduled helicopter flights from JFK to other New York airports and Manhattan. British Caledonian upped the ante with door-to-door limousine rides to and from the airport in London, as well as all five of its

American gateways. SAS offers comparable limo service. And if you happen to reserve at one of 43 SAS-owned hotels, they'll check your baggage straight through to your room. Other carriers will probably be forced to match these service leaders. Ask— don't wait for them to offer.

Airport Amenities

Separate lounges for business-class passengers are standard operating procedure these days, particularly in an airline's hub airport. But not all lounges are created equal. Singapore Airlines has a fabulous facility, complete with showers, at the Singapore airport. Pan Am has converted its old terminal at JFK into a plush business and first class waiting area, with check-in on the spot. Canadian Pacific's Attaché Class offers "trickle boarding," a leisurely 20-minute boarding period in which passengers are free to dawdle.

And the best? Thai International and SAS are trying hardest. Some of the others have such high standards of service that they are candidates even without stand-out frills. Lufthansa, Swissair, KLM, Varig, Singapore, and Cathay Pacific certainly fit the description. But the winner is a carrier some veteran flyers have never heard of: Virgin Atlantic.

Virgin Atlantic is a tiny British carrier that has been serving the Newark-London route daily since 1984. Miami-London service was added in 1986. By the time these words are published, there will also be 747 service on the London–Los Angeles and London–JFK routes.

The brainchild of Richard Branson, rock and roll mogul, travel packager and world-class balloonist, Virgin Atlantic filled the discount-carrier void left by the bankruptcy of Laker Airlines Economy Class is cheap, reliable, and somehow avoids the cattle car ambience of most carriers. But Virgin Atlantic's pride and joy is its business class.

Required by British authorities to fly into London'? Airport, and thus unable to provide efficient air conne rest of Europe, entrepreneur Branson understood he would have to provide very special service to attract business travellers. His answer: Upper Class, the equivalent of first-class service at business class prices.

The sleeper-style seats with footrests are two-abreast, natch. And with 55 inches between rows (compared to the 38-inch pitch on the typical transatlantic business class service) there is plenty of room to recline. The cuisine may not be in the same league as Thai International, but there is plenty of champagne and smoked salmon to go round, and it's served on Wedgwood. Two lounges (one on each deck) offer the opportunity to stretch, drink and socialize.

Travellers have a choice of airport limo service or first-class rail tickets from Gatwick into central London. And as a final bonus, Virgin Atlantic offers what is surely the most generous frequent flyer program in the air. No clubs to join, no miles to accumulate. Every Upper Class passenger gets a free, transferable economy class ticket on every trip, good for one year.

Travel agents write tickets for Virgin Atlantic, of course. Or book direct by calling (212) 242-1330 or (800) 867-8621.

THE BEST
American Champagne
· ·

What's champagne? A very special wine from a very special hundred square miles of vineyards to the south and west of the city of Reims, insist the French; not just any old fermented grape juice with fizz.

They're right, of course. But pedantry is getting them nowhere. As with Xerox, Kleenex, Scotch tape, and Jell-O, the success of the generic has eroded the meaning of the name. There is no legal definition of champagne in America. And with few exceptions, sparkling wines made anywhere in the 3,600,000 square miles to the south and west of Caribou, Maine, are called American champagne. Happily, quite a number of them are very good wines indeed.

When the microbes in yeast digest the sugar in grape juice, they produce carbon dioxide bubbles along with alcohol. With still wine, the bubbles escape before the cork goes on the bottle. But with sparkling wine, the gas is trapped.

Inexpensive American champagne—all the stuff under five dollars—is brewed in bulk in steel tanks, then siphoned into bottles while still under pressure. It ought to be possible to make excellent "bulk process" champagnes. One American bulk-process brand, Angelo Papagni Sparkling Chenin Blanc, is in fact pretty good wine. But at nine dollars a bottle, Angelo is not a bargain. And no other bulk-process wine even pretends to quality.

Classier American champagnes, like their French namesakes, are made by the "méthode champenoise." Here, the wine is bottled in still form after the gas escapes, and a second round of fermentation is allowed to take place. The debris created in this second fermentation is collected at the cork end of the bottle, then removed in a tricky process that preserves most of the bubbles.

The second fermentation consumes virtually all the sugar in the champagne. Wine shipped in this state is labelled "natural." But you won't find many natural champagnes on the supermarket shelf. Just as well: The grapes used in American champagnes rarely taste good when they are finished as dry as, say, French Chablis.* So ordinarily, a dose of table sugar is added. Mediocre champagnes tend to be relatively sweet; sugar does wonders in covering up the sins of the winemaker. The very best have just a hint of sweetness, and are typically labelled "brut." Just to confuse things, "extra dry" means sweet—too sweet to accompany food. "Semi-dry" or "demi-sec" translates as extremely sweet.

French champagne must be made from one or more of three grape varieties: chardonnay, pinot noir, and pinot meunier. In America, anything goes. But first-rate brands all have a lot of chardonnay, or pinot noir, or both. Chardonnay-based champagnes are pale in color and delicate in flavor. They are often called "blanc de blanc," though the phrase has no legal meaning in the United States. American champagnes made from pinot noir blends have more color and body. Wines labelled "blanc de noir" are often made from 100 percent pinot noir grapes and have a deep reddish hue. Don't confuse them with pink or rosé champagnes, which typically get their color from the addition of a dollop of red wine.

So much for the preliminiaries. Which American champagne is the best? Twenty years ago the answer would have been easy. The Korbel Winery pioneered The American Style: méthode champenoise wine with a simple, fruity taste, and without the whiff of yeast characteristic of French champagne aged for several years before it is bottled. Korbel Brut is still America's most pop-

*The notable exception: Hanns Kornell Sehr Trocken. This dry natural champagne is a touch bitter to some palates, but it certainly is a decent wine.

ular quality champagne, and a bargain at about seven dollars a bottle. But recently, California champagne makers have begun to succeed with less fruity and more complex styles.

Schramsberg was the first of this new wave. President Nixon put the Napa Valley winery on the map by taking its Blanc de Blancs to China. Today the best of the Schramsberg products is the vintage Reserve, a very subtle (and overpriced) wine that is aged much longer than most American champagnes. Mirassou Vineyards in Santa Clara County has also successfully made the transition to the new style with its vintage Brut and vintage Blanc de Noirs.

Chateau St. Jean, a big Sonoma County winery owned by Suntory, the Japanese spirits conglomerate, produces a lovely vintage Brut. So does Piper-Sonoma, a joint venture between the French champagne maker Piper-Heidsieck and a big American wine importer. Gloria Ferrer Brut, the sparkling wine made in Sonoma County by the Spanish Freixenet family, is first-rate. But our favorite comes from the DOMAINE CHANDON.

Opened in 1977 in Napa by the makers of Moët & Chandon French champagne, Domaine Chandon has been an overnight success. The company did not attempt to duplicate its French style. A different mix of grapes is used and the taste is bolder. For greater consistency and flexibility, vintages are blended and sold without dates. The Blanc de Noirs is excellent. But the real pride of the house is the Anniversary Reserve and Special Reserve. The former is exceptionally delicate, with a faint rosé blush. The latter, sold only in double-size magnum bottles, is heavier, yeastier, and more complicated. These are probably the best sparkling wines made outside of France.

The winery, incidentally, runs a very fine, very expensive restaurant near the town of Yountville, an hour or so northeast of San Francisco. For a preview of heaven, reserve an outdoor table for lunch on a warm summer day. Call 707-944-2892.

Evidence That American Education Is Turning Back to Basics

. . . .

*I*n 1984, The Future Farmers of America chapter in Princeton, California, collected $7,087 in federal crop subsidies for growing 60 acres of rice. "This gives them experience, a learning experience," explained Andy Ferrendelli, the group's teacher and advisor at Princeton High School. "They go out and get loans and farm the land, just like the other farmers around here."

Beer

. . . .

S tart with a bucket of barley; add water, and allow it to
sprout.   Prepare "malt" by roasting the sprouted barley
long enough to caramelize some of the starch.   Dump the malt
into hot water, adding corn or rice if you want to cut costs or
create a paler-colored brew.   Cook this "mash," then filter out
the floating debris.   What's left is a carbohydrate-rich liquid called
"wort."

Boil the wort with hops, a bitter-tasting plant that is a key to
the final flavor of the beer.   Filter and cool.   Now add brewers'
yeast and allow the microscopic bugs to convert the carbohydrates
in the wort to alcohol and carbon dioxide.   Age for days or even
months, depending on taste.   When it's ready, allow a second,
brief fermentation to create fizz, or simply carbonate it like soda
pop.   The result is beer.

Brewing sounds simple, and it is.   Simple enough, anyway, to
have flourished long before humans first put pen to papyrus to
write down the recipe: the Babylonians are known to have made
homebrew from grain some 8,000 years ago.   During the Middle
Ages in Northern Europe, beer accounted for much of the caloric
intake of the 90 percent of the population that did 99 percent of
the work.   Their yeasty, easily spoiled homebrew probably wasn't
all that tasty—but, then, neither was the rock-hard black bread
that accounted for most of the other half of the calories that kept
them plowing.   Beer, at least, had a kick.

Today, beer is made just about everywhere* except Libya, Iran, Saudi Arabia, and other benighted lands where the devil and his alcohol are unwelcome. Several thousand brands are sold—1,500 in Germany alone. But the majority are forgettable variations on some dozen traditional styles. In fact, as recently as a decade ago, there was reason to fear that really fine brew was headed for extinction, victim to mass marketing that favored bland, stable beers over distinctive regional styles.

Fear no more. In England, drinkers are in open revolt against the six national breweries that own most of the pubs. Tiny independents, featuring fragile, unpasteurized, unfiltered brews, are flourishing, and the big six have been forced to compete in kind. In the U.S., "boutique" breweries from Seattle to Eau Claire to Manhattan have slurped up much of the market for tasty, complex beers previously left by default to imports. And suddenly, exotic beers from Belgium, Germany, England, and Australia that bear little family resemblance to Budweiser or Heineken are finding an international market.

With literally hundreds of good beers to choose from, which ones stand out? Consider some remarkable candidates:

Dortmunder Kronen Classic

Foreigners think of Munich when they think of German beer. But the greatest German beers come from the city of Dortmund. This one, made by the oldest brewer in the city, is an all-barley beer with a lot of hops and a faintly sweet aftertaste.

Lindemans Gueuze

A fine "lambic" beer, and one of the few available outside Belgium. Lambics are made without brewers' yeast, depending en-

---

*Even, if you wish, in your own basement. Old World Brewing Supplies, 117 Alter Hills, Staten Island, NY (718-667-5164), sells kits for easy home brewing for about $70. The American Homebrewers Association, in Boulder, CO (303-447-0816), offers information on brewing techniques and sources of materials.

tirely on microscopic, airborne fauna to cause fermentation. The basic ingredients are barley and wheat; hops are used sparingly. The end product, a blend of beers of several ages, is unlike anything else you've ever tasted. The color is cloudy peach; the scent is fruity and tart. The taste ... find out for yourself.

Anchor Steam

A delightful, copper-colored brew made in San Francisco by Fritz Maytag of washing machine fame. Unlike all but a handful of American beers, it is fermented at high temperature, entirely from barley malt. The result is a very rich, malty beer balanced by a lot of hops. Almost certainly America's best bottled beer.

Thomas Hardy's Old Ale

Created in the 1960s by the Eldridge Pope Brewery in Dorchester, England, this is a remarkable re-creation of a 19th-century brew. It's reddish brown and intensely flavored; a newly opened bottle simply explodes with the scent of hops. Thomas Hardy's is about 10 percent alcohol, more than double the average beer and enough to keep it stable in the bottle for decades. In fact, the brewer recommends that it be aged, like good red wine, for about 10 years.

Guinness Extra Stout Draught

The standard against which stouts—dark beers with a dry, bitter taste—should be compared. Try the draught version (available both in Ireland and abroad), rather than the bottled sort. It is creamier, less carbonated, and somehow more mellow.

Molson Brador Malt Liquor

The beers from the oldest Canadian brewer are all a cut above the mass-market North American beers. Brador is Molson's best, fermented with a lot of hops to make a very dry, very tasty beer. The name "malt liquor" is a bow to the fact that it has a higher alcohol content than ordinary North American beers.

Pilsner Urquell

For our money, though, the best beer—the quintessential beer—is PILSNER URQUELL from Czechoslovakia. Pilsen is a town in Bohemia, and Pilsner is the style of beer that made it famous. Pilsners are pale, dry, lightly carbonated, and delicately flavored, with the hops dominating the taste of malt. The Urquell Brewery makes the best, probably because it is careful to use only hops from the Saaz region. Take extra care in buying and storing Pilsner Urquell. The brew is less stable than most and develops a faint papery taste when it is over the hill.

Bicycle

. . . .

*P*rofessional racers think of fine bicycles as tools of their trade, the thin edge between winning and losing in the most physically demanding of the big-money sports. A new breed of mostly urban, mostly affluent amateurs say they want fancy bikes for the exercise and the pleasure of competition. You may have heard the bit: Bicycling is easier on the knees than running, less damaging to $50 haircuts than laps in a chlorinated pool, and requires less advance planning than tennis or squash or skiing.

All this is true. But there's an added kick to bicycling that probably explains why dermatologists, management consultants, and investment bankers by the thousands are lining up to buy bikes that cost as much as a week at the Ritz in Paris. The bicycle, they have discovered, is accessible, unfrustrating, hands-on technology.

An $8,000 stereo may sound better than an $800 model, but not one college-educated owner in a hundred has even the faintest idea why, or could understand if an electronics engineer tried to explain. Even the automobile is slipping beyond the comprehension of ordinary mortals. Mechanics now have to service them the way kids paint with numbers.

Bicycles, by contrast, are intuitive: Push here, it moves there; push harder, it moves more; push too hard, it breaks. Simple enough for almost anyone to tinker with, yet far from perfected. The bicycle, in other words, is an excellent candidate for the ultimate adult toy.

Some basics. The lighter the bike, the easier it is to pedal; this counts double for the rotating parts. Much of the effort (and the money) in design goes into reducing a bicycle's weight without reducing its strength or durability.

The stiffer the frame, the less pedalling energy is dissipated in the act of twisting metal. But stiff is a mixed blessing. A frame that is truly unyielding will transfer road shock to the fragile wheels, or the rider's yet-more-fragile behind. So one of the games bicycle makers play is to experiment with designs and materials that improve the tradeoff between efficiency and comfort.

Cycling is easiest when the rider can pedal at a steady cadence with constant effort. A bicycle with a wide range of gears will thus be more accommodating on varying terrain. But the wider the range, the less smooth the transition from gear to gear. One way around the problem is to have a lot of gears. But racers looking for that vital edge of pedalling efficiency at high speed go a step further, narrowing the range by raising their lowest gear.

Moving parts should perform crisply, reliably, and with minimal friction. Brakes should engage and disengage smoothly, and push out of the way for easy wheel changing; brake pads should be big enough for comfortable stopping power. The derailleur, the mechanism that shoves the chain from gear to gear, should feel precise, like a good manual shift on a car.

Twenty-five years ago, first-rate bicycle components were very expensive and all European. American bikes dominated the low end—the kids' market, where no one worried about gears or weight or fancy paint jobs. Then Asian imports blew the American, as well as the less expensive European, models off the road. Excellent, durable bicycles that will satisfy anyone who rides 20 or 30 miles on a weekend are now easily had for $300. Look for one of dozens of machines that specify double-butted, chrome-molybdenum steel frames; aluminum rims; cotterless, aluminum cranksets; quick-release mechanisms for both front and rear wheels; sidepull brakes; quill pedals, and clincher tires. The weight should run about 25 pounds, give or take two.

Bicycles in this category include models by Bridgestone, Sunk-

yong, Takara, Zebra, and lots more. Where you purchase the bike
probably matters more than which brand. Department stores are
a no-no, since they won't match the frame to your body size, and
won't put the pieces together for you. Go to a bicycle shop, preferably one where the guy behind the counter looks like an enthu-
siast. Tell him how you plan to use the bike. That way, you'll be
steered toward a "sport-touring" model with a relatively soft ride,
a wide gear range, and unskittish, forgiving steering.

Now for the fun part: the no-compromise bicycle for riding on
good roads as fast and far as possible. Like cars and politicians,
bicycle frames seem to reflect national character. Italy still dominates the high end, with elegant, beautifully finished designs.
France is into clever engineering. Japanese designs are always intelligent and reliable, but often a little dull. Americans aren't predictable.

The battle right now centers on materials: steel alloy vs. up-
and-coming aluminum vs. titanium vs. carbon fiber composites.
Very light, perfectly finished chrome-molybdenum frames, like the
top-of-the-line bikes from Cinelli, are the conservative choice.
They are steadily losing favor, though, to frames made from oversized aluminum tubing—frames by the American maker Klein, for
example. Aluminum is never as pretty as steel, but it can be
made lighter and stiffer than steel, reducing the workload of the
rider. And it absorbs shock better, easing the pain on bumpy
roads.

Superlight titanium alloy, prized in jet fighters for its strength at
very high temperatures, may yet give steel and aluminum a run for
the money. Thus far, though, titanium frames have been prone to
stress cracks. So for the next few years, anyway, the very best
frames will be made of carbon fiber composites.

Carbon fiber is lighter and stronger than other materials.
Bonded with resins, it can also be made stiffer. Best of all, carbon
fiber frames absorb shock even better than aluminum, providing a
silky ride. If money is no object, consider the Vitus Plus-7 Car-
bone model from France.

Drivetrain parts, wheels, and brakes should be the top of the line from Campagnolo, the Ferrari of component manufacturers. This, admittedly, reflects conservatism—no, call it snobbery. Everyone now agrees that the Shimano components are just as good. Actually, Shimano has surpassed Campagnolo in one component, the derailleur. Its 600 SIS model clicks crisply from gear to gear, eliminating the usual guesswork.

Pedals: Campagnolo and Shimano dominate sales at the top of the line. But there are remarkable superlight pedals from Look and AeroLite, really shoe and pedal combos that work like ski bindings. Seat: Specific choices here would be misleading because everything depends on the shape of your bottom. Those who are particularly tender may wish to add a Spenco saddle pad to whatever they choose. Spenco, by the way, is the shock absorbent used for inner soles in good running shoes.

The total weight of this svelte bomb should run about 19 pounds. Expect to pay about $2,000 for it, or half that much if you are willing to settle for a fine steel frame and a less glitzy paint job.

THE BEST
Bicycle Helmet

· ·

*D*ark cloud: Each year 1,000 Americans die in bicycle accidents, three out of four from head injuries.

Silver lining: The use of well-designed helmets could virtually eliminate the serious head injuries, saving about 750 lives annually.

Modern bike helmets all work the same way. A hard outer shell spreads the shock over a wide area. A stiff but crushable inner shell gives the brain a precious fraction of an inch to slow down gradually, absorbing the energy of impact without tissue damage. The bare head hitting asphalt from a drop of five feet must go from 12 miles an hour to zero in just five ten-thousandths of a second. But an inner shell, with close to a half-inch of crush space, gives the head about seven times as long to decelerate. That extra three-thousandth of a second is the difference between almost certain death and a nasty headache.

Two groups, the American National Standards Institute and the Snell Memorial Foundation, set protection standards for bike helmets. ANSI drops helmets from a height of 39 inches onto a metal surface and measures the maximum acceleration rate on a model head inside. If the average of four shocks is less than 300 times the acceleration of gravity (300 g's), the helmet passes.

Now, 300 g's is rarely enough to kill, but can be enough to injure. Most people, moreover, fall farther than 39 inches when they flip over the handlebars, and thus take a harder pounding when they land. So while it's good to know that virtually all the helmets on the market meet the ANSI standard, it would be nice to do better. That's where the folks at Snell fit in.

Bell Vı-Pro bicycle helmet (Courtesy of Bell Helmet Company)
. . . .

They test their helmets from twice the height—higher than an
adult handlebar vaulter. To pass, the average shock must not exceed 300 g's, and the shock on any single trial drop must not exceed 300 g's. Judging by tests performed in 1986 by *Bicycle Rider*
magazine, a number of helmet makers probably meet this tougher
Snell standard, among them Bailen, Hanna, OGK, and Vetta. But
to date, only models from the **BELL HELMET COMPANY** carry
Snell's sticker of approval.

The Bell Ovation (about $65) has an inner lining of expanded
polystyrene foam for shock absorption, plus a wafer-thin outer
shell for impact protection. Low weight (a mere 10 ounces) and
oversized air vents make it one of the most comfortable helmets
available.

P.S. Bell also makes the L'il Bell Shell (about $35) for kids who
ride in back. It, too, meets the rougher Snell safety standard.

THE BEST
Bird Feeder

. . . .

S ome bird feeders look like miniature ski chalets, little
wooden A-frames with plate-glass windows and a deck for
the feathered guests to stand on. Others are cylindrical, clear-
plastic jobs, vertical villages with multiple perches and feeding stations. Both types do the job—birds, it seems, care less about the
ambiance than the cuisine. But both share one glaring failing:
They are easy prey for pillaging squirrels.

Over the years, strategies have emerged for coping with the
squirrel menace. You can mount a plastic hood over a hanging
feeder. You can grease the pole of a standing feeder to make it
difficult to climb. You can lie in wait for the rodents with a
water pistol, hoping that a wet lesson or two will frighten them
away. Or you can find solace in religion or drink or Valium, for
nothing really deters a hungry squirrel.

Nothing, that is, except the **HYLARIOUS BIRD FEEDER,** the virtually foolproof invention of Norman Graham Carlson of White
Bear Lake, Minnesota. The Hylarious is a clunky steel box that
holds a generous two gallons of bird seed, and comes ready to be
mounted on a two-by-four post. The steel bar serving as a perch
on the business end of the box is also the handle of a lever attached to a door covering the feeding area. Birds aren't heavy
enough to move the lever. But the moment a squirrel hops on,
the door slides shut. The amount of weight it takes to close the
door can be changed by adjusting a counterweight on the other
end of the lever arm. So the feeder can be fine-tuned to allow
small birds to dine, yet keep out the pigeons and crows.

Norman Graham Carlson died nine years ago, but his son Tom carries on the mission with the help of his wife and a half-dozen employees. Hylarious feeders can be found in fine garden stores in the East and Midwest. If your fine garden store isn't among them, write Tom for a flyer at the Graham-Carlson Company, Box 10571, White Bear Lake, MN 55110. The feeder is available by mail order for about $52.50.

. . . .

Hylarious Bird Feeder (Courtesy of Graham-Carlson Company)

THE BEST
Boondoggle

. . . .

*F*ed up with a boss who expects you to laugh when she repeats the same old Polish jokes? Tired of working eight days a week for a salary that barely covers the kid's orthodontia bills? Had it up to here with traffic that turns a commute into a twice-daily nightmare?

You need a large, secure income. You need clean, fresh air. You need time to reflect on the mystery of nature. You need to become a wheat farmer in Saudi Arabia.

That's right: a wheat farmer in Saudi Arabia. Consider the case of Mohammed Ali Motlaq, a former officer in the Saudi security forces who has retired to the land of his father and his father's father. Mr. Motlaq's family used to eke out a living growing dates on a patch of desert near the village of Buraida in the Central Qasim province. But back in the early 1970s, the Saudi government worried that countries supplying food to the desert kingdom might take offense over the size of their fuel bills and do something dastardly. Like forming a cartel, perhaps, and claiming that a bushel of grain was worth at least as much as a barrel of crude oil. So the Saudis decided to spend whatever was necessary to grow their own.

First the government dug wells to reach underground aquifers hundreds, sometimes thousands, of feet below the sand. Then they offered interest-free loans to anyone who would use the water to cultivate wheat. Lest anyone fear the business might still prove to be unprofitable, they guaranteed to buy the grain for five times the world price. Mr. Motlaq, among other farmers, took the government up on its offer. His family date patch has grown to a 9,000-acre spread equipped with the best equipment that rivals can buy. Mr. Motlaq, of course, is too rich to get his hands dirty; the work is done by Filipino laborers, directed by American managers.

The program has worked well—much too well. Last year the desert yielded two million tons of wheat, twice as much as the Saudis could choke down with their mutton. Yet government attempts to cut back the subsidies met with very little enthusiasm from this new breed of rural capitalist. So the Ministry of Agriculture is looking for places to sell the surplus. Perhaps they'd like to trade some for oil. . . .

THE BEST
Bottled Water
. . . .

*J*ulius Caesar drank the saline waters of Vichy—for his health, one presumes, since it couldn't have been for the taste. Pliny the Elder was partial to the slightly effervescent water from Ferrarelle. Michelangelo was convinced that the pleasantly taste-less water from Fiuggi cured his kidney stones. Peter the Great, never one for moderation, reportedly drank 21 daily glasses of H_2O lugged from Bru, in Belgium.*

The 19th-century bourgeois custom of taking the cure at some splendid palace of sulphur water and quackery has largely disap-peared. Annual traffic at Vichy has fallen from a peak of 300,000 in 1865 to just 20,000 today. But Europeans retain a soft spot for natural spring waters, bottled or al fresco. Italy has 260 brands, Germany, 300. France consumes the most per capita: about 80 quarts a year. French physicians still occasionally prescribe min-eral water cures, and medical insurers still reimburse the "curistes" for their expenses.

In recent years, moreover, Americans have come to appreciate the pleasing combination of asceticism and chic that comes with substituting bottled water for stronger stuff. Rodeo Drive in Bev-erly Hills, trendsetter for mass culture, now has a water bar called Ixiz, where 51 brands from 18 countries are served. Under the New Prohibition, Ramlosa with a twist rates an A, the white wine spritzer a B. Liquor, especially the brown kind, is a serious no-no: Any Fortune 500 CEO caught ordering a double Cutty-on-the-

*Apparently, it didn't do the trick. Peter gulped his last gulp at age 43.

rocks as an aperitif would be stripped of his golden parachute before the raspberries with crème fraiche made it to the table.

It should hardly be surprising, then, that designer water has become big business. Most of the old spas are being refurbished as luxury fat farms—pardon, health resorts (see "The Best Health Spa"). In France, Perrier, Evian, and Vittel struggle for volume the way GM, Ford, and Chrysler used to slug it out for market share. Perrier, the biggest vendor at home, is also the biggest abroad. It now controls the distribution of 10 French and three Spanish brands, plus Calistoga and Poland Spring in the United States. Vittel has the upper hand in the Middle East, with stakes in Lebanon, Egypt, and Kuwait.

Which is the best? Much depends on which itch you mean to scratch. If your idea of water is medicine, a psychic cure for hepatitis or gout or constipation, it presumably pays to stick with a brand that is chock-full of minerals and tastes like it. The really loathsome concoctions can only be purchased on site at the springs. And for good reason: drunk in sufficient quantity, some are actually poisonous. Among tamer bottled brews, consider Contrexéville from the Vosges hills of France. Or Adelheidquelle from southern Germany. Each liter of the latter contains 4,000 milligrams of bicarbonates, sulphates, chlorides, potassium, and other assorted soluable chemicals. Watch out, though; among the mineral goodies in a liter of Adelheidquelle is 973 milligrams of sodium, enough to ruin any low-salt diet. The Soviet Union exports a yet more mineralized water called Borjomi. It weights in with 6,000 milligrams of dissolved rock, including 1,500 of sodium.

If the idea is refreshment, a substitute for sweetened or caffeinated thirst quenchers, consider the highly carbonated waters with a low mineral content. There's Perrier, of course. Poland Spring, from Maine, has a nice CO_2 zip and practically nothing else. But why pay top dollar when carbonated, high-quality tap water, otherwise known as seltzer, is available in every supermarket? Virtually any brand will do. The name seltzer, incidentally, is a corruption of Selters, one of the first German bottled waters.

Probably the best reason to drink bottled water is to complement food. And here, the lightly carbonated, lightly mineraled waters come into their own. Bru (or its twin, Spa), spring water from the Ardennes forest with almost no sodium, has a lovely, subtle bite. But our own favorite is **BADOIT,** a tingly, naturally carbonated water from the hills above Lyons. Louis Pasteur sipped it with dinner. Perhaps you should, too.

THE BEST

Evidence That Britain Isn't Part of Europe

. . . .

*E*ver since Napoleon, British and French entrepreneurs have dreamed of building a tunnel under the English Channel. And now, with the formal agreement of the two governments, the "chunnel," or "fixed link" as the bureaucrats prefer to call it, is about to become a reality. But not everyone is enthusiastic. According to the *Folkstone Herald*, a newspaper in one of the big channel ports, 88 percent of the respondents to a local survey believe that the sea barrier is needed to prevent packs of mad dogs from overrunning Britain. After the chunnel, Folkstonites say, rabies will be "virtually unstoppable."

Business School

· ·

*F*ashions in business schools move as rapidly as hemlines in
Milan. Harvard's vaunted "case method" dominated the
1970s, as competitors rushed to market their own versions of how-
to-earn-more-in-your first-job-than-dad-made-at-40. Then somebody—to be fair, it was the president of Harvard University—discovered that the school was churning out soulless Brooks Brothers
types who knew a lot about leveraged buyouts and deferred stock
options, but relatively little about the business of making things.

Exit the era of competitive problem-solving in small groups.
Enter the era of the computer jocks. Carnegie-Mellon in Pittsburgh led the trend with a curriculum heavy on "quantitative
methods." Carnegie-Mellon graduates, most of whom had under-
graduate degrees in engineering or science, proved to be very good
at managing researchers in high-tech industries. But they offered
no special expertise in the day-to-day routine of juggling commit-
tees, troubleshooting assembly-line snafus, or snowing the Wall
Street analysts.

Exit the number crunchers. Enter the new organization men.
He (or almost as likely, she) knows enough to second-guess the
accountants and engineers, yet is smooth enough to finesse a television interviewer, tough enough to break a union, and kind
enough to command loyalty from subordinates.

Now, you may argue that such people are made by God, not by
business schools, and you may be right. But that isn't stopping
the B-schools from trying. Course work is becoming more eclectic. Advanced Balance Sheet 301 and Nonlinear Programming

Methods are out. Crisis Management, International Trade Law, and Business Ethics are in. Carnegie-Mellon, spiritual home of the digit pushers, offers The Gold Collar Workers, a course on how to motivate "knowledge workers."

How, then, to choose among the best? First consider some classy also-rans. The University of California at Berkeley, especially strong in finance, is the best value: tuition is less than $6,000, half the tab of schools with comparable status. Yale has the most radical, hands-on management curriculum, and the strongest commitment to admitting women. Chicago and M.I.T. (Sloan) are closely aligned to top-of-the-line graduate programs in economics, and are thus fine places to launch a teaching career. Duke (Fuqua) is the only élite business school that is still expanding, and is thus the easiest to get into. The very best, though, is surely one of the big three: Harvard, Pennsylvania (Wharton), and Stanford.

Harvard stumbled out of favor. But under the aggressive leadership of Dean John McArthur, it is on the road back to supremacy. Two facts virtually guarantee its continuing success:

(1) A $200-million endowment, more than that of all other B-schools combined. What doesn't gravitate naturally to Boston can always be purchased.

(2) An army of 33,000 graduates, an incredible percentage of whom are well up the corporate ladder. According to a recent survey, half the members of the class of '49 are now chief executives. And Harvard graduates, it is reasonable to assume, are inclined to hire other Harvard graduates.

The Wharton School at the University of Pennsylvania fell earlier and further than Harvard. But it has been hustling like crazy in recent years, and now probably has the most distinguished faculty of any business school. To the surprise of some, a 1985 poll of corporate recruiters ranked Wharton as Numero Uno.

But the present and, probably, future king is STANFORD. It was the first to strike a balance among number-crunching, case method exercises, operations skills, and people management. It is supported by superb graduate programs in computer science, law, and economics. It is so small (300 in a class vs. Harvard's 780 and Wharton's 700) and so well regarded that it can afford to be very picky: In 1985, just 9 percent of applicants were accepted, compared to 18 percent at Harvard, 29 percent at Wharton. Perhaps most important, it overwhelms rivals in the region. Those applying for jobs in the Sun Belt are likely to be judged by Stanford graduates.

Car

· ·

Remember the bad old days, when Los Angeles commuters shot it out for tankfuls of unleaded and Arab sheiks discovered the joys of wintering in Monaco? Everyone assumed that driving would never be the same.

Everyone was right, though the changes have been surprisingly painless. Cars were forced onto crash diets, stripping them of great cast-iron engines, overstuffed bench seats, and baroque trim. Happily, less has proved to be more. Even the humblest of the new cars handles better, takes bumps without inducing motion sickness, and is far kinder to the spine. And, thanks to a dozen tricks for pushing more air and gasoline through smaller engines, the best of this fuel-efficient breed are every bit as muscular. Sample the wealth:

The Hyundai Excel ($6,000)

The basic engineering, licensed from the Japanese giant Mitsubishi, is short of state of the art. And the engine is startlingly underpowered. But this first Korean car to be exported offers quiet, comfortable, hassle-free transportation. Adjusted for inflation, the price of this reliable little subcompact is lower than a 1966 VW Bug!

The Ford Taurus ($14,000)

It's been a long, hard winter for Detroit. American cars have gotten better, but so has the foreign competition. And after decades of being outclassed at every price point, you just had to wonder whether Big Auto would ever catch up.

Wonder no more. The Taurus and its twin, the Mercury Sable, are splendid cars—as comfortable and roomy as the road hogs they replaced, yet as agile and fun to drive as some of the expensive European touring sedans. Best of all, the Taurus's aerodynamic body shape looks great. Now if Ford drops one last vestige of monstermobile ugly, the strip of fake plastic wood on the dash, the triumph will be complete.

The Honda Acura Legend ($20,000)

To judge by the sheet metal, the Legend is just another bland Japanese sedan. But beneath the plain face lies the ultimate in refined, user-friendly small sedans. Fine handling, plenty of acceleration (from a 150 horse-power V-6), an interior as handsome as it is comfortable. And remember, this is a Honda: They do it right the first time.

The Saab 9000 Turbo ($26,000)

Another car that can't be judged on first appearances. Like all Saabs, and many cars in this price class, it's quiet, comfortable, and designed with driving enthusiasts in mind. What makes the 9000 Turbo stand out is the most sophisticated small engine in autodom. Four cylinders, with a displacement of just 2.0 liters, manage 21 EPA city miles to the gallon. Yet they generate 160 horsepower, enough for zero to 60 in 7.5 seconds and a top speed of 140 miles per hour. The secret is four valves per cylinder, and, of course, turbocharging. Strikingly, there's virtually no lag before the characteristic turbo-surge.

The Audi 5000 CS Turbo Quattro ($33,000)

Buyers have been lapping up the $22,000 economy version of this sleek, silent, very German sedan. In fact, it's developed a reputation as the poor man's Mercedes. But customers haven't been flocking to the more expensive Turbo Quattro, the technological wonder of the Audi fleet. Full-time four-wheel drive permits true sports-car cornering and a sense of solidity on any driving surface. Turbocharging and intercooling provide plenty of snap. And the computerized anti-skid braking system extracts professional performance from panicky amateurs.

The Citroën CX 25 GTi Turbo ($35,000)

Plucky Citroën builds the oddest cars in the world, and is proud of it. The company was first by a decade with front-wheel drive, four-wheel disc brakes, and hydraulic suspension, not to mention aerodynamic body shapes. This latest (now 13-year-old) design isn't nearly as daring as the DS or Citroën-Maserati sedans were in their time. But the CX is a fine car, with the great Citroën ride and rationally eccentric Citroën controls. Equipped with a turbocharger, anti-lock brakes, and a sweet five-speed transmission, it is better than fine. Buy it in America to be the first on your block—after a 13-year absence, Citroën is making an unofficial comeback in the U.S.A. Or buy it in Europe, where a much lower price tag makes it excellent value.

The Jaguar XJ6 ($40,000)

What more can you say about a 17-year-old sedan that was the sleekest on the road until Jaguar made it even sleeker with a facelift this year? The interior is almost as elegant as the sheet metal. The suspension is as smooth as Devon cream, offering a fine compromise between the American luxury ride and the no-nonsense firmness of a Mercedes. And factory quality control is now up to the standards set by the design. Compare it to the big Mercedes S-Class and BMW 7 Series, which cost more and lack the classic good looks of Britain's great touring sedan.

The Bentley Eight ($95,000)

A Bentley, so the hoary joke goes, is a Rolls-Royce for the diffident. This Bentley is indeed a Rolls-Royce—the entry-level Silver
Spirit model, modified with a tighter suspension, wider tires,
sportier interior trim, and more complete instrumentation. The
idea is to appeal to a younger class of fogies, the sort who'd welcome the symbolic baggage of the Bentley nameplate but prefer
driving to being driven. All that bulging sheet metal still looks
stodgy, though, and the handling is no better than good. Without
a turbocharger (available on domestic versions), the Eight is underpowered. But there is something amazing about these stately
dreadnoughts of the motorways. And just think: At about $20,00
less than the comparable Rolls, it is practically a bargain.

The Mercedes Benz 560 SEL ($70,000)

Feature by engineering feature, the Mercedes S-Class sedans have
only one rival for best large sedan: the newly designed 12-cylinder
BMW 750iL. We'd stick with the Mercedes, if only because of
its superior reputation for reliability and workmanship. Its mas-
sive aluminum V-8, rock-tight steering and miraculous suspension
make a 560 SEL going 100 mph feel like a Cadillac at 60. The
automatic transmission is the absolute peak of the industry. And
few cars come close on safety. Every big Mercedes comes with
driver-side airbags and anti-skid brakes.

Just a quibble or two. The long wheel base and heavy curb
weight put physical limits on its agility. The smaller, lighter
Mercedes 300E and compact 190E 2.3-16 have a spryness lacking in
the 560, and pack a lot more punch besides. But the 300E is as
spartan as a bottom-of-the-line K-car—the green plastic upholstered kind, favored by elderly insurance salesmen and the U.S.
Army. The 190 is a very small car, with a backseat suitable only
for midgets. And neither has a really first-rate manual gear shift.

Why couldn't Mercedes build a sedan with the understated luxury of a 560 SEL, the legroom of a 300E, and the hot performance of the 190 2.3-16?

AMG Mercedes Hammer

Believe it or not, such a Mercedes is available—one even better than our hypothetical sedan. But Mercedes doesn't build it. This supercar, called the AMG MERCEDES HAMMER, is an amalgam of Mercedes parts, with additional modifications for performance and style.

AMG is a German company that has been customizing Mercedes for racing (and other vanities) for 20 years. This time, however, it has gone all the way, stuffing a souped-up version of the giant 5.5 liter V-8 from the 560 into the body of a 300E. The steering and suspension have been modified, and fat, road-hugging Pirelli P700 tires substituted for the factory standards. The sheet metal on the rear deck has been reworked and skirts added to reduce air drag. Cushy, electrically adjusted, all-enveloping Recardo bucket seats come both front and back.

The result is a comfortable, beautifully appointed luxury sedan with the silky manners of a Mercedes 560 in city driving and the highway performance of a great Italian sports car. Speed? Try zero to 60 in 5.0 seconds with an automatic transmission, and a top velocity of 178 miles per hour. Braking? Try 70 down to zero in 165 feet. That's better than a Lamborghini Countach or a Ferrari Testarossa. Road-holding? Not quite the equal of the Lamborghini on a ski-pad, but better than a Porsche 911 Turbo.

An AMG Mercedes Hammer, ready to use on American highways with full factory warranty, costs about $135,000. A little rich for your blood? For just $90,000, AMG of North America will build you a Hammer, using the body and chassis of your own Mercedes 300E. For details, contact AMG in Westmont, Illinois, 312-971-0500.

Champagne

. . . .

S tart by narrowing the field. Sparkling wines from California can be very good. So can sparklers from the Seyssel commune in southeastern France. Ditto for Spanish espumoso—Gran Codorniu comes to mind. But without doubt, the great champagnes are true champagnes, from the Champagne region of northeastern France.

Some basic distinctions. Champagne without a vintage label is a blend of wine from several different years. Vintage blending assures consistency, but it also puts a cap on potential quality. That's why the very best champagnes are dated. In poor years—a rarity now, thanks to new technology—no vintage wine is bottled.

Like many other French wines, most good champagnes are made from a blend of grape varieties. White chardonnay grapes add lightness and bouquet; red (yes, red) pinot noir grapes provide the body and the dominant flavor. A few of the traditional houses produce wines from a single grape: blanc de blancs solely from chardonnay, blanc de noirs from pinot noir. These unblended champagnes are usually excellent and always interesting. Other delightful oddities: rosé champagnes (colored pink with a dash of red wine), crémant champagnes (just half the carbonation; good as an aperitif), tête de cuvée champagnes (from the juice of the first pressing) and R.D. champagnes (aged longer for extra body and bouquet).

Champagnes labelled "nonvintage brut" are the Chevys of the line—good, all-purpose sipping wine at half the price of the luxury model. Brut, meaning dry, is a term of art, not a legal definition. Some, like Louis Roederer Brut Premier, are very dry indeed. Others, like Taittinger, are soft and distinctly sweet. Both Roederer and Taittinger, incidentally, are excellent champagnes; the choice is a matter of taste.

That, of course, is no barrier to strong opinion; here are mine. Among the less expensive champagnes (under $20), nonvintage Perrier-Jouët Grand Brut is most likely to please. It is lighter and slightly sweeter than average, with more taste of grape.

Where price is no limit, the choice becomes more difficult. The two most widely available prestige labels, Louis Roederer Cristal and Moët & Chandon's Dom Pérignon, are good but over-rated—A-minus champagnes at A-plus prices. Two well-known blanc de blancs, Dom Ruinart and Taittinger, come closer to the ad copy. Feather-light, they are the essence of what most people want from champagne.

For our money, though, the very best champagnes come from the house of **BOLLINGER.** Made with a higher proportion of pinot noir grapes and aged longer than most, Bollinger vintage champagnes are dark, heavy, and complex. Since very little sugar is added to the finished wines, they are extremely dry, almost austere in quality. Try the Bollinger Tradition R.D. for the experience. Or go all the way with Bollinger Vielles Vignes. This is the ultimate boutique wine, champagne made entirely from pinot noir grapes from two tiny vineyards totalling just one acre. The vines themselves are exceptionally old, yielding tiny, highly flavored grapes in very small quantity. Don't expect to find Vielles Vignes at every corner liquor store, though. In an average year just 2,000 bottles are produced, of which just 500 end up in America.

THE BEST
Cheap College

· ·

At Stanford, your bio professor may be a Nobel Prize winner. At Swarthmore, your roommate probably will be. Brown is neo-yuppie, sign–me–up–for–Goldman Sachs. Yale had Jodie Foster, Jennifer Beals, and still has pretty architecture. Amherst has prettier lawns. Sarah Lawrence is only a 25-minute commute by Porsche from the East Village. But all cost at least $15,000 a year—closer to $18,000 if you spring for an occasional Calvin Cooler, or prefer to dry-clean your jeans.

What's the alternative? Residents of the dozen or so states that take public education seriously are able to save $5,000 to $6,000 in tuition without skimping on standards. Rutgers, Virginia, Texas, North Carolina at Chapel Hill, Wisconsin, and the State University of New York at Binghamton (yes, Binghamton) are very good. Berkeley, Michigan, and Illinois at Urbana are even better.

If you like cold showers and are eager to improve your posture, you could try one of the military academies. All four provide free tuition; room and board is on the house. Congress even throws in $500 a month to cover R & R, an occasional bottle of Absorbine Jr., and the like. Standards in engineering and the sciences run just short of the élite private universities. The drawback, of course, is that Uncle Sam expects graduates to wear uniforms.

Prospective architects, engineers, and artists have a very interesting option. Cooper Union for the Advancement of Science and Art has neither dorms nor cheerleaders. In fact, the private college barely has a campus: classrooms, labs, and cafeteria are housed in three cramped buildings in lower Manhattan. But Cooper

Rice University (Courtesy of Rice University)

· · · · · · · · · · · · · · ·

Union does have a first-rate faculty, adequate technical facilities, and students whose average math SAT score is 720. Best of all, it's tuition-free.

Trinity University in San Antonio charges about $5,000 tuition, which by Texas standards is steep. But the brash little university (3,000 students) is in a hurry to improve its already pretty good academic standards. So it offers fat scholarships to kids with good grades and Board scores, even to kids whose parents can afford to pay the full freight.

Still another off-the-beaten-path bargain is The New College of the University of South Florida. Founded as a private liberal arts college in 1960, the Sarasota school was meant to be a cross between hippie Santa Cruz and earnest Oberlin. But The New College ran out of granola (and money) in 1975, and was only saved from bankruptcy by union with the State University system.

Happily, the marriage seems to have done it no harm. The low-rise campus on Sarasota Bay is charming and informal. Classes are tiny, the faculty young and accessible. Out-of-state tuition is just $3,000, and living costs are roughly half those of urban campuses in the north and west.

But for all their virtues, none of these institutions comes close to the best of the low-cost schools: RICE UNIVERSITY in Texas. Its 300-acre campus in Houston is an oasis of quiet courtyards and neoclassical architecture. The humanities and social science departments are excellent, the science departments even better. Students complain about the academic pressure, but most of them wouldn't have it any other way.

What makes Rice special is the combination of a super faculty, first pick of Texas high school seniors, and pots and pots of money. Created by the will of the fabulously wealthy William Marsh Rice, the 84-year-old school has never had to grub for pennies. Only Princeton and Harvard have larger endowments per student, and they must bear the far higher expenses that come with large graduate departments in the humanities.

Until 1965, Rice was tuition-free. Now the school charges about $4,500 to those who can afford it. Roughly 80 percent of the students receive financial aid, though, with an average grant of about $5,000.

THE BEST
Chinese Restaurant in America
. . . .

C hinese food in American has evolved a long way from the primordial ooze of overcooked omelettes (egg foo yung) and breaded pork in vinegar and Karo Syrup (sweet and sour sauce). In the sixties, Joyce Chen's handsome Cambridge restaurant won the hearts and minds of the Aquarian generation with "Peking" specialties—mu shu pork, shrimp in black bean sauce, etc. Yalies impressed their parents back home with tales of Mongolian hot pot and fried dumplings with pepper oil, from Blessings in New Haven. Then, suddenly, in less time than it takes to stir-fry broccoli in sesame oil, American Chinese made a great leap forward.

Once-proud owners of Cantonese restaurants were forced by their creditors to add the word "Szechuan" to their names. Campy Hawaiian-Chinese restaurants that specialized in mai tai's with paper umbrellas learned to barbecue lamb Hunan-style. Plumbing contractors and dental surgeons talked knowingly of the differences between Fukienese, Shanghai, and Hakka food.

Don't misunderstand; the ends did justify the means. Many fine restaurants have survived the rigors of the long march to authentic regional cuisine. Consider the pleasures of The Beijing Duckhouse (144 E. 52nd St., 212-759-8260) and Shun Lee Palace (155 E. 55th St., 212-371-8844) in New York, Uncle Tai's Hunan Yuan in Houston (1980 South Post Oak Blvd., 713-960-8000), The Mandarin in Beverly Hills (430 N. Camden Dr., 213-272-0267). The rediscovery of dim sum, the brunch treat from discredited Canton, brought hoards of gourmands back to The Silver Palace in

MENU FOR LUNCH AND DINNER

Appetizers:

1. **Onion Cake** 1.50
   Thin flour cakes with egg & green onions or deep-fried.

2. **Dumplings** 3.00
   Crescent dumplings filled with chopped meats & vegetables and served with condiments (with or without hot sauce).

3. **Diana's Special—Delicious Meat Pie** 4.95
   Deep-fried flour cakes filled with meat sauce, Parmesan cheese, vegetables and condiments. (with or without hot sauce)

Soups (Dinner only):

1. **Mo Si Soup** .... 3.00 - 5.75 - 8.75
   With eggs, pork, vegetables, bean curd and delicious wood ears!

2. **Hot and Sour Soup** .... 3.00 - 5.75 - 8.75
   With eggs, pork, bean curd, wood ears and bamboo shoots

Famous Hunan Salads
(Served Cold)

1. **Chicken Salads** 6.50
   Shredded chicken mixed with cucumber strips, lettuce, shrimp noodles and garnished with specially prepared sauce. It is a delicious treat at any time.

2. **Bean Sprout Salads** 4.00
   Bean sprouts, cucumber strips mixed with specially made sauce. A traditional deep-down-cooling-off dish for Hunan farmers.

3. **Eggplant Salads** 4.50
   Eggplant mixed with hot and sour sauce. A delicious dish for summer time.

Entrees
(Hot & Spicy Country Style Dishes)
A LA CARTE

1. **Harvest Pork** 5.00
   Slices of pre-cooked pork sauteed with onions, cabbage, and celery-like roots. During the winter season, our workers work so hard that they need some kind of spicy & nutritious food to revive their utterly exhausted body. This dish serves the purpose.

2. **Shredded Pork & Celery** 5.00
   Shredded pork cooked with shredded celery, bamboo shoots, hot and spicy sauce. This dish is served all year around. It is commonly catered at country fairs to attract customers.

3. **Bean Curd with Meat Sauce** 5.00
   Bean curd stewed with delicious meat sauce, hot bean sauce, and green onions. A real treat.

4. **Deep-Fried Shredded Pork with Vegetables and Hot Bean Sauce** 5.25
   Deep-fried shredded pork with bell peppers, carrots and bamboo shoots sauteed in hot bean sauce.

5. **Sliced Pre-Cooked Lean Pork with Hot & Garlic Sauce** 5.95
   A popular dish in Hunan. (Served cold.)

6. **Hunan Spareribs** 5.50
   Marinated spareribs cooked with bell peppers, onions, garlic, ginger, hot black bean sauce.

7. **Hot & Sour Beef** 5.75
   Sliced beef sauteed with sliced carrots, onions and hot & sour sauce. A nutritious dish usually served on the "Double Ninth" festival day. A tradition of climbing to the high places on that day.

8. **Shredded Beef with Bell Peppers** 5.75
   With shredded beef, bell pepper, bamboo shoots and delicious hot sauce.

9. **Hot & Sour Chicken** 5.75
   Diced boneless chicken sauteed with bamboo shoots, bell pepper, sliced carrots, hot & sour sauce, and minced fresh ginger. A breathtaking dish for your dining pleasure.

10. **Stewed Chicken with hot Curry Sauce** 5.95
    Diced boneless chicken cooked with chicken, bell peppers and Indian hot curry sauce. (super hot)

11. **Braised Rock Cod Fillets** 5.95
    With bean curd, vegetables and hot bean sauce.

12. **Braised Fish Balls with Vegetables** 5.95
    Home-made fish balls made of rock-cod and cooked with vegetables. Bamboo shoots and green onions. Delicious.

13. **Whole Fish** .... 9.00 - 12.00
    Rock cod cooked in spicy hot sauce.

14. **Hunan Shrimps** 7.25
    With onions, bell peppers, bamboo shoots in hot bean sauce.

15. **Hunan Scallops** 7.25
    With onions, bell peppers, bamboo shoots in hot black bean sauce.

16. **Henry's Special** 8.95
    Chicken, shrimps, scallops, and vegetables with hot bean sauce. (A most delicious dish)

SMOKED SPECIALTIES

Smoked meats are prepared at this premises according to the old way in Hunan province and all have a very strong smoky taste.

17. **Smoked Ham** *(hot or not hot. Let us know in advance.)* 6.25
    Sliced smoked ham sauteed with bamboo shoots, bell pepper, onions, sliced carrots and hot pepper sauce. A very popular dish in Hunan.

18. **Smoked Chicken** *(Smoked with bones; hot or not hot)* 6.25
    Chopped smoked chicken cooked with bamboo shoots, carrots, bell pepper, and hot sauce. A delicious dish.

19. **Half of a Smoked Duck** *(cooked with bones; hot or not hot)* 10.50
    Deep-fried smoked duck cooked with bamboo shoots, onions, bell peppers, carrots, fresh garlic, ginger and hot black bean sauce. A delicious treat.

20. **Marty's Special** 6.50
    Smoked ham and diced boneless chicken cooked with bell peppers, onions, bamboo shoots, carrots and spicy hot black bean sauce.

SPICY, BUT NOT HOT DISHES

21. **Shredded Pork with Pickled Vegetables** 5.00
    A very popular dish in Hunan.

22. **Fresh Bacon, Hunan Style** 5.50
    Sliced fresh bacon cooked three times, boiled/deep-fried/steamed with pickled vegetables. A popular dish for Hunan farmers in winter.

23. **Sliced Beef with Green Onions** *(see hint)* 5.75
    A spicy but not hot dish specially prepared for those who do not take hot pepper.

24. **Stewed Beef Chunks** 5.00
    Beef chunks around 40 pounds cooked in a sealed pot for hours. It is tender and delicious.

25. **Diced Boneless Chicken with Fresh Garlic Sauce** 5.75
    A spicy dish cooked with bamboo shoots, bell pepper, carrots, and fresh garlic sauce. A delicious dish for those who do not like hot pepper.

VEGETABLE DISHES

26. **Bean Curds with Pickled Vegetables and Bamboo Shoots** 4.25
    A popular dish in Hunan.

27. **Sauteed De Luxe Vegetables** 4.25
    Hand picked vegetables cooked with bamboo shoots, bean curd and sliced carrots.

28. **Bean Sprout Salads** 4.00
    Bean sprouts, cucumber strips mixed with specially made sauce. A traditional deep-down-cooling-off dish for Hunan farmers.

29. **Eggplant Salads** 4.50
    Steamed eggplant mixed with hot and sour sauce. A delicious dish for summer time.

Steamed Rice for each person .... .50

Occasional Dishes!

Occasional dishes require special preparation and depend greatly upon the daily availability of ingredients in the market. Hence, we cannot maintain these dishes on a day-to-day basis. Kindly ask your waiter about them.

1. **Fresh & Crispy Squid** 7.25
   Fresh squid cooked with onions, bamboo shoots, bell peppers and black bean sauce.

2. **Kung Pao Chicken** 6.25
   Diced boneless chicken cooked with scorched whole red hot peppers, onions, bamboo shoots, bell peppers, minced garlic and ginger, roasted peanuts and hot bean sauce.

3. **Henry's Shredded Pork** 5.95
   Shredded pork cooked with wood ears, scallions, spinach, scrambled eggs and special sauce. (hot or not hot)

4. **Five Spiced Bean Curd with Shredded Pork** 5.25
   Five-spiced dehydrated bean curd cooked with bell peppers, scallions, bamboo shoots and black bean sauce.

5. **Spicy & Hot Rock Cod Fillets** 7.50
   Deep-fried rock-cod fillets cooked with hot bean sauce, minced ginger and garlic, hot peppers and scallions.

6. **Eggplant with Meat Sauce** 5.25
   Eggplant cooked with minced garlic and ginger, scallions, meat sauce, hot peppers, a touch of vinegar and hot bean sauce.

7. **Dry-Sauteed String Beans** 5.25
   Tender string beans cooked with black beans, red hot peppers, garlic, ginger and meat sauce.

8. **Bean Curd, Silver Threads & Vegetables** 5.00
   All three stir-fried and stewed with scallions and black bean sauce.

Hunan Restaurant (San Francisco) menu (Courtesy of the Hunan)

. . . .

New York (50 Bowery, 212-964-1204) and Asia Garden (736 Pacific Ave., 415-398-5112) in San Francisco. Today just about every suburb in America has a restaurant serving passable boiled dumplings and eggplant with garlic sauce.

The relentless process of natural selection continues, of course. Chinese seafood has made a big splash in Los Angeles: Mon Kee's (679 N. Spring St., 213-628-6717) and Diamond Seafood (724 N. Hill St., 213-617-0666) stand out.

New York's Chinatown is also rediscovering its roots in the more sophisticated Cantonese cuisine brought over in recent years by wealthy emigrées from Hong Kong. Try 20 Mott St., (212-964-0380), creator of ethereal minced conch with ham and mushrooms. Uptown, Pig Heaven (1540 Second Ave., 212-744-4333) proves nightly that Chinese food need not be diet food. For this eater, however, one well-established but decidedly untrendy restaurant stands above all the rest: Henry Chung's HUNAN, in San Francisco.

Henry Chung was not born to the wok. Son of a soldier, great-grandson of a tea exporter, graduate of the National Central University in Chungking, he fled China after the war. The first stop was Tokyo; the second, Houston, where for a decade he presided over The Mellow Dip, a frozen custard drive-in. Later he moved with his family to San Francisco to become an office worker.

But destiny finally called. In 1974, at the age of 54, Henry Chung opened a restaurant serving dishes based on his grandmother's recipes. Kearney Street, with a half-dozen formica-topped tables and counter space for 10, was an instant success. In 1979, he opened a second and much larger establishment on Sansome Street with an identical menu. The place on Sansome is less hectic and better ventilated, and it sports a wonderful NO MSG banner spoofing the style of the Red Guards. But we'll stick with the original, if only because the stir-frying is 50 feet and a few seconds closer to the tables.

Expect to wait a bit: the lines are often long, but they move fast. Start with the onion cakes: multilayered, feather-light deep-fried pancakes filled with chopped scallion. But don't pass up the other appetizer, fried dumplings filled with pork and cabbage and served with the trademark red hot sauce of Hunan.

Now the choices become agonizing. Among the hot, country-style dishes, the hot and sour chicken seasoned with lots of ginger is to kill for. Ditto, the braised rock cod balls with bamboo shoots and green onion, the shredded pork in hot bean sauce, and the stewed chicken flavored with curry. Henry offers a unique thrice-cooked bacon with pickled vegetables, and a spicy (but not hot) boneless chicken with more garlic than you can imagine. There's also the option of Hunan-style smoked meat—the ham dish edges out the chicken. And don't forget the cold salads. Mashed eggplant with a rich hot and sour dressing is lovely; bean sprouts with cucumber go nicely with all the hot stuff.

Wash it all down with beer or tea. And pause a moment at the cash register to watch the stir-frying behind the counter. If you've been inspired, buy an autographed copy of Henry's cookbook. Oh yes, the check: Figure $14 a person if you're careful, or $20 for an ultimate blowout. The Hunan is located at 853 Kearney St., 415-788-2234.

Chocolate Chip Cookie

· ·

R ecreational sex is out because of fear of disease. Smoking
is out; so is getting drunk."

"What's left?" asks Faith Popcorn,* President of Brainreserve,
Inc., and America's leading trend finder. "Cookies."

Ms. Popcorn's pessimism seems a bit premature. Still, it's nice
to be prepared for any eventuality. Ms. Popcorn also says that
America is in for a long bout of "cocooning"—"going into the
house and pulling the covers over our heads." So rather than expose readers to the myriad hazards of driving down to the mall to
buy cookies from David's or Mrs. Fields, we offer the ultimate
chocolate chip cookie in recipe form.

That cookie, in case you ever doubted it, is the ORIGINAL TOLL
HOUSE. First created by Ruth Wakefield in 1930, it was named
for the restaurant she owned in Whitman, Massachusetts. Legend
has it that Ruth was working on a variation of a then-popular
cookie confection called the Drop-Do. She assumed that broken
pieces of chocolate would blend into the dough as the cookies
baked. She assumed wrong. But the resulting melange of buttery
dough and partially melted chocolate was an instant success. And
a very easy one to reproduce.

---

*No kidding. She's a real person and that's her real name. Don't ask why.**

**All right, ask. She says her Italian grandfather was named Corne. When they
asked him his name at Ellis Island, he responded, "Poppa Corne." Told you not to
ask.

Original Toll House Cookies

½ cup (¼-lb. stick) butter, softened to
   room temperature
6 tablespoons sugar
6 tablespoons dark brown sugar
1 egg
½ teaspoon vanilla

1 cup plus 2 tablespoons unbleached flour, unsifted
½ teaspoon baking soda
¼ teaspoon salt

1 cup (half a 12-oz. package) real (never
   chocolate-flavored) semisweet chocolate chips
½ cup pecan pieces (optional)

Preheat the oven to 375 degrees.

Cream the butter, sugar, brown sugar, and vanilla until fluffy. In a separate bowl, combine the flour, baking soda, and salt. Add a bit at a time to the butter mixture, mixing until smooth. Stir in the chips and nuts.

Drop rounded teaspoonfuls onto ungreased baking sheets (preferably ones made from black-finished steel), leaving about three inches between batter lumps. Bake for 9 to 12 minutes, until light brown. To avoid breaking the cookies, allow them to cool a few minutes before removing them from the sheet. Makes about three dozen cookies.

Serve with cold milk or lemonade. Coffee is too adult. Electric blanket and "Leave It to Beaver" reruns optional.

City Bicycle

· ·

N eed a bike to commute to work on city streets? Perhaps a
jaunt to a neighborhood park to watch your daughter
pitch in the Little League?

The common choice is a touring bicycle, the kind with ten
speeds and tires the width of your knuckle. Touring bikes are
maneuverable and demand modest pedalling effort. What's more,
they are generally good value—$250 buys a fine one. But with
very little rubber to protect against road shock, potholes can be
agony and curb-jumping is an invitation to disaster. The gears can
only be changed while you pedal, a serious inconvenience in stop-
and-go traffic. Low-set handlebars force you to lean forward,
straining neck and shoulder muscles. And the absence of a chain
guard or fenders practically guarantees stained clothing.

One alternative is an all-terrain bike, a delightfully light, delightfully comfortable version of the fat-wheeled, indestructible
models kids used to deliver afternoon newspapers (when there still
were afternoon newspapers). All-terrain bikes can stop speeding
bullets and leap tall buildings without bending their wheels or
stretching the cables on their oversized brakes. Their handlebars
and gearshift levers are nicely positioned for riding upright.
But they don't resolve the axle-grease-on-business-suit or the
downshifting-at-the-red-light problems. And their two-inch-plus
balloon tires create a lot of pedal resistance once you're moving at
a good clip.

It's still possible to buy an old-fashioned three-speed "English
racer," and in many ways that isn't a bad choice for city biking.

The gears are in the rear hub, making it possible to shift without moving the bicycle. Fenders and chain guard offer a first defense against mud and grease. But flimsy construction makes them vulnerable on bad roads, and quickly transforms them into rattletraps. Flexible, low-strength steel frames, along with inexpensive crank-and-chain sets, create a big drag on pedal power. And the three-speed gear range doesn't go low enough for steep hills, or high enough for the occasional dash on smooth, level pavement.

The solution: a top-of-the-line "city" bicycle, combining the rugged, space-age construction of an all-terrain bike with the simplicity and familiar comforts of a three-speed. One of the very best is the METRO 5, sold by the Sterling Cycle Company of Philadelphia.

Like most other high-quality modern bikes, the Metro's frame is made from rigid, chrome-molybdenum steel alloy; the 27-inch wheels from strong, aluminum alloy; the 36 spokes per wheel from stainless steel. This expensive combination keeps the weight down to about 28 pounds—six or seven more than a decent racing bike, but ten fewer than the one-speed delivery bikes of yesteryear.

Pedals and cantilever-type brakes are sturdy imports by Shimano. The Metro 5 comes with 1⅜-inch tires, wide enough to survive an occasional jumped curb, but narrow enough and hard enough (recommended pressure: 75 pounds per square inch) to keep rolling resistance fairly low. The combination of wide tires and nicely sprung leather saddle makes for a very comfortable ride.

Gearing is five-speed, with a range just short of the standard ten-speed and more than adequate for city use. As important, there's no derailleur to change gears; the Sturmey-Archer mechanism is inside the rear hub, just like a three-speed. Shifting is done with idiot-proof thumb-levers on the handlebar. The handshift system makes it possible to cover the entire length of chain with a flexible plastic tube, eliminating cuff stains. Feather-light fenders can be ordered to take care of the general mud problem.

The Metro's design puts the crank just 10½ inches off the ground. That means the seat is two or three inches closer to the

Sterling Metro 5 bicycle (Courtesy of Sterling Cycle Company)
· · · · · · · · · · · · · · · · ·

ground, too, making it easier to balance the bike at low speeds and a snap to hold the bike upright at stoplights.

Options include a powerful Velo-Lux headlight with recharger and an amber strobe light to guard the rear. Oh yes, there's a clip for carrying a U-shaped Kryptonite lock. You'll probably want the lock—the Metro retails for $600.

THE BEST
Civilian Application of Defense Research

. . . .

*E*verybody knows the space program brought us Teflon and
scratch-resistant sunglasses. But what, besides $640 toilet
seats, has the Pentagon provided us with lately?

Crispy microwave pizza.

As every modern chef knows, microwave ovens cook without
warming the plate because microwaves pass harmlessly through ceramics or clay. That's great at clean-up time, but guarantees that
the crust of a frozen pizza will remain soggy long after the topping
has been steamed to inedibility.

Enter the Defense establishment, fresh from technological
triumph on the Air Force's Stealth Bomber. Stealth, the scientists
pointed out, is nothing more than an airplane coated with materials that absorb radar waves rather than bouncing them back
to a receiving antenna. And radar waves are nothing more than
microwaves. That inspired Pillsbury to design the first "stealth"
pizza box.

The inside of the pizza package is coated with a high-tech metallic film that efficiently absorbs microwaves, and quickly becomes
hot to the touch. The result: a crust that bakes nicely, and in the
same time it takes for the fixings to melt.

As often happens, of course, the solution to one technological
problem leads to another. "I can see the Russians coming over
and ordering two million pizzas," worries one consulting engineer,
"then peeling back the film and putting them on their airplanes."

Compact Disc Player

· ·

*I*magine a 70-minute sound recording small enough to fit in your palm, rugged enough to survive a dousing of Tab, yet capable of reproducing a stunning range of frequencies and sound levels with no perceptible background noise. Imagine that the machines to play the recordings are as trouble-free and easy to operate as good record players, and run about the same price. There's no longer any need to imagine this miracle, of course, when you can buy one at any electronics store. The cheap, high-quality compact disc or "CD" player has arrived, and stereo will never be the same.

Tapes and records contain a shorthand picture of the music, etched mechanically or magnetically on their surfaces. Machines that can translate this picture back into music with great accuracy are expensive and delicate. Unless one is careful, dirt or heat or magnetism will muddy the picture. And no matter how carefully handled, the image is damaged a little each time it is viewed.

CDs, on the other hand, capture sound "digitally," coded as a long series of numbers. The numbers are read off the surface of the disc by reflecting a narrow beam of light through a protective transparent coating. Reading the numbers with cool, reflected light (at the incredible rate of 44,000 numbers per second) doesn't wear the disc the way a phonograph needle damages vinyl. And because redundant numbers are cleverly spread through the sequence, specks of dirt or scratches on the disc's surface must be quite large to make a noticeable difference in sound reproduction.

CDs do have their critics. Audio perfectionists point out that the CD digitally samples the music rather than continuously scanning it, and thus can't attain the accuracy of extremely well made records played on the very finest sound system. They're right about the current generation of CD players: The very best records played on the very best equipment reproduce the subtlest music— say, a Beethoven piano sonata interpreted by Horowitz—with greater depth and character. But unless you are prepared to spend $1,000 or more on a turntable, tone arm, and cartridge* and then treat your vinyl records like Rembrandt originals, CDs have the edge. In the $200 to $300 price range where most of us live, CDs are spectacularly better.

What to look for:

Sound Quality

All CD players can reproduce music without adding background noise. All reproduce music with an icy clarity, as if a layer of cloth had been removed from the speaker grills. But less expensive players have a slightly harsh sound—an excessive brightness. Most people can hear the difference when machines are played side by side, through excellent amplifiers and speakers. But the differences are modest, and the only judge of what's good enough for you is your own ear.

Error Correction

Virtually all CD players sail through the occasional fingerprint or dust speck without skipping a beat. But some have special circuitry to compensate for greater surface damage, and some are built with scanning mechanisms that are less likely to be disturbed by vibration. If you're in the market for a more expensive model, it

*Ready for the plunge? Try a SOTA Star Sapphire Turntable ($1,600) with an SME V magnesium tone arm and matching Virtuosi DTi moving coil cartridge ($1,200). Figure another hundred dollars for connectors. Even this sum will be wasted, though, if you don't match the turntable with an expensive amplifier and speakers.

Meridian 207 Pro compact disc player (Courtesy of Madrigal Audio Laboratories)
. . . .

may pay to invest in a test disc (available in upscale audio stores) that can put a CD player through the extremes.

Versatility

Home units generally have the dimensions of a large, thick college textbook. Portables are just a quarter of that size, weigh about two pounds with battery packs, and plug into a stereo receiver with a single jack. CD players for cars are considerably more expensive than basic home or portable models because they must be specially protected against road shock. Some companies are now selling both home and car CD players with automatic changers, allowing you to play as many as ten discs without interruption.

Features

Just about every player these days lets you program tracks out of the prescribed order, and most provide an audible scan through music at double or triple time. Additional frills may include wireless remote control, a volume control for headphones, a display of total time remaining on the disc, and fast access that finds a new track in one or two seconds, as opposed to four or five.

Among portables, the Sony Discman D-15 (about $300) holds an edge for compact size, and built-in rechargeable batteries. At the economy end of the home players, it would be hard to beat the NEC CD-500E (about $275). This model has competitive if not exceptional sound quality, all the standard convenience features and, wonder of wonders, remote control. Probably the cheapest entries into noticeably better compact disc sound are the Magnavox CDB-650 (about $350) and the Pioneer PD-9010X (about $400), both all-frills machines with extremely tight specs.

Now quality becomes entirely subjective. Some ears prefer the sound of the super high-tech Nakamichi OMS-7AII (about $1,600, undiscounted) or the Sony CDP 705ESD (about $1,500, undiscounted). Our own choice is the **MERIDIAN 207 PRO** (about $1,500, undiscounted), from the little company that invented high-end CD players. The 207 Pro looks a little different, housing the electronics separate from the vault-like player box. What makes it very special, though, is the sweet, sweet sound that comes close to the audiophile standard for turntables.

Consolation Prize

· ·

*I*t was fun while it lasted. Lured away from mighty I.T.T. in 1974, Michel Bergerac did his best to put the Revlon Corporation back on its feet. In 11 torrid years of jetting around the world in his Boeing 727, he managed to transform the fatigued cosmetics manufacturer into a diversified purveyor of health-care products.

Sales exploded from $500 million to $2 billion. Trouble is, profits imploded, falling to $125 million in 1985 from a peak of $192 million. So it did not come entirely as a surprise when Ronald Perelman, the chairman of Pantry Pride, wooed and won over Revlon's stockholders for a cool $2.7 billion.

Pauvre Michel is now out of work. But unlike many 54-year-olds on the wrong end of a pink slip, he is not likely to have a problem making ends meet in his golden years. His original employment contract called for five years' severance, worth $7 million. Stock options exercisable at departure were worth another $13 million. And then there was the tidy little termination package created by the board of directors for Revlon's cherished employees in 1983, in case someone should have the bad taste to buy out the company. Mr. Bergerac's ermine parachute: $15 million. Total take: $35 million.

Was it worth $35 million to Revlon stockholders to ease his return to the real world?

"How do you judge these things? I don't know," opines a modest Bergerac. "We wanted Michel to feel he was wanted," explains a member of Revlon's compensation committee.

Convertible

. . . .

*T*hinking convertible? You're not alone. Since the ragtop was brought back to life by Chrysler in 1982, sales have gone through the . . . skyrocketed. Some 20 models are now available, ranging from the dowdy Renault Alliance to the sheik's special, the $170,000 Rolls-Royce Corniche II.

For value and safety, you can't beat the Volkswagen Cabriolet, a peppy little econobox with a built-in roll bar to save your neck in a crash. For sport touring, there's the Saab 900 Turbo or the BMW 325i. And for letting the gold chain crowd know you've really arrived, it would be hard to beat Detroit's new hybrids, the Cadillac Allante and the Chrysler Maserati. But for pure, innocent fun, nothing matches the last unpretentious convertible, one of the Ford MUSTANGS made between 1964 and 1968.

The first Mustang, introduced at the New York World's Fair in April 1964, was little more than a gussied-up Ford Falcon compact—underpowered, poorly suspended, and wall-to-wall plastic. But Mustangs were cheap ($2,665, factory list for the convertible), came in the neatest candy colors, and over the years have proved to be quite durable. Ford couldn't turn 'em out fast enough.

By the late '60s, the thrill was fading and Ford shifted its marketing focus from Sweet Sixteen to Muscle Car. Mustang engines got bigger, suspensions were toughened, and the sheet metal took on a thuggy, I'm-meaner-than-you-are look. But tens of thousands of the early models survive, many restored to mint condition by car buffs who can't afford real antiques. Parts and accessories still come cheap, and are easy to find through a dozen mail-order distributors specializing in Mustangobilia.

A 1967 or 1968 model in excellent condition will set you back a mere $7,000 to $10,000—perhaps $500 more if you insist on the original "Playboy Pink" paint. A Mustang of this vintage is probably a poor investment; there are too many around. But there's simply no better time machine for a leisurely drive to the beach.

Mustang Monthly—that's right, a monthly magazine for Mustang enthusiasts—has classified "for sale" listings. A year's subscription runs $24. Write *Mustang Monthly*, PO Box 6320, Lakeland, FL 33807. Or, for serious networking, join the Mustang Club of America, PO Box 447, Lithonia, GA 30058. A sample copy of the newsletter costs $2.

. . . .

Ford Mustang convertible (1964) (Courtesy of the Ford Motor Company)

Cooking Pans

· ·

Your grandmother probably used cast iron; your mother, cast aluminum. Cooking magazines are full of ads for stainless-steel cookware layered with other metals. Meanwhile, the three-star French chefs who ought to know are always photographed with copper pans in their hands. Which is really best?

Depends what's cooking. A pan capable of searing a steak to a crunchy black is almost useless for simmering a delicate buerre blanc sauce. The right pan for low-fat cookery just won't do for deglazing meat essences. And while department stores and interior decorators simply adore matched sets, serious cooks can't afford to put form over function.

The Pan for Sauces

The key to sauce cookery is even heating, plus the ability to reduce temperature quickly. Copper is ideal for the job because it conducts heat very well, yet cools quickly because the metal stores very little heat. Copper reacts with acids in foods, so copper pans are lined, usually with tin. The best lining material, though, is nickel. It is more durable—a tin lining must eventually be replaced—and won't melt or blister if the pan is allowed to overheat.

Most copper pans are French imports from Harvard, Lefevre, or Mauviel. But don't worry about brand names; look for copper that is at least one-eighth- and preferably one-quarter-inch thick.

Figure on spending $80 to $100 for a pan eight inches in diameter and three inches deep.

The Pan for Searing

Cast-iron pans weigh a ton, take ages to heat, and require a lot of care. But heavy-gauge cast iron has one great virtue: it stores heat very well.

Throw a big steak into a hot aluminum or copper or steel pan, and the meat will instantly cool the metal. Result: gray steak. Dump the same size steak into a cast-iron skillet heated to the same temperature, and the meat will sizzle brown. That's why cast iron is indispensable for sealing in the juices of pan-grilled meats and thickly sliced fish steaks.

Cast iron is relatively cheap. Just $15 buys a large pan from General Housewares or one of its competitors. Wash cast iron with a soapy brush (never Brillo; the scratches will rust) and keep it "seasoned" with a light coat of cooking oil to prevent food from clinging.

The Pan for Counting Calories

Serious cooks used to turn up their noses at Teflon-lined pans. Most were cheap, thin aluminum, which heated unevenly. To keep the soft coating from scratching, special nylon or plastic utensils were needed. And once the coating began to wear—no matter how cautious the cook, it never took more than a few years—the pan was worse than useless.

But time and technology marched on. The new polymer and silicone coatings (SilverStone Supra, Super T-Plus, Greblon) are much tougher—tough enough, in fact, to last four or five years with minimal care in handling. And they are now available on high-quality aluminum and cast-iron pans. Use the nonstick surface for conventional frying with less butter or oil. Or try "flash-sautéing" meats and veggies at high heat with no fat at all. One

Cuisinart Commercial cooking pans (Courtesy of Cuisinart, Inc.)
. . . .

of the better brands, the Bourgeat heavy-gauge aluminum frypan coated with SilverStone, runs about $50 in the 11-inch size.

The All-Around Sauté Pan

So much for specialized uses. What's best for knocking around the kitchen? Solid stainless steel is good-looking, incredibly durable, nonreactive with foods, and a snap to clean. But it heats unevenly and changes temperature slowly. Nickel-lined copper is gorgeous and quite versatile, but it is very expensive and a real pain to keep shiny. Heavy-gauge, black-finished aluminum (Calphalon, Magnalite Professional, Leyson) has won over a lot of cooks, and for good reason. It's light, heats evenly, and requires no heroic care. For our money, though, we'll go with stainless steel with a copper core.

A sandwich of copper and stainless steel (lots of copper inside, thin stainless outside) retains most of the virtues of each metal. It is as easy to clean, as nonreactive with foods, and almost as durable as solid stainless steel. Yet it heats almost as evenly and cools almost as rapidly as nickel-lined copper. The only serious drawback is price: nothing, other than the best copper, is as expensive.

If you do go to for steel/copper, go for broke with the rugged, high-style CUISINART Commercial line. The surface is fine "18-10" stainless,* and the copper core comes right out to the sidewalls for optimal heat distribution. The stainless-steel handles can go into the oven and emerge unscathed. And unlike many other brands, Cuisinart lids fit quite snugly, sealing in moisture and sealing out air. Steel yourself to spend about $80 for a 10-inch pan and lid.

*Meaning the steel is alloyed with 18 percent chromium and 10 percent nickel. "18-8" is virtually as good. Cheaper steel alloys used in cookware may be stainless in the sense that they won't rust, but they may darken with use.

THE BEST
Corkscrew
. . . .

T here are a hundred devices for removing corks from wine
bottles, and almost none of them work very well. The
standard folding opener, the one with the little knife for cutting
the foil, is compact and businesslike, but it takes considerable care
to center the screw and a great deal of muscle to extract a tight
cork. The most popular openers, the ones with little wings that
act as levers once the screw is engaged, solve the muscle issue.
But, as often as not, they break long corks, leaving a mess of
scraps behind.

Alternatives? Remember Corky, the little pump that forced air
through the cork with a hollow needle? Sounds like a great idea.
But sounds, alas, don't remove stubborn corks. Then there's the
sort with two blade-like prongs—just wedge and wiggle. Sometimes it works like a champ. But, then, sometimes the check
really is in the mail.

Enter Herbert Allen, retired oil service executive, trained engineer, and lover of good wine. A proper corkscrew, he figured,
should automatically center for the tightest possible grip and least
chance of tearing a fragile cork. It should be long enough to penetrate the entire length of the extra-long corks used in the best
red wines. It should bite into the cork with minimum fuss.
And—here is the conceptual breakthrough—it should take modest
force to operate. If it is too hard to pull, it isn't doing the job.
If it is too easy to pull, a single impatient jerk may break the cork.

The result of Mr. Allen's basement tinkering is the disarmingly
simple **SCREWPULL.** The Screwpull's hard plastic lip fits over the

wine bottle for accurate centering every time. The long helical screw is coated with slippery DuPont SilverStone Supra (Silver-Stone wears better than Teflon). The continuous turning motion provides steady pressure, adequate to budge a machine-compacted cork but rarely enough to break it. Not the perfect corkscrew perhaps, but a major advance in the technology.

Many buyers resent the $12 to $15 price tag: $12 is a lot for a couple of pieces of molded plastic and a coil of coated steel wire. But this is not the place to become pennywise. Screwpull can pay for itself on one good bottle. Besides, genius deserves reward.

Cruise Ship

. . . .

*F*or organized frenzy—if this is midnight it must be time for aerobic backgammon—you can't beat what the ad agencies call the "fun" ships. And among the vessels catering to nonstop partying, it would be hard to beat the Carnival Line's *Tropicale*. Built in 1982 to carry 1,200 passengers on short cruises, it features the usual pocket-sized swimming pools, bars specializing in Hawaiian Punch with rum, food with a capital Q for Quantity, and exercise classes to relieve guilt. What makes the *Tropicale* stand out from the crowd, though, is its maniacal devotion to The Good Time: The Vegas-style floor shows, chrome-on-chrome casino and discos (open till six A.M.) live up to the billing.

A variation on the "fun" ship is the "high density" ship, where the sheer size of the crowd creates unusual opportunities for singles. Consider the *Norway*, a downscaled, redesigned version of the great 67,000-ton ocean liner, the S.S. *France*. Configured for 2,000 passengers, it is awash with pick-up spots ranging from bars to ice-cream parlors to Italian cooking lessons to boutiques. Nobody, alas, has figured a way to increase the ratio of unattached males to females.

The *Queen Elizabeth 2* is about the same size as the *Norway* and offers almost as many attractions—among them, a branch of the lusher than lush Golden Door Spa (see "The Best Health Spa"). But the ship aims for more staid, wealthier types than the *Norway*. The best suites in what used to be first class are knockouts. And the kitchen for the two élite dining rooms (reserved for the folks who pay premium rates for the formerly first-class suites) produces some of the best food in the world. Even without access to the top restaurants, the polished service and spaciousness of the better cabins arguably make the *QE2* the choice for long cruises.

Moving down in size but not in class, one must fit in a mention of the 25,000-ton *Sagafjord*. This new acquisition of the Cunard group may not provide the most or best of anything in particular. But it is so comfortable and so flawlessly run that it has gained exceptional loyalty among repeat cruisers.

Searching for something entirely different? Small ships for specialized cruises are definitely in. The *Delta Queen*, built in 1927, is the last mint-condition paddle-wheel steamboat offering lazy days on the Mississippi. Lindblad Travel charters the *Kun Lun*, a 2,300-ton ship to carry just 36 passengers up the Yangtse River. Originally designed to pamper VIP guests of the People's Republic, it is now the nicest way for Western tourists to see the heartland of China. The *Maxim's des Mer*, a converted military patrol boat, is

. . . .

Sea Goddess **cruise ship (Courtesy of Cunard Sea Goddess)**

very small (15 suites), very upscale ($5,000 a week per person), and promises ultimate luxury on short Caribbean and Mediterranean cruises.

The *Society Explorer*, owned by Society Expeditions, is small enough to go 2,500 miles up the Amazon and tough enough to survive the occasional nudge from an iceberg. It is also luxurious enough to please passengers who want smoked salmon and Perrier-Jouët with their adventure. The *Pacific Northwest Explorer*, a 97-ton vessel with a yacht-like, seven-foot draft, was built for very comfortable cruising along the rivers and coastal channels of the Canadian northwest. The *Wind Star*, a dazzling little ship propelled by computer-controlled sails rather than engines, offers romance along with the traditional cruise comforts.

But for those who want a cruise on which every need is anticipated and no legal pleasure is far from hand, it would be hard to beat the SEA GODDESSES. Identical ships, the *Sea Goddesses I* and *II* are the brain children of a group of executives of the big Norwegian Caribbean Lines. This very profitable cruise company (which operates the *Norway*, among other ships) has never had much success attracting wealthy clients. And the execs set out to discover why.

Their market research showed that people with six-figure incomes don't like organized fun and games—and don't like to rub shoulders with people who do. So a group of Norwegian investors put Ronald Kurtz, one of the NCL executives, in charge of designing a cruise line for the Faubourg St. Honoré/Rodeo Drive crowd. The first vessels, launched in 1984 and 1985, are really oversized yachts—$34 million, 4,000-ton pleasure palaces that bear about as much resemblance to the average cruise ship as the Staten Island Ferry.

Each is fitted with 58 very large, virtually identical suites decorated in white oak and pastel fabrics. Each has a queen-sized bed with down pillows, a big picture window, generous closet space, a safe for valuables, and a full-sized bathroom supplied with goodies ranging from Mary Chess soap to René Guinot sunscreen. The refrigerator contains pretty much anything you'd like to drink; passengers fill out a questionnaire listing preferences before boarding. And like virtually everything else on the *Sea Goddesses*, the Chivas and Chandon are included in the price of the ticket. There's a VCR in each suite and a big library of current tapes on board (rated PG to X). Room service is available 24 hours a day and tipping is discouraged.

Life on board is no more structured than days spent at a super-luxury hotel. There are no seatings at meals, no assigned tables, and no maître d' eager to shut up shop before the last guests have wandered in. Any meal, of course, can be had at any time in your suite—even pecan waffles to satisfy the three A.M. munchies.

Lunch (weather permitting, in the outdoor cafe) leans toward cold lobster, seasonal salads, fresh berries, and excellent pastries. Dinner in the main dining room is generally nouvelle continental, modified on request to suit meat-and-potatoes tastes. The china is Hutschenreuther, the crystal Villeroy and Bosch, the silver Felix Frères. And the only better eating to be had at sea is at the Princess Grill of the *QE2*.

Interior public spaces—two salons, three bars, a library, a glassed-in atrium—are light and airy; fresh flowers are everywhere. There is a standard pool, Jacuzzi, and gym. And unstandard access to the water from a special platform on the stern. Passengers are welcome to swim, snorkel, and windsurf. There are even two power boats for water skiing.

Those who wish may gamble in the pocket-sized casino, or dance to a combo after dinner. But what the *Sea Goddesses* offer that is hardly ever found on a cruise ship is real privacy—peaceful space to watch the stars, or do anything else that comes to mind.

The price of paradise is high. At about $1,200 a day per couple, the *Sea Goddesses* run about 20 percent more than comparable-sized quarters on the *QE2*. To soften the blow, the company offers special discounts on the Concorde to Europe. For information and reservations, write Sea Goddess Cruises, 5805 Blue Lagoon Dr., Miami, FL 33126, or phone 800-458-9000.

THE BEST
Decaffeinated Coffee

. . . .

*O*nce upon a time they could send a man to the moon, but they couldn't make a decent cup of decaffeinated coffee. Now the jury's out on both.

Your average cup of 100 percent Colombian coffee, brewed by the filter method, contains about 65 milligrams of caffeine. African "robusta" beans, used to make instant coffee or to blend with Latin varieties for less expensive supermarket brands, contain about 130 milligrams per cup. Yet in caffeine-sensitive adults, as little as 200 milligrams is enough to produce symptoms ranging from restlessness to heart palpitations.

That explains why Ludwig Roselius became rich inventing a chemical process to remove the caffeine. And it explains why General Foods purchased both the patent and the trademark "Sanka" (as in the French, "*sans* caffeine"). What it doesn't explain, though, is why the consumption of decaf has quadrupled since the mid-1960s, while sales of the real thing have fallen by 40 percent.

Is caffeine dangerous? It is certainly a no-no for pregnant women: There is evidence that it causes defects in puppies born in laboratories. And since it is a central nervous system stimulant that temporarily raises pulse rate and blood pressure, researchers have been looking hard for a link to heart attacks. What they've found, though, is considerably less than a smoking gun. Two California studies suggest that two cups of coffee a day, with or without caffeine, raise blood cholesterol levels in sedentary, middle-aged men. More cholesterol probably increases the risk of arterial disease.

The story is also inconclusive for caffeine and cancer. A couple of studies link coffee drinking (not caffeine consumption) to malignancies, particularly bladder tumors. But a couple of other studies found no evidence at all.

Still, a lot of people who would rather play it safe are cutting back on both coffee and caffeine. And coffee distributors, eager to avoid bankruptcy, are filling the shelves with 97 or 98 percent caffeine-free versions of the standard brands. If your goal is merely to find one that tastes better than the dread instant Sanka, the task is easy. Every brand of pre-ground decaf is more coffee-like than any brand of instant decaf, whether the latter is freeze-dried, spray-dried, or aired out in Juan Valdez's own backyard.* Finding a decaf that will please the tastebuds of a coffee lover is a bit more difficult.

Among lightly roasted supermarket brands, Melitta, Savarin, and Brown Gold hold an edge over Chock Full O' Nuts and Hills Brothers, and a wide margin over Sanka, Brim, and Folgers. They are all a bit flat, though, short on aroma and body. It helps to brew them extra strength—double the standard coffee measure—but it doesn't help enough. Dark, espresso-style roasting does mask this inherent weakness of decaf. In fact, MEDAGLIA D'ORO is probably the only supermarket decaf that could pass for real coffee.

To do better, move up in price to coffees sold in the bean by specialty stores. Decaffeinated beans vary widely in quality, depending on freshness and the method of decaffeination as well as the country of origin. Generally, you'll do best buying decaffeinated 100 percent Colombian, and at a store that roasts the beans on the spot rather than purchasing them roasted from a wholesaler.

---

*Some folks claim a taste for Hag, a decaf instant imported from Germany at roughly double the price of instant Sanka or Brim. Don't waste your money.

Beans labelled "water-process" have been decaffeinated with hot water rather than chemicals. That's somewhat reassuring, since the commonly used chemical is methyl chloride, a solvent that causes cancer in high doses. The Food and Drug Administration limits residues of methyl chloride in coffee to 10 parts per million, and typically the brewing process cuts the residue below one part in a million. But even the hint of methyl chloride scares some people enough to opt for water-process. Unfortunately, there's no free lunch: Water-process decafs run an extra dollar or two a pound, and rarely taste as good.

If local stores can't satisfy you on bean quality, roasting style, or decaffeination process, there's always mail order. Zabar's, a giant fancy-food store in New York, sells both methyl chloride and water-process decafs in a number of blends. The coffee is always fresh and considerably cheaper than in smaller stores. For specifics, call 800-221-3347 or 212-787-2000.

Defense Against the Lone Ranger

. . . .

*A*n enterprising engineer at Northwestern Bell Telephone is
selling underwear impregnated with particles of metallic
silver. The silver, she says, protects against harmful radiation leak-
ing from video display terminals. Panties, camisoles, and T-shirts
run about $25. They're perfect for both home and office—but
not, perhaps, for airports.

THE BEST
Diet Pill

· ·

Wanna lose weight the easy way?

Who, besides the occasional masochist, high school dietician ("just eat sensibly and avoid between-meal treats") or sumo wrestler doesn't? But as countless dieters find time after time, most diet potions don't work. And most of the ones that do work are too dangerous to use.

Starch blockers, somewhat mysterious substances extracted from beans, were all the rage a few years ago. They were supposed to inhibit the absorption of carbohydrates in the gut. They probably do, but not in doses that are healthy for adults and other living things. If you haven't tried starch blockers already, you're not likely to: They've been off the market since 1982, when the Food and Drug Administration told manufacturers to prove the chemicals safe and effective, or take the first bus out of town.

Fiber pills, the ones so relentlessly promoted in the backs of women's magazines, are almost certainly harmless. In fact, the fiber may be useful in reducing colon cancer. But few people other than the cheerful, bikini-clad housewives in the ads find that the filling effect reduces the urge to eat.

Amphetamines were once routinely prescribed for dieting because they are very effective appetite suppressants. They also make you very, very happy; then, very, very sad. And sometimes very, very paranoid. With cocaine, at least, you can invite your friends in for the party.

But two other pills, chemically related to the amphetamine family, are legal, sometimes effective, and available without prescription in drug stores from Kauai to Key West. Benzocaine, the topical anesthetic used in everything from Anbesol to Lanacane, apparently reduces the incentive to eat by deadening the taste buds. If this scorched-earth approach to dieting doesn't appeal, consider phenylproponalomine (PPA). It is a standard ingredient in over-the-counter decongestants that also seems to reduce interest in food.

There are catches, however. Neither benzocaine nor PPA works for everyone; many dieters don't even notice the difference. Second, neither chemical can be considered absolutely safe. PPA is a definite no-no for anyone taking drugs for the treatment of depression. Moreover, lots of people are apparently tempted to exceed the recommended dose of PPA on the theory that a lot will work better than a little. The result can be dizziness and heightened blood pressure.

Benzocaine and PPA rate only a D for definite-maybe; amphetamines, an F for foolhardy. What's better?

According to new research, that familiar urge for a mid-afternoon Twinkie is sometimes related to the decline of a critical brain chemical called serotonin. Typically, the body responds to the deficiency with cravings for sweets and starches, which help right the imbalance. But a drug called dextro-fenfluramine can serve the same purpose, restoring willpower at crucial moments. It has been successfully tested at a number of research clinics, including one at M.I.T. And it is now being sold in France under the trade name Isomeride. When, or if, Isomeride will cross the Atlantic is not yet known.

However, another new diet drug, fluoxetine, is further along in the American licensing process, and may be available by prescription by the time these words are published. Fluoxetine (trade-name: Prozac) was developed by the Eli Lilly Company as an anti-depressant. But, like Isomeride, it also seems to ease the compulsion to eat carbohydrates by changing the brain's chemical balance. Junk food will be with us always, but this could turn it into a declining industry.

Dog Food

. . . .

*I*t all began with a fast-talking entrepreneur named James Spratt. A native of Cincinnati, Spratt spent the better part of 1860 touring the English countryside in an unsuccessful effort to sell lightning rods. His companion, a dog whose pedigree is lost to history, proved almost as hard to please as the farmers. The pup would only eat ship's biscuit, the mealy wedges of unleavened carbohydrate fed to sailors on long voyages before the age of canning.

That inspired the dog-loving Spratt to cook up a more nutritious variation on the biscuit theme, a blend of grain, vegetables, and meat which he called Spratt's Dog Cake. Packaged by the tony London firm of Walker, Harrison and Garthwaite, it proved a hit with the fox-and-hound set. Dog Cake soon crossed the Atlantic; the first factory was located on East 56th Street in New York.

Spratt's Cakes provided a more balanced diet than the scraps, and probably increased the stamina of working dogs. But the idea of buying separate food for Fido didn't catch on big until 1957, when Ralston Purina began selling Dog Chow in supermarkets. And the real boom came only in the '60s, when the giant people-food processors—Campbell, Lipton, Post, General Foods, Mars, Carnation—sunk their teeth into the market. Today, 50 million dog owners in America spend over $3 billion a year for six billion pounds of the stuff.

Actually, it's not as easy to peddle dog food as you might guess. At the heart of the matter is a contradiction: Dogs eat dog food, but people choose it. It doesn't help to create a formula that drives Spot wild if Spot's owner gags at first sniff.

In the 1970s, the marketeers at the food conglomerates decided to treat Spot as if he were human. Dry dog food was out: Would *you* eat the slop? So was canned dog food that smelled like a barnyard. Cans were lined with white enamel to achieve the sanitary look. Peas and carrots were added to the blends to suggest stew. Flavors, running from liver to chicken to cheese, were added to the lines with appropriate doses of food coloring.

It doesn't take a degree in veterinary medicine to know that dogs are color-blind, and thus utterly immune to the lure of Red Dye Number 16. Nor is it hard to guess that every dog worthy of his or her hyena genes loves an occasional whiff of dead prey. Strikingly, dog owners proved to be less gullible than the manufacturers assumed. Fake-human dog food at human prices* generated a lot of cute advertising copy, but not much in the way of profit.

The peas and carrots are now gone. So are the white enamel liners. And it is no longer considered a form of animal abuse to serve plain old dry dog chow. Television ads still offer up the occasional sheepdog wearing a clown suit, but the emphasis in dog-food marketing has shifted to the three basics: price, price, and price.

Price does matter, of course, but so should nutrition. The first step in finding the best is learning to read the code words on the package. If the label doesn't certify that the product is "complete and balanced," you can be certain the mixture doesn't contain enough protein, carbohydrate, fat, fiber, vitamins, and minerals to sustain health.

Unfortunately, "complete and balanced" isn't necessarily good

---

*In case you were wondering, some people do buy dog food for their own consumption, usually on the assumption that it is cheaper than people food. Dry dog food is a bargain, if not a delight to the tastebuds. But it's easy to exceed the nutritional value of "gourmet" canned dog food with rice and beans, or Cheerios and milk, and at much lower cost.

enough. Dog-food makers can meet the standard with a simple chemical analysis. No one specifies the source or type of nutrients included, and no one is very fussy about the relative proportions. Thus a manufacturer can meet the protein standard with wheat, which is difficult for dogs to metabolize, or casein (from milk), which is very easy. Carbohydrates may come from grains, which also add valuable fiber to a dog's diet, or they may come from milk sugar (lactose), which causes diarrhea in puppies. It's not unusual, moreover, for "complete and balanced" dog foods to contain inadequate or excessive amounts of utilizable vitamin A, calcium, phosphorus, zinc, and copper.

The only absolute guarantee of nutritional sufficiency, then, is a feeding trial—and preferably not one you perform on your own dog. Ralston Purina and Gaines have led the pack here, testing to make sure their foods produce healthy animals before marketing the formula. Most brand-name manufacturers have fallen into line. Today, every top-of-the-line dog food, dry, moist, or canned, is good enough.

A formula good enough for all dogs, however, can't be best for dogs in specific stages of life. Puppies, working dogs, and lactating dogs need a higher proportion of fat and protein in their diets. Hence the logic behind Gaines Cycle I, Hills Science Diet, and Purina's Hi Pro and Puppy Chow. On the other hand, older dogs are susceptible to kidney damage from excessive protein. They're better off with a low-fat, low-protein formula like Cycle-4 or Fit and Trim. These are also good foods for overweight dogs because they substitute fiber for calories, making it easier to control appetite.

THE BEST

Estimate of the Time and Place of the Next Great California Earthquake

. . . .

*E*very resident of lotusland vaguely understands the threat. But earthquakes are like airplane crashes, hot-tub burns, and killer bees—it's hard to get worked up about a disaster that will probably happen to somebody else. Now, thanks to modern science, the excuses for ignoring the earthquake threat are running out. Seismologists have a pretty good idea when the quake will happen, and where. And, kid you not, the end is disturbingly nigh.

First things first. A few billion years ago the cooling surface of young planet Earth fractured into great tectonic plates. These plates now drift on the currents of the red-hot, semi-fluid mantle below, ever so slowly making and unmaking oceans, continents, and mountain ranges.

Most of California is part of the North American plate. But the western edge of the state, from Humbolt County to the Baja, forms the eastern edge of the Pacific plate. And it is grinding northward at an average rate of two inches a year. The border between the two plates forms the 650-mile-long San Andreas Fault, visible in some places as a barely healed gash on the landscape.

Movement along the fault is not continuous—there, in fact, lies the rub. Friction locks the plates together until the gradual accumulation of pressure ruptures a weak place. Then, unimaginable masses of rock slip by each other with a great thud, radiating unimaginable amounts of energy outward as shock waves.

Where the rough edges give easily under the strain, the plates slip a few feet every 20 or 30 years. Pent-up energy is relatively small and the earthquakes do relatively little damage. But along big chunks of the fault, the plates haven't moved for many decades. By no coincidence, these are the sites of the monster quakes of the past.

In 1857 a huge earthquake ripped along the lightly populated southern portion of the fault, from Parkland to San Bernardino. In 1906 the entire 240-mile-long northern section of the fault ruptured, virtually levelling San Francisco. Each of these quakes released about a million times more energy than the moderate tremors that rattle windows and overturn vases in California every few months.

Geologists long ago pinpointed the long-quiet (and therefore riskiest) portions of the fault. But they didn't have a clue as to whether it would take another two years or 200 for the rock to snap again—at least they didn't until Kerry Sieh came along. Sieh, a Cal Tech graduate student, discovered a spot 55 miles north of Los Angeles where periodic slippage of the fault had left a 1,700-year record in the sediments collected along a creek bed. Similar evidence has since been gathered for the northern (San Francisco) portion of the fault.

The next San Francisco earthquake is likely to be a mammoth one, equivalent in power to the 1906 quake. But happily, the day of reckoning is probably far away: The U.S. Geological Survey reckons the odds of a rupture in the next 30 years as less than 5 percent. Los Angeles, on the other hand, isn't likely to make it nearly so long. Sieh found evidence of 12 more-or-less regularly occurring earthquakes, one approximately every 150 years. And since the last one occurred in 1857, time is running out.

The Geological Survey puts the probability of a giant quake centered somewhere within the Los Angeles sprawl at 2 to 5 percent within one year, 50-50 by the turn of the century. When the quake does hit, it will be a doozy. In order to relieve the accumulated strain, the plates would have to slip about 15 feet along a 250-mile section of the fault. That's not quite up to the 1906 San Francisco standard. But the State of California estimates it would be enough to kill 14,000 people if it occurs on a weekday afternoon, when the most people would be working in large buildings or riding on the streets. Property damage at any time of day could exceed $20 billion.

These estimates, made before the Mexico City catastrophe in 1985, may be on the conservative side. Damage in Mexico was far worse than expected, in large part because the loose soils beneath the city magnified the impact of the shock waves. Los Angeles, alas, is similarly vulnerable.

The danger to people, of course, would be much smaller if the timing of the L.A. quake could be predicted in advance. Seismologists have, in fact, accurately forecast big ones in China and Mexico. They've based the predictions on a compilation of evidence ranging from the release of radon gas from stressed rock, to laser-detected ground elevation along the fault, to clusters of barely detectable micro-quakes. But the scientists have missed as often as they've succeeded. And politicians are sure to think twice about evacuating Los Angeles for a week on the basis of anything less than a sure thing.

What could be done now, though, and probably will be done in the next few years, is to build a short-term warning system. Shock waves from a quake move only about 10 miles a minute. Computers linked to hundreds of sensors along the fault could sound the alarm in time to preserve computer records, isolate gas mains, perhaps even give people a few minutes to get away from the most vulnerable structures. Not much to work with, perhaps, but it sounds a whole lot better than waiting for Armageddon.

Evidence That Big Brother Is Still Loving, Feeling, Caring

· ·

W hat with highways crumbling, terrorists rampaging, and missile sites unhardened, there's little government money left over these days for human needs. How refreshing, then, to report that the California Legislature has managed to set aside a few nickels for the State Task Force to Promote Self-Esteem and Personal and Social Responsibility.

Sponsored by Assemblyman John Vasconcellos (formerly into "personal emotional work" at the Esalen Institute at Big Sur), the Task Force is charged with spending $245,000 to discover how self-esteem is "nurtured, harmed, rehabilitated." That may be a lot of fluff to swallow in one gulp. But Mr. Vasconcellos, a man who has "explored a lot of alternative ways of being and relating," is not a man who backs away from a challenge. Back in 1984, he suffered a heart attack. Where others might have experienced only pain and fear, Mr. Vasconcellos saw an opportunity to be and relate. He asked his friends to stop what they were doing each day and visualize themselves as little brushes scraping away the plaque in his arteries.

It didn't work—Mr. Vasconcellos was forced to resort to conventional bypass surgery. Still, the experiment was a bit like the Task Force on Self-Esteem: Trying may be its own reward.

Fast Food

. . . .

Wendy's makes the best burgers, buns down. But a lusciously greasy Wendy's Single with cheese (there's also
a Double and Triple) contains a death-defying 550 calories.
McDonald's is still champ on the thin fries front, probably because
it cooks them in artery-clogging beef tallow. Roy Rogers's Hot
Ham and Swiss is a decadent, chewy delight, with a distinctively
undelightful 1,400 milligrams of salt per six-ounce serving. Pop-
eye's Creole-Style Chicken beats homemade, but you don't even
want to guess what's in it.

Government health types recommend that roughly 43 percent of
daily calories come from complex carbohydrates (bread, potatoes,
etc.); at most, 30 percent from fats. But according to *Consumer
Reports*, your average cheeseburger-fries-shake combo runs 43 percent fat and just 23 percent complex carbos. The easier they go
down, it seems, the harder they are to live with.*

Well, not always. Consider **XIAN CHINESE EXPRESS,** a popular
take-out chain in Chicago. Xian (pronounced see-an) is the creation of Anthony Chan, a cardiologist with the dream of selling relatively cheap, tasty food that serves the body as well as the soul.
His dishes, based on family recipes, all improve upon the American
Heart Association's goals for fat, cholesterol, and sodium consump-

---

*No kidding; fun food may be taking its toll. On average, professional men and
women in their mid-30s weigh about six pounds more than they did just a decade
ago. Nobody really knows why, but here's a clue: A pint of boring old Sealtest ice
cream contains 800 calories, while trendy Häagen-Dazs contains 1,400. "We don't
hunt food anymore," one physician told *Forbes* magazine, "it hunts us."

tion.   Frying is done in corn oil, which is low in saturated fat. Only very lean cuts of meat are used; chicken skin, the part of the bird with most of the fat, is removed.   And MSG, source of sodium and throbbing temples, is never used.

The 30-dish menu contains information on calories, salt, and fat content.   Even at its best, Xian's Chinese food can't compete with the élite of New York or San Francisco's Chinatown.   But the egg rolls and almond chicken are much better than passable; the Hunan Beef merits a detour.   Actually, you may not have to detour much longer.   Xian is busily signing up franchises to bring healthy fast food to the hinterlands.

Film Noir

· ·

N̲o matter what you do, fate sticks out its foot to trip you."
These words, spoken—make that snarled—by Ann Savage in the B-movie classic *Detour*, sum up the doom-laden sensibility of the typical film noir. Sure you've got the brains and you've got the guts, it taunts, but sooner or later life will catch up to you, too.

The world of the film noir is littered with hard-boiled gumshoes, two-faced women, con artists, gangsters, and gunsels. What few decent, well-meaning folk there are can usually be bought (cheap). But even if they struggle to maintain their integrity, they don't stand a chance. They're bound to end up in a web of deceit and broken dreams. In *DOA*, Edmund O'Brien is a hard-working detective stiffed with a slow-acting poison intended for someone else. Just minutes after the film's opening, a doctor informs him of his fate. "Mister, you don't get it," he tells him flatly. "You've been murdered."

You won't find much in the way of heroism in the film noir, unless it's inadvertent: Sentimentality is for suckers. Whether guilty of corrupting himself and others, or simply as a victim of circumstances, the film noir hero is fated to take it on the chin. "Blame me," John Garfield tells his girlfriend in *Force of Evil*. "Everybody does."

This unofficial genre (first appreciated by the French, but don't hold that against it) contains some of the most transcendent movie moments of all time: Lee Marvin scalding Gloria Grahame's face with a pot of boiling coffee in *The Big Heat*; Cloris Leachman tortured to death with pliers in *Kiss Me Deadly*; Ann Savage locking her lover in a hotel room while she goes out on the town in *Detour* ("I don't like your attitude, Roberts," she tells him when he protests. "All you do is bellyache.").

How, then, to pick the best? You don't have to get it right the first time out. In fact, you'll probably have more fun if you save the best for last.

Start with *The Big Sleep* and revel in the screen's quintessential Philip Marlowe, Humphrey Bogart. Stick with Bogie for *Key Largo*, *The Maltese Falcon*, and *Dark Passage*, all classics of the genre. Less romantic, but in many ways more interesting, is the little-known *In a Lonely Place*, wherein an alienated (and weathered) Bogart plays an alcoholic Hollywood screenwriter whose neuroses may have driven him to murder.

Bogart's the ideal film noir hero. Everybody responds to his softie-with-a-brittle-veneer. John Garfield is not quite as accessible. With Garfield, you get the feeling that underneath the chip on the shoulder lies hidden an even bigger chip. See him buck the odds (and blow it) in *The Postman Always Rings Twice* and *Force of Evil*.

You can't go wrong with classics like *Double Indemnity* (worth the price of admission for Barbara Stanwyck's wig alone), *Sunset Boulevard*, or *The Third Man*. But you'll have just as much fun with such lesser-known novelties as *Lady in the Lake*, *Ride the Pink Horse*, *The Big Clock*, *Criss Cross*, *Scarlett Street*, *The Lodger*, *Hangover Square*, *Brute Force*, *Knock on Any Door*, *Ruthless*, *Cornered*, *The Mask of Demetrius*, or *Where the Sidewalk Ends*.

Having made your way down the rain-slicked, lamplit side streets, you're ready for the best film noir ever: OUT OF THE PAST (1947), featuring the greatest star in the noir pantheon, Robert Mitchum. Always languorous and vaguely threatening no matter what the role, Mitchum's world-weary manner conveys an overriding fatalism. You get the feeling life is something he can take or leave. And, as we all know, no one's more dangerous than someone with nothin' left to lose. No one, that is, except Kathie Moffat, played to double-dealing perfection by Jane Greer. Greer's Kathie may be the most cunning and carnal woman ever committed to celluloid.

The plot revolves around the romantic triangle of Kathie, hard-guy Whit (Kirk Douglas), and a private dick, Jeff Markham (Mitchum). Markham, hired to retrieve Kathie for ex-lover Whit, ends up falling for her. After successfully hiding out from Whit for months, the lovers are discovered by Jeff's former partner. When he threatens blackmail, Kathie summarily kills him. Stunned, Jeff conceals the crime, but calls it quits with Kathie. Using an assumed name, he begins a new and happy life with Nice Girl Ann—only to be unearthed by Whit, who has once again taken Kathie as his mistress. Now the plot takes another twist . . . enough. No need to derail the suspense.

Incidentally, Taylor Hackford directed a 1984 remake of *Past*, titled *Against All Odds*. Vincent Canby called it California Noir. After a look at the original, you'll probably call it a disappointment. Hackford discarded the key elements: extensive narrative flashbacks, pulp fiction imagery, shadowy lighting, Expressionist compositions and camera angles. And while the sexual confrontations are more (much more) explicit, *Against All Odds* doesn't begin to touch the sexual intensity of the original. Most damning, the plot has been softened to appeal to audiences already brain-damaged by the likes of *Rocky*.

Although not nearly so well known as *The Maltese Falcon* or *Double Indemnity*, *Out of the Past* is beloved by cinéastes, baby moguls, and the kind of devoted film freak who spends hours a day at the Titus Theater at New York's Museum of Modern Art. You might catch it on the late show. But better to see it on the big screen, sans commercials, where you can properly experience director Jacques Tourneur's poetic pessimism and Nicholas Musuraca's relentless gray-on-gray cinematography. The next best bet is a

video rental.   Or purchase your own copy for $39.95 from The
Nostalgia Merchant, 6255 Sunset Blvd.,* Suite 1019, Los Angeles,
CA 90028.

*Where else?

Fly-fishing Rod

*I*f you think fly-fishing is just an excuse to go wading, make
life miserable for a bunch of hungry trout, and then brag
about it over a six-pack, think again.

For thousands it is the platonic sport, one that demands more
coordination than strength; intelligence and intuition as well as patience. A good fly-fisherman needs to know where the fish are
likely to be and what sort of "fly," or artificial lure, is likely to
attract them. With a flick of the forearm, he or she must be able
to cast to a target 100 feet away with an absolute minimum of
disturbance to the water. Folks who are hooked on fly-fishing
think nothing of journeying to Alaska or Scotland in search of the
perfect trout stream. So it shouldn't be surprising that the sport
has spawned an enthusiasm for good equipment, and in particular,
a fascination with rods that borders on cult.

Some basics. A fly rod should be strong, flexible, and elastic.
Yet it must be light for easy maneuverability, and it must offer a
consistent feel that is individually tailored to the taste and casting
technique of the user. Inexpensive rods—less than $100—are
generally made of glass fiber. Glass is very strong. But it is less
than the ideal for elasticity or flex, and rods made of glass are
relatively heavy.

Graphite fiber, the same stuff they use for jet fighter parts,
tennis racquets, and golf clubs, now dominates the market for
medium-priced ($200–$400) rods. Graphite is feather-light and
very elastic. One brand, Sage's Graphite II (9630 N.E. Lafayette
St., Bainbridge Island, WA 98110), is often cited as the finest of

the type. But graphite isn't strong enough for the longer rods used for ocean-casting. Boron fiber, or graphite reinforced with boron, is needed for landing big fish. And in any case, the most discerning fly-casters think graphite and other synthetics lack the finesse needed for the ultimate in accuracy.

The very best rods are made from bamboo—not just any bamboo, mind you, the species "arundinaria amabilis" or "tonkin cane" from Southern Asia. Tonkin cane is not as light as graphite, but it is stronger. And it practically glows when finished with good varnish. Most important, cane imparts a very consistent, predictable feel that makes it the material of choice for expert fly-casters.

Cane rods run three to five times as much money as graphite, and for good reason. The bamboo itself is costly. But most of the expense is in the 30 to 100 hours of highly skilled labor needed to fashion a good rod from the raw bamboo. Only a dozen or so companies—really artisans' shops—make cane rods. The best come from American craftsmen.

Ask aficionados for their favorites and you're likely to hear the names Thomas and Thomas, Orvis, Winston, Howells. Collectors (rods have become investments as well as sports equipment) pay as much as $4,000 for pristine examples of the work of the late Pinky Gillum or Jim Payne. But the most skilled rodmaker working today is probably **WALT CARPENTER** (PO Box 405, Chester, NY 10908).

Carpenter's custom-made cane rods are six-sided solid core laminates bonded with modern phenolic resins to form remarkably strong units. They weigh three to five ounces, depending on the length and desired strength. Rods can be (but rarely are) constructed as single pieces. Virtually all break down to two or three sections for portability. The male-female plugs, or "ferrules," that snugly join the sections are made of "nickel-silver," an alloy of copper, nickel, and zinc.

The guides that channel the line are made from super-hard tungsten steel. The "seat" for attaching a reel can be the traditional nickel-silver, or Carpenter's own version in aluminum. The

Walt Carpenter at work on his fly-fishing rod (Courtesy of Walt Carpenter)

. . . .

grip is made from cork, cut with the grain running vertically to minimize moisture penetration.

Carpenter's best model is hand-rubbed to a deep brown with four coats of marine varnish. An extra tip (the most vulnerable piece) is included. At $1,450 perfection doesn't come cheap. Or fast: Because he works alone, expect to wait two years for your custom Carpenter rod.

An example of Marie-Claire Montanari's nude studies (Courtesy of
Marie-Claire Montanari)

. . . .

Gift for a Lover

· ·

*L*ike many professional photographers who are serious about their art, **MARIE-CLAIRE MONTANARI** specializes in studies of the female anatomy. Unlike most others, her nudes are also her clients. You could be one of them.

Montanari isn't into cheesecake. She studied under *Harper's Bazaar* photographer Lisette Model, and her work shows it. The effect is sensual but subtle. "I record the moment when a woman feels good," she explains.

Women of all ages have posed for Montanari. Sessions usually last three hours. A portfolio of five 11 x 14 prints in black and white costs between $650 and $1,000. For information, write her at 60 East 12th St., New York, NY 10003, or phone 212-473-1566.

Way to See the Grand Canyon

. . . .

*M*ost folks join the mob in Grand Canyon Village, a little patch of tourist heaven on the south rim of the canyon. The views from the rim road, leading east and west, are great. The views of the sunburned kids whining for Cokes and the pudgy guy with the "Kiss Me, I'm Albanian" T-shirt aren't.

Thrill-seekers can do better by taking the 45-minute joy ride on Grand Canyon Airways (602-638-2407). It isn't very safe, and it isn't cheap (about $50). But it is a stunner. Of course, you can also beat the crowds by viewing the canyon from the less popular lookouts on the north rim. The North Rim Lodge at Bright Angel Point (800-634-6951) offers decent rooms and fabulous vistas from the hotel patio. Better still, check out the scenery from isolated Point Sublime, accessible by a 17-mile dirt road from the north rim entrance station.

Then there's the four-legged option. One-day mule rides go down as far as Plateau Point, roughly 3,000 feet below the rim and 1,500 feet above the Colorado River. Two-day mule trips from the south rim go all the way to the bottom of the canyon and back, with an overnight stop at the Phantom Ranch cabins. Info and reservations (months in advance, please): 602-638-2401. Not recommended for those with a fear of heights or an aversion to temperature extremes.

Hardy souls can hike the seven miles (and 4,600 vertical feet) down the South Kaibab Trail, from the south rim to Phantom Ranch, then hike back up on the less arduous ten-mile Bright

Grand Canyon Dories (Courtesy of Grand Canyon Dories)
. . . .

Angel Trail. Don't even consider trying the round trip in a single day.

But if you have the time, money, and sense of adventure, don't drive or ride or walk. See the world's greatest natural wonder from the bottom up—from a boat floating down the Colorado River. About 20 companies offer river trips, providing guides, transportation, and camping supplies. Some outfitters use giant motor-powered rubber rafts which carry 20 to 25 people. These "baloney" rafts are an efficient way to cover a lot of territory, but the trip is noisy and impersonal. Wiser outfitters employ smaller, oar-powered craft. The very best, **GRAND CANYON DORIES,** uses 17-foot wooden boats to make the 277-mile voyage from Lee's Ferry to the deep green waters of Lake Mead.

John Wesley Powell, a one-armed Civil War veteran with a lust for romance, was the first Anglo to travel the length of the canyon in 1869. During 25 days on the river with eight companions and three boats, his "joy was almost ecstasy." Martin Litton, founder of Grand Canyon Dories and a passionate conservationist, seeks to give his customers a similar (though safer and more comfortable) experience.

Dory groups typically consist of 16 paying guests, four to a boat, plus a crew of seven. Extra supplies for the trip are packed on a rubber raft, which also carries two cooks. If speed were the idea, the river could be run in six or seven days. One doryman, in fact, managed it—rapids and all—in under 40 hours. But speed is anything but the name of the game. The dories dawdle the canyon in 18 days, slowing time to a child's perspective.

A typical day might go like this.

Seven A.M. (give or take a half-hour): Out of the sleeping bags to the murmur of the cooks and the smell of fresh coffee. Copious breakfast in the dawn quiet, as the sun changes the canyon walls from browns and grays to a hundred shades of orange and red. A quick rinse of plates and cutlery—the staff does the real cleanup work. Time to chat or read or wander the riverbank. Then, a few minutes to pack the boats, leaving not a scrap of evidence of human presence.

Ten A.M.: Buckle on an orange life vest and settle down for a few hours of drifting, punctuated by occasional minutes of thundering white water and 10-foot waves. The first time through the rapids is terrifying. But terror soon gives way to delight, even pride of accomplishment. The real credit, of course, goes to the immensely skilled boatmen who never lose their cool and make it all look easy.

Noon: Lunch on the narrow riverbank, shaded from fierce desert heat by a towering outcropping of black rock. The heat would be a bigger problem were it not for frequent dips of hats and T-shirts in the 55-degree water. Lunch is light—sandwiches of cheddar, smoked meats, bean sprouts grown during the trip. Maybe a chilled Coors and kid-dessert of apples and Mint Oreos. Time now for a climb to a waterfall, a naturally warm Jacuzzi cascading from the mountainside. Or perhaps a hike along a cliff to study the variety of rock formations from up close.

Three P.M.: Back on the river for an hour or two of hypnotic drift. Or a chat with boatmates; passengers rotate boats so that everyone has a chance to meet everyone else. Sprawling seating arrangements make silence a socially acceptable alternative. If the water is calm, adventurous campers may paddle alongside in inflatable kayaks.

Five P.M.: Stop for the night. Half hour of housekeeping: unloading the boats, setting up individual campsites, inflating air mattresses. Tents are available, but usually not needed. Then a quiet drink or two, watching the water run past and the light change to dusk. Dinner at sevenish—perhaps chiles rellenos and a salad, or chicken with Chinese vegetables. Time now to catch the first stars in the desert sky.

To make shorter trips possible, Grand Canyon Dories allows exits and entries at two points along the 18-day course. The middle segment probably offers the best mix of vistas, side trips, and white water. To catch the boats en route, you ride (a mule) or hike down to Phantom Ranch. After the week on the river, a helicopter lifts you out of the canyon to an isolated airstrip on the north rim. Then an hour on a chartered plane brings you back to Las Vegas. Rates run roughly $125 a day per person, with virtually everything (even sleeping bags) included. Write or phone for details, and book well in advance for a trip during the April–October season. Grand Canyon Dories, PO Box 7538, Menlo Park, CA 94026. Phone 415-854-6616.

Health Spa

· ·

*T*hese used to be dreary places, where the aching and overweight gulped foul-smelling water and wallowed in mud
baths in penance for overindulgence. Some spas still push the cu-
rative properties of sulphurous spring waters. And as Freud might
have predicted, mud is holding its own. But happily, the emphasis is shifting from masochism to the pleasanter themes of stress
reduction and body worship.

The Last-Year-at-Marienbad look is out; California Chic is in.
The white-coated quacks who prescribed upper colonics and injec-
tions of monkey gland extract have been deported to Transylvania.
In their place, enthusiastic instructors in pastel leotards explain the
delights of aerobic exercise, fiber-rich foods, and boutique cosmetics. Consider some of the more alluring options:

Eugénie Les Bains

This pleasant resort in a pleasant village near the Spanish border
has the requisite mineral spring, swimming pool, exercise classes,
and country roads for jogging. What makes it extraordinary is the
kitchen. Home of Michel Guérard's *cuisine minceur*, it is weight-
watcher heaven. Sample sweetbreads with wood mushrooms, eggs
with lobster and truffles, an ethereal apple tart—all on the 1,300-
calorie regimen. Watch it, though: Monsieur Guérard operates a
three-star restaurant on the same property, where a single night of
indiscretion could wipe out a week's good works. Write Eugénie
les Bains, 40320 Eugénie les Bains, France. Or phone 58-58-19-01.

Royal Club Evian

Probably Europe's snazziest and most expensive garden of healthy delights, located in a once-grand 19th-century resort town on the French side of Lake Geneva. Handsome sports facilities in a manicured park . . . beauty treatments ranging from marine-algae wraps to ozone steamings . . . a pretty good low-calorie restaurant . . . old-fashioned hydrotherapy featuring Evian water . . . new-fashioned computerized "rejuvenation" therapy featuring heaven knows what . . . and to keep the wallet in trim, a fully equipped casino. Write Royal Club Evian, Rive sud du Lac de Génève, 74500 Evian-les-Bains, France. Or phone 50-75-14-00. In the U.S.A.: 800-223-6800.

Canyon Ranch

The place for serious jocks who don't mind a spot of luxury on the side. This lovely desert resort at the foot of Arizona's Santa Catalina mountains offers a heavy menu of hiking, running, mountain biking, swimming, racquet ball, tennis, and weight training. For the mud-wrap set, there's a delightfully hokey "Parisian Body Polish"—massage with a mixture of body cream and crushed pearls. Canyon Ranch, by the way, is one of the few American spas where there are likely to be as many male guests as female. Write Canyon Ranch Vacation and Fitness Resort, 8600 E. Rockcliff Rd., Tucson, AZ 85715. Phone 602-749-9000.

New Age Health Farm

Wonder what happened to flower power in the era of creative selfishness? It's alive and well, and moved to the Catskills. New Age, set on 155 acres of meadow and woodland, is a touch short on creature comforts but long on spiritual awareness. Yoga, organic veggies, meditation, all-natural cosmetics—the whole holistic bit, offered with flair and disarming sincerity. Medically super-

Rancho La Puerta (Courtesy of Rancho La Puerta)
. . . .

vised, all-juice fasting for those in a hurry to harmonize this year's body with last year's swimsuit. Write New Age Health Farm, Neversink, NY 12765. Phone 914-985-2221.

La Costa

The health spa for people who aren't sure they want to be at a health spa. This glitzy resort, sprawling over 1,000 acres of suburban San Diego, features 36 holes of golf, 23 tennis courts, five swimming pools, every conceivable exercise machine with trainer attached, a movie theater, and live Las Vegas–style entertainment. If you're serious about losing weight, the spa cuisine awaits. If not, you'll have no difficulty tracking down the lobster and Dom Pérignon. Write La Costa Hotel and Spa, Costa Del Mar Rd., Carlsbad, CA 92008. Phone 800-542-6200.

The Greenhouse

With three staff members for each of the 39 guests in the mansion (women only), this place offers the ultimate in pampering. Float your way through the week of breakfast in bed, water exercises, massage, loofah baths, hot oil manicures, fashion shows, and advanced courses in skin care and makeup. Top it off with a shopping blowout at Neiman-Marcus in Dallas, round-trip—did you doubt?—by limousine. Write The Greenhouse Spa, PO Box 1144, Arlington, TX 76010, or phone 817-640-4000.

The Golden Door

Easily the prettiest, most fashionable, and (next to The Greenhouse) the most luxurious of American spas. A visit to this 177-acre Japanese-style oasis of calm is an annual ritual for overweight movie moguls and overwrought Palos Verdes socialites. Lots of exercise under the polite bullying of a very well-trained staff. Light, healthy food. And plenty of time to do absolutely nothing,

beside the pool. Most of the year, it's reserved for men or women only; total capacity is just 35. But The Door has recently advanced to couples. Write The Golden Door, PO Box 1567, Escondido, CA 92925, or phone 619-744-5777.

Rancho La Puerta

No spa, though, is the equal of **RANCHO LA PUERTA** in Tecate, Mexico, just across the border from San Diego. This understated desert resort can't match the diversions of La Costa, the womb-like comfort of The Greenhouse, or the drop-dead chic of The Golden Door. But the handsome guest houses, pools, and courts set amid 150 acres of lush gardens radiate serenity and good taste.

Mucho opportunity for rigorous exercise here: swimming, tennis, volleyball, running, weight training, aerobics, boot camp hikes over mountainous terrain. Or, if one were so inclined, the day could be entirely filled with massages, hot tubbings, manicures, pedicures, and herbal wraps. This is a resort for adults. Every activity is voluntary, and there's no cruise director to keep score.

Most of the 100-or-so guests at Rancho La Puerta hope to lose weight, and most do take off four or five pounds in a week. The food is vegetarian, tasty, filling, and faintly Mexican. Signs in the dining room suggest the portions for a 1,000-calorie diet. But traditional American breakfasts are available on request, as are rice, bread, and butter at lunch and dinner. Some guests even bring wine.

Entertainment? Conversation, video movies, books, the view of the stars in the smogless desert.

Prices run from $1,000 to $2,000 per week. All accommodations are in private cottages. The resort provides transportation for the 45-minute trip from the San Diego Airport. Write the reservations office at Rancho La Puerta, 3085 Reynard Way, San Diego, CA 92103. Or phone 619-478-5341. And try to plan ahead: The place is usually booked three months in advance.

Hospital

· ·

*T*wenty or thirty years ago, when physicians were gods and hospitals their temples, the pecking order was simple. Hospitals serving the faculties of the Olympian medical schools had a virtual monopoly on top talent and technology. Everybody else settled for what the deities sent their way.

But something democratic has happened on the way to lithon-tripters and positron emission tomography. The old-line teaching hospitals are still among the best. However, as medicine has grown more expensive, it has grown dependent on Washington to finance the experimental, high-tech procedures. Lobbyists now hustle for hospital and med school grants the way they scrap over defense contracts. And, no surprise, the blue chip medical centers of the Northeast and Midwest have had to share the wealth and glory with Sun Belt upstarts.

The other big change in medicine is the drive for specialization. Practice makes perfect, even where procedures have almost be-come commonplace. A hospital with 200 coronary bypass cases each year is likely to achieve a higher survival rate than a hospital performing the surgery on 20 patients. What's more, it is likely to manage the job for less money. So patients (and insurers) are sometimes better off sacrificing Dr. Kildare–style personalized care for the statistical success of the assembly line.

Begin with an abbreviated list of the specialists, the places where you are most likely to be treated by men and machines on the leading edge of the technology:

Experimental Cancer Treatment: National Cancer Institute, National Institutes of Health, Bethesda, MD; Biotherapeutics, Inc., Franklin, TN.

Childhood Leukemia: Sidney Farber Cancer Institute, Boston, MA.

Kidney Stone Treatment: Baylor College of Medicine and Hospitals, Houston, TX.

High-Risk Pregnancy: Brigham and Women's Hospital, Boston, MA.

Blood Diseases: University of Minnesota Hospitals and Clinics, Minneapolis, MN.

Allergy and Immunology: University of California—Davis Medical Center, Sacramento, CA.

Liver Transplants: University Health Center, Pittsburgh, PA.

Heart Transplants: Stanford University Medical Center, Stanford, CA.

Pancreas Transplants: University of Minnesota Hospitals and Clinics, Minneapolis, MN.

Bone Marrow Transplants: University of Washington Affiliated Hospitals, Seattle, WA.

Pediatric Surgery: Children's Hospital of Philadelphia, Philadelphia, PA.

Vascular Surgery: New York University Medical Center, New York, NY.

AIDS: University of California—Los Angeles, Los Angeles, CA.

Diabetes: Joslin Clinic, Boston, MA.

Chronic Pain: Comprehensive Pain Center, University of Miami Affiliated Hospitals, Miami, FL.

Rehabilitation: Howard Rusk Institute for Rehabilitation Medicine, New York, NY.

For all the specialization, there are still some hospitals where you can hardly go wrong in any department. The University of Alabama Medical Center in Birmingham runs the gamut from the genetic cloning of tumor-specific antibodies to pediatric cardiology to arthritis rehabilitation. Johns Hopkins Hospital in Baltimore ranks near the top in internal medicine, neurosurgery, pulmonary medicine, and gastroenterology. Massachusetts General in Boston is the primary teaching center for the Harvard Medical School, and probably the most prolific producer of new technology in diagnostic medicine, burn care, and surgery.

But for breadth and depth, the MAYO CLINIC is probably without peer. The Clinic, part of the Mayo Graduate School of Medicine in Rochester, Minnesota, is deservedly famous as a diagnostic center, one of the few places where 200 specialists are within practical reach. It is also an élite treatment center, providing everything from sound-wave destruction of kidney stones to transplants for the nerve-deaf to radiation treatment after cancer surgery. And it has an enormous research commitment, offering patients the bonus of being where great technology is born.

Admissions to Mayo and the choice treatment centers are by physician referral. Don't assume, however, that your family doctor will automatically direct you to the best. Inertia—or ignorance—may leave you stranded in a second-rate facility. For an exhaustive list of the best hospitals by specialty and state, see *The Best in Medicine* by Herbert Dietrich and Virginia Biddle (Harmony Books, 1986).

THE BEST
Hotel
. . . .

*O*nce upon a time, grand hotels really were grand. Writers from Proust to Hemingway soaked up their best material at the Ritz bar. The fate of Eastern Europe was periodically decided over schnapps at The Adlon in Berlin. The exiled younger sons of British dukes dreamed opium dreams of cricket triumphs and former mistresses under the ceiling fans of Raffles. Everywhere the rich chose to dawdle, there were servants in profusion to unpack steamer trunks, plump feather pillows, and walk Pekingese.

Today, it is hard to find a hotel that offers a decent quail egg, or even a hall porter who understands the difference between black and white tie. But there are compensations. Hundreds of hotels reliably provide the bourgeois basics: fast service, new mattresses, silent air conditioning, decent food, a convenient place to jog. Dozens manage all that with understated style—the real luxury in an era in which everything serviceable, from nouvelle cuisine to local television news shows, is quickly cloned.

Europe still has a disproportionate share of these special urban retreats. London shines with The Dorchester, gussied up in pale shades of silk. The Connaught remains the distinguished city home for country gentlemen. The Berkeley, shunned by snobs as nouveau, is one of the nicest modern hotels anywhere. At Claridge's, royalty is still treated royally. You may not be so fortunate.

Paris has many good hotels and two great ones: the sleek, always up-to-date Plaza Athénée and, *évidement*, The Ritz, an island of calm on the busy Place Vendôme that simply envelops guests in service. Vienna has The Imperial, roccoco opulence worthy of courtiers to Franz Josef. The Hassler in Rome, at the top of the Spanish steps, is a well-oiled machine of luxury. The Gritti Palace in Venice, a 16th-century palazzo on the Grand Canal, is a legend. The legend, alas, suffers from the hint of indifference that comes from serving too many one-time visitors.

America, once thought too innocent, too democratic, and in too much of a hurry to care about sophisticated luxury, is doing better these days. New York has always had The Pierre and The Carlyle. Now it has two hotels that are better: The Mayfair Regent and an Americanized version of The Plaza Athénée. Chicago's Ritz-Carlton is modern and cheerfully efficient. Dallas boasts of two winners. The Fairmont maintains a level of service almost inconceivable in an American hotel with 600 rooms. The much smaller Mansion on Turtle Creek is luxury, Texas-style—one part Louis XIV, two parts down-home comfort.

The Rodeo Drive crowd may debate the relative merits of The Beverly Wilshire and The Beverly Hills. Those who don't like crowds prefer the Four Seasons. Business travellers to San Francisco are hooked on the effortless efficiency of The Stanford Court. We'd opt for The Four Seasons-Clift, with its palatial rooms and knockout bar in the lobby.

Visitors to Asia are often struck by the gaudy overkill of the new luxe hotels—The Shangri-la in Singapore, for example, or The Hilton in Seoul. But there are still some super places to choose among. Tokyo has The Okura and The Imperial. Both are a shade impersonal, but both provide service that belies their immense size.

The Hong Kong Regent, often cited as Asia's best hotel, is a monument to Chinese entrepreneurship and adaptability. The Peninsula, across the bay in Kowloon, is the last bastion of British colonial elegance. Unfortunately, The Strand in Rangoon is a threadbare ruin. Forget Raffles in Singapore: all that remains is the name, a few scruffy palm trees in the courtyard, and Churchill's picture over the bar. Stay instead at The Goodwood Park, a splendidly kept colonial establishment that is the second home of East Asia's oil potentate, the Sultan of Brunei. Or follow the example of Somerset Maugham and savor the bustle of Bangkok river life from the veranda of The Oriental.

Yet for all their splendor and efficiency, these great hotels lack one crucial ingredient: a sense of romance, a hint of adventure. The Oustau de Baumanière, a converted 400-year-old olive mill in the shadow of the medieval ruin of Les Baux in southern France, fits the category. So does The Ram Bagh Palace Hotel in Jaipur, India, a former Maharajah's palace with drop-dead formal gardens and a fabulous indoor pool. So, too, does Peponi's, a white-washed, Bogart-style backwater in Lamu, on Kenya's steaming tropical coast. But our favorite is **THE TAWARAYA** in Kyoto, Japan's foremost traditional inn and a shimmering monument to Japanese culture and hospitality.

Founded by a textile merchant named Wasuke Okazaki, management of the tiny "ryokan" has remained in the same family for almost 300 years. The building was damaged by fire in 1788 and again in 1864, but has been lovingly restored. Happily, important concessions have been made to modern convenience: The plumbing, heating, telephones, and central air conditioning work very well. But the current owner, Mrs. Toshi Okazaki Sato, is devoted to maintaining a sense of continuity.

A first impression of The Tawaraya is the Zen simplicity of the tiny stone lobby leading to an interior courtyard in subtly contrasting greens of moss and maple. Guest suites—virtually empty rooms in light wood, partitioned with delicately patterned shoji screens—have floor-to-ceiling windows overlooking the gardens. The futons, assembled each evening and whisked away in the morning, are so comfortable that one forgets why Westerners sleep on mattresses. Each of the 19 suites has a private bathroom plus a Japanese bath made from fragrant cedar.

Service is beyond impressive: Clothing is quickly folded and stored out of sight; giant, fluffy towels are changed after each use;

freshly pressed kimonos and hot tea await each time you return from a foray into the ancient city. Traditional Japanese breakfasts (salted salmon, rice, pickled veggies, bean soup . . . it grows on you) and dinners are choreographed by your own servant.

Robert Oppenheimer, Stephen Sondheim, Jean-Paul Sartre, Isaac Stern, Yoko Ono, Willem de Kooning, Walter Cronkite, Alfred Hitchcock, and the King of Sweden have stayed at The Tawaraya. If you choose to pay the price (figure $500 a day for two with meals) and reserve early enough, you could, too. Write The Tawaraya, Fuyacho, Oike-Sagaru, Nakagyo-Ku, Kyoto 604, Japan. Telex: 5423-273.

THE BEST
Ice Cream
. . . .

*S*ome ground rules. By ice cream, we mean ice cream, not the ambrosial gelato that is the center of civilized life in Italy. This may be an arbitrary distinction—gelato and American ice cream are made from similar ingredients. But it is a necessary distinction if we are to maintain even the pretense of suspense. For everyone who has tasted it knows that Fiocci di Neve in Rome (51 Via Pantheon) makes the best frozen dessert, bar none. This precious substance, which bears the same name as the shop (translation: snowflake) is rather rich, lightly sweetened, and flavored solely by its primary ingredients: cream and eggs.*

Back to cold, hard (and excessively sweet) reality. Mass-produced ice cream has come a long way from Howard Johnson's and Baskin and Robbins. The first big improvement was the rediscovery of heavy cream: ordinary brands contain 10 percent butterfat, the legal minimum to be entitled to the generic name ice cream. Now every freezer case is chock full of "super premium" brands containing at least 16 percent butterfat; Bassett's, the pride of Philadelphia, boasts of 18 percent. Add any more fat, by the way, and the product develops a not altogether pleasant greasy-crumbly texture.

Next, ice cream makers focused on "overrun," a measure of how much the volume of the finished product has been increased

---

*Fiocci di Neve also makes a series of gelato flavors with rice mixed in. That's right, rice—it's really no more radical than crushing Reese's Pieces into Steve's vanilla. The rice adds texture, producing a delightful cross between ice cream and rice pudding.

by the incorporation of air. Breyer's, typical of better supermarket brands, has always had a 90 percent overrun, meaning it contains 47 percent air. Sealtest, a tad downscale, has 100 percent overrun, or 50 percent air.

Now, air has an honorable role to play as an ingredient in ice cream. It makes the stuff easier to scoop when very cold. More important, it gives ice cream a fluffy consistency; many discriminating foodies consider a 50 percent overrun to be ideal. But try telling that to the folks who market ice cream. Low overrun has worked wonders for sales of Häagen-Dazs (the Scandinavian ice cream made from a secret Bronx recipe). Competitors like Frusen Glädjé (the Scandinavian ice cream made from a secret New Jersey recipe) and Ben and Jerry's have chosen to match Häagen-Dazs with a minimal 20 percent overrun in a 16 percent butterfat product. The result is very dense and very rich—typically more than 1,100 calories a pint.

There is more to good ice cream, though, than butterfat and air. Freshness is critical, for both the texture and taste of ice cream deteriorate if it is stored for very long. This explains why vanilla ice cream made at home with cream, eggs, sugar, and bottled vanilla flavoring straight from the supermarket can be so delicious. And it is a key to success for many local ice cream stores. The University Creamery in State College, Pennsylvania, for example, sells an otherwise ordinary ice cream (14 percent butterfat, 80 percent overrun) that is exceptionally tasty because it is never more than a few days old.

Last, but far from least, is flavoring. Makers of virtually all the high fat super premiums avoid artificial anything. But compared to proper Italian gelato, the final product is bland and unsubtle. That reflects marketing strategy, not lack of skill or an attempt to save money on ingredients. For, while much of it is eaten by adults, ice cream is still sold as kid food—cool, sugary stuff meant to reawaken comforting memories of life before the onset of mortgage payments and lower back pain.

Happily, a handful of local ice creameries aim at more sophisticated palates. Neal's, with stores in both Houston and Waco, makes an intense chocolate named after the great Roman gelateria, Tre Scalini. Fono's, in Palo Alto, California, comes close to reproducing a good gelato. Robin Rose, a chain in southern California, gets fine results by adding liquors and puréed fruit to good ice cream bases. Toscanini's in Cambridge, Massachusetts (the city with the highest per capita consumption of ice cream in the country), produces a killer white chocolate flavor. But the most distinctive ice creams are made by NEW YORK ICE, in New York City.

New York Ice started doing business in 1980, with tart fruit ices reminiscent of the great sorbets from Berthillon in Paris. Two years later, the company expanded into ice cream. Most flavors are 16 percent butterfat, but "feel" considerably lighter in the mouth because they average a 40 to 50 percent overrun. What makes New York Ice so special is its flavors: zabaglione, espresso, rum raisin, a superbly subtle vanilla. Best of all are the baci, a mild chocolate with hazelnuts, and the crème caramel, real caramel ice cream with chunks of freshly made pecan praline. New York Ice is available for retail licking at Paradice, 444 West 43rd Street, near 10th Avenue.

Investment Adviser

. . . .

Ralph, your know-it-all brother-in-law, rode a stock called BioPharmoGenetics all the way from 2⅜ to 16. When you broke down and purchased 1,000 shares, the Food and Drug Administration announced that BioP's cure for hay fever caused varicose veins in laboratory mice. . . .

Cousin Millie's broker, the one who called the big turn in interest rates in 1979, was crazy about distillery shares. Now everybody has switched to Perrier with a twist, liquor stocks are on the rocks, and Millie's broker has moved to Fort Lauderdale. Doesn't anybody really know about investing?

Lots of people do. The only catch is that the ones who know this year probably won't know next year. Most investment advisory services build a following by hammering at simple, dramatic themes: "Buy gold before the coming monetary crisis," or "The future is in Asia," or "The planet is running out of energy." When gold (or Asia or oil) gets hot, the services offer wise interviews to *The Wall Street Journal*, and the sheep flock for shearing.

Once assembled, moreover, the flocks are remarkably loyal. Investors, like other gamblers, prefer to remember the winners and forget the losers. Newsletter writers oblige by bragging about the glory days and hedging their current advice by keeping it as unspecific as possible.

That is where the *Hulbert Financial Digest* fits in. It, too, is a newsletter. But rather than following stocks, bonds, or pork bellies, Mark Hulbert keeps track of 80 investment services, rigorously tracking their performance since 1980. Where the advice is vague, Hulbert does his best to tailor a portfolio to the spirit of the prose.

As of April 1986, the most successful newsletter over the previous six years was *The Prudent Speculator* (PO Box 1767, Santa Monica, CA 90406; $150 a year). If you had used the service since July 1980, reinvesting all earnings, you could have turned $10,000 into $71,940.* That works out to an average annual return of 40 percent, or nearly triple the return that you would have earned by investing in the broad range of stocks tracked by Standard and Poor's 500 index.

Another service, however, may prove as appealing over the long haul. *The Growth Stock Outlook* (PO Box 15381, Chevy Chase, MD 20815; $175 a year) has managed an average return of 24 percent by following the fundamentalist, look-for-underlying-value technique they teach in business schools. And unlike *The Prudent Speculator, The Growth Stock Outlook* seems to be a consistent money maker in all sorts of markets: No single year's advice in the six examined by Hulbert was a loser.

Our own favorite is yet another advisory service, THE VALUE LINE INVESTMENT SURVEY. This venerable weekly ranks some 2,000 stocks in five categories, from most to least timely to own. Ratings are based on what some experts call an "earnings momentum" model, where a stock's growth in earnings is compared to the market in general.

Value Line's system strikes the B-school types as simplistic. But the proof is in the numbers: *Value Line*'s top-category stocks have done well over the six-year period, chalking up a compounded annual return of 26 percent. Much more important, "category I" stocks have been doing very well for a very long time. If you had

---

*The least successful, by the way, was *The Granville Market Letter*, whose reverse alchemy would have transformed $10,000 into $5,470 in the five years between July 1980 and July 1985.

started with $10,000 in 1965 and consistently followed *Value Line*'s advice, you would have had $547,600 to your name by the middle of 1985!

At $495 a year, *Value Line* isn't cheap.   But you can try it out for 10 weeks for a mere $60.   Write to *Value Line* at 711 Third Avenue, New York, NY 10017, or phone 800-633-2252, extension 281.

Kitchen Knife

. . . .

*P*icking good kitchen knives is simple—and would be simpler still if food snobs stopped parroting one another's outdated advice. The basics:

The Blade

The best-selling knives are made from low-carbon stainless steel. They look good, require little care, and can be had for a song. The only catch: They don't hold an edge very well and are a bear to sharpen. Two weeks after you've brought them home, they're next to useless. Equally cheap, high-carbon steel knives do hold an edge. They remain the standard in restaurant kitchens, where quality tools at minimum price are just what the chef ordered. But ordinary high-carbon steel must be stored dry to prevent rust. And no matter how carefully they are handled, the knives quickly tarnish gray-black.

That's why most knowledgeable foodies treat themselves to the small luxury of high-carbon stainless knives. High-carbon stainless looks good, and though a bit harder to keep sharp than ordinary high-carbon steel, holds an edge equally well. You can't tell the difference between high- and low-carbon stainless simply by look-ing. But cutlery makers aren't diffident: If the label doesn't say high-carbon, it probably isn't.

The Handle

Handles on all good knives used to be made of wood, with three rivets showing to prove the metal "tang" extended the full length.

But wood isn't particularly durable. It can be ruined in weeks if—heaven forbid—you run knives through the dishwasher. Today, some of the best brands come with handles made from slip-resistant, heat-resistant polypropylene plastic. One reputable manufacturer, Gerber, uses an odd but functional aluminum handle coated with epoxy resin.

As for the "full" tang with triple rivet—forget it. The handles on all good knives are built to stay attached to the blade. If knives are in other respects equal, pick the handle that feels best in your palm.

The Balance

One reason some knives feel better in the hand than others is weight distribution. Some manufacturers tinker with the balance by adding weights to the handles of long-bladed knives. This can make a difference, particularly with knives for dicing and mincing. But so can the design of the handle; cut before you buy.

The Grind

"Hollow ground" blades are thinnest at the business edge, and therefore are good for slicing; they also take the sharpest edge. "Saber ground" blades are thickest, and thus best (sturdiest) for chopping. You need both kinds for kitchen work, and perhaps a compromise "taper ground" blade for cutting crisp veggies. Most manufacturers don't bother to specify the grind; but, chances are, they'll match the design to the function of the knife.

Which to buy? Virtually all knives made from high-carbon stainless are better than okay. One reasonable strategy is simply to pick the cheapest high-carbon stainless line that feels good and looks rugged. Two relatively inexpensive brands, Chicago Cutlery and Alfred Zanger, fit this category, but so do many anonymous imports. If you're prepared to pay considerably more for good looks and the guarantee of high quality, go for one of these name-brands: Gerber, Henckels, Marks, or Wusthof. Better yet, wait for a sale: All these well-made but overpriced lines have factory-supported markdowns a couple of times each year.

At bare minimum, a set should include one paring knife with a three- or four-inch blade, one slicing and dicing knife with a six-inch blade, a six-inch boning knife with a heavy, narrow blade, and a 10-inch carving knife. Figure on spending $125, or as little as a third that much for generic brands.

It is nice to add a matching serrated blade for cutting bread. But if money is an issue, any old $4 hardware store version will do just as well. Invest the savings in a foolproof sharpening machine (see "The Best Knife Sharpener").

Knife Sharpener

. . . .

According to the U.S. Census Bureau, the average American family owns 3.4 knife sharpeners, none of which works.

Only kidding. The Census Bureau has yet to take the issue of dull knives as seriously as it ought. But if it did, the results of the survey would not be in doubt. The drawers of American kitchens are cluttered with discarded gadgets guaranteed to restore a razor edge every time. ("If not completely satisfied, simply mail to our customer representative in Oaugadoughou for a full refund . . .")

In theory, knife sharpening should be child's play: Rub a blade against a harder surface and bits of steel will wear off, creating a sharper edge. Sharpeners made from heat-treated steel alloys and ceramics are most common, but even a smooth piece of quartz rock or the back of a bone-china plate will do. It turns out, though, that hardly anyone has the patience, light touch, and steady wrist to draw the blade across the sharpening surface at a consistent angle for a long enough time.

Enter the CHEF'S CHOICE DIAMOND HONE SHARPENER, creation of a Delaware company called Edgecraft. The little electric counter-top machine has three sets of slots that guide a knife blade against rotating stones covered with diamond dust. Slowly drawing the blade through the first set reshapes the cutting edge, removing burrs and nicks. Repeating the process with the second set of slots grinds the edge on a finer surface. The third set of slots guides the edge against a yet-finer surface, finishing the job.

At $80, the Chef's Choice is no small investment. Still, why bother paying as much or more for fancy knives if you don't plan to keep them sharp?

THE BEST
Kosher Wine

. . . .

*E*verybody knows that kosher wines are sweet, syrupy concoctions that taste like Welch's Grape Juice laced with essence of old inner tube. Everybody used to be right. The wines
drunk by Americans who honored Jewish dietary restrictions were
typically fermented from Concord grapes, a fruit whose only
known virtue is that it can survive the long, frigid winters of
northern New York State. Concord wines are undrinkable unless
they are heavily sugared to mask the characteristic "foxy" taste.
Even with a good dose of sucrose, they are pretty terrible.

But nothing in religious law says that kosher wines must be
cloyingly sweet or concocted from inferior grapes. The only requirement is that each person who touches the grapes or the wine
before it is bottled must be an observant Orthodox Jew. The
Concord connection dates from Prohibition, when only sacramen-
tal wines were legal and the only grape varieties available were
sweet eating grapes.

Before World War II, European Jews drank high-quality red
and white wines made from standard European wine grapes. Pro-
ducers usually met the koshering rules by leasing portions of existing vineyards, plus the necessary equipment. Now, with the rise
of a new class of affluent, worldly, yet religious Jews in the United
States, quality kosher wines are coming back.

Two tiny California wineries, Hagafen Cellars in Napa and
Weinstock Cellars in Sonoma, are producing decent varietals from
chardonnay, sauvignon blanc, and Johannisberg riesling grapes.
Weinstock even markets a white zinfandel, a medium-dry, pink

"blushing" wine that looks great and tastes pretty good.

From Bordeaux comes Château Le Pin, a B-plus dry red. From Hungary, there's the Egri brand Cabernet Sauvignon, an earthy wine resembling a pleasant Spanish rioja. One Italian shipper, Bartenura, is exporting a light Valpolicella and a Soave. But fittingly, the very best of the new kosher wines are Israeli.

THE YARDEN WINERY is located on the Golan Heights, on territory captured from Syria during the 1967 war. Until the late 1970s, the land was used by eight cooperatives to grow fruit—mostly apples. Then, at the suggestion of a visiting American wine expert, the co-ops started experimenting with wine grapes on the cool, misty plateau. With financial backing from the government, they hired a winemaker and a consultant from the University of California and imported equipment from Italy and France. Shimshon Welner, the Israeli manager, lugged 10 cases of the 1983 vintage Sauvignon Blanc to America for critical tastings. The rest is history.

Yarden Sauvignon Blanc, sold almost exclusively in America, is delightfully fruity, with enough acid to cut the relatively high sugar content. Compared to California, Italian, and French wines in the $10-a-bottle class, Yarden may not be a bargain. But it is excellent wine by any standard, and by far the best kosher wine now available. Two other Yarden wines are worth a try, too. The Cabernet Blanc, a rosé made from red wine grapes, is tart and refreshing. The Muscato d'Gamla is a very sweet wine comparable to dessert wines from Italy and Hungary.

Light Beer

. . . .

Y our standard brew, be it Beck's or Bud or Ballantine, contains about 150 calories per 12-ounce bottle. Good German
bock, a dark, malty, high-alcohol beer, contains double the calories. Yet makers of "light" beer claim fewer than 100 calories.
How do they manage?

Some do it the easy way, diluting ordinary medium-calorie beer
with no-calorie tap water. If you're already plastered, or happen
to be deeply engrossed in a discussion of Marx's concept of surplus value with the blonde on the adjacent stool, such watery
brew may suffice. But thanks to modern science and the relentless drive for profit in the beverage industry, better light beers are
now available.

All beer contains alcohol, carbon dioxide bubbles, flavorings, and
a bit of malted grain left over from the fermentation process.
Virtually all the calories come from the alcohol and the malt residue, which contains a little protein and a lot of carbohydrates. So
it's a matter of arithmetic: To cut the calories you have to cut the
alcohol or cut the malt.

In regular beer, fermentation stops when the little yeast bugs
run out of digestible food in the malt. By adding an enzyme discovered by a Danish high-tech firm in the 1970s, the indigestible
dextrins in the malt are transformed into digestible sugars, allowing virtually all the carbohydrates in the malt to be converted to
alcohol and carbon dioxide. The brewer then adds a dollop of
water to dilute the extra alcohol, ending up with a mix that contains about 100 calories, virtually all of which come from the alco-

hol. To make "superlight" beers, the sort with just 70 to 80 calories a bottle, still more water is added.

Light beers made this way have less body than ordinary beer because they contain little or no malt residue. Much of the art of making low-carbohydrate beer, then, is to use ingredients that fool the mouth and nose into tasting what is no longer there in ordinary quantities.

Few brewers, it seems, are artists. Many low-carbo beers—Miller Lite for example—taste like a mix of ordinary beer and club soda, even though they aren't. But this may be more a triumph of marketing than a failing of brewer's skill. When Miller popularized light beer in the 1970s, it created a whole new market. Lots of light beer converts actually prefer washed-out beer because they never liked the flavor of beer in the first place. Lots of other drinkers operate on an implicit pain-pleasure principle: If it tastes too good, it must be bad for you.

Sample around, though, and you will find a few low-carbo brands with character. Among the domestics, Heileman's Light and Stroh Light are worth a sip. Both are nicely balanced beers in the American style, as tasty as the blander, more calorific brands like Budweiser and Schlitz. Among the imports, Amstel Light, a Dutch brand made by Heineken, is good. Nordic Wolf and Molson Light are even better.

If Molson doesn't satisfy, consider a light beer that sacrifices some of the alcohol rather than most of the malt. The big brewers make reduced-alcohol beers crafted along the lines of the "near-beers" sold in states that never got over Prohibition. Unfortunately, each is blander than the next. But one little company, Grant's Brewery in Yakima, Washington, does make a delicious, full-bodied beer with 2 percent alcohol and about 100 calories per 12-ounce mug. **GRANT'S CELTIC ALE** is made entirely from barley malt to give it a tangy flavor and deep copper color. Like true English ales, it is top-fermented at high temperature with a lot of locally grown hops, briefly aged, and delivered to bars and restaurants unpasteurized. Which brings up the only catch: Celtic Ale is currently available only in the Seattle area.

P.S. All bottled beers deteriorate with age and exposure to heat; low-carbohydrate beers are especially sensitive. So a very fresh bottle of a mediocre brand is generally better than a poorly preserved bottle of the best. Buy beer from stores with lots of turnover. And when you have the option, choose bottles from the refrigerator case.

THE BEST
Managed Company
· ·

*T*he giants in the high-profile glamour industries get most of
the attention—companies like:

Royal Dutch Shell, the British-Dutch-American behemoth that has no
peer in its ability to find oil and develop reserves;

Sony, the electronics maverick that combines the best of Japanese
manufacturing and marketing skills with an American sensibility
for gadgets;

Wal-Mart, America's most profitable discount retailer, in a business
crowded with savvy, cutthroat operators;

Schlumberger, the super-lean multinational that over the last few decades has led the world in petroleum engineering technology—not
to mention return on invested capital;

Hyundai, an amazingly efficient producer of everything from computer chips to compact cars to ocean-going tankers, and a perfect
symbol of South Korea's economic renaissance;

Swissair, the private European airline that goes head-to-head with
subsidized, state-owned carriers and makes money every time;

Gannett, the American media conglomerate that gave new life to
small-town newspapers by cutting costs, often without cutting
quality; and

IBM, no longer Numero Uno in every niche of the computer and office-equipment business, but still the player to beat in every new game in town.

Our own choice, though, is **NUCOR,** an American company that prospers in the least glamorous and least profitable of industries, steel. The secret behind the Nucor miracle: A revolutionary combo of ascetic, hands-on management, a compulsion to lead in technology, and an innovative labor policy that might have been inspired by Charles Darwin.

By all the usual measures, Big Steel is in a hopeless position. Productive capacity exploded in the 1960s and '70s, as every newly independent country with an airline and a Coca-Cola bottler rushed to join the club of steelmakers. Meanwhile, the demand for steel stagnated as manufacturers discovered cheaper or lighter substitutes. Aging plants in Europe, America—even Japan—have been scrapped, and the bloodletting is sure to go on for another decade. How, then, can Nucor consistently turn a profit in the most fiercely competitive of national steel markets?

Begin with technology. Nucor's founder and chief executive, F. Kenneth Iverson, refuses to go head-to-head with the big, integrated iron and steel makers like USX, Bethlehem, and Nippon. Nucor makes only a limited number of steel products in small mills, using relatively cheap electric furnaces. That permits Iverson to buy completely new technology every 10 years, half the average life for steelmakers' equipment. By no coincidence, Nucor's "minimills" are as modern as the newest plants in South Korea and Brazil.

Most American and European steel companies are locked into high-wage contracts and union-negotiated work rules. Nucor has avoided serious confrontation with the steel unions by siting its plants in places like Darlington, South Carolina, and Jewett, Texas, where organized labor is viewed with great suspicion. But engineer Iverson is no union-baiting ideologue; he knows there's more to high productivity than holding organized labor at bay. Iverson uses a startlingly direct blend of carrot and stick to get the most from his work force.

The base wage at Nucor averages a subsistence-level six dollars an hour. But employees can add twice that much in incentive pay to their take-home if their production "teams" work to full capacity. In Japan, the team concept is used to apply group pressure to perform. Iverson takes the idea a step further: A worker gets just four "forgiveness" days a year. Any absenteeism or lateness beyond that number, for any reason including illness, and the individual forfeits a full week's incentive pay.

This survival-of-the-fittest system isn't easy on employees, particularly older employees. But it sure gets the job done: Nucor averages about 800 tons of steel annually per worker, comparable to Japanese productivity. Average pay in a good year exceeds $30,000—a quarter more than unionized steel workers receive in the Rust Belt, and roughly double the industrial wage in Nucor's little mill towns.

Modern plants and motivated workers are just two parts of the Nucor formula. In fact, the first two probably wouldn't be possible without the third: committed management.

No bureaucracy stands between executives and the shop floor. Nucor's entire corporate staff consists of 16 people. Secretaries are scarce; perks like executive dining rooms and first-class air travel, nonexistent. Every Nucor employee, including Iverson, receives the same number of vacation days. And white-collar compensation is locked to corporate performance. Executives earn incentive pay only if profits exceed a target return on capital. In 1983, the target was missed and the chief executive of America's ninth-largest steel company took home just $106,000.

Is Nucor the model for the revitalization of ailing Western industry? Heavy investment in technology . . . smart, flexible management . . . a ferocious work ethic, practiced from the top down. . . . One could imagine worse.

Market for Prune Juice

. . . .

According to Selling Areas-Marketing, a subsidiary of Time Inc. that advises companies on where to focus their sales effort, Miami is the prune capital of the hemisphere.

That makes sense, as does the special appeal of roach spray in New York and Houston, and the popularity of candy bars in alcohol-free, caffeine-free Salt Lake City. But why is Savannah the best market for meat tenderizers? Atlanta for antacids? Indianapolis for shoe polish? Portland for dry cat food? Seattle for toothbrushes? Philadelphia for iced tea? Grand Rapids for rat poison? Dallas for popcorn?

These, and other mysteries, solved at eleven. . . .

Motorcycle Gang

. . . .

C onfess. You like the studded-leather look, but would turn
to jelly at the first sight of a switchblade. You enjoy an
occasional chug of beer, but always call a taxi if you're having
more than one. You'd get a kick from the throaty purr of a giant
engine between your legs, but have no interest in discovering what
it feels like to go 110 on the Santa Monica Freeway. Don't hide
your ambivalence—flaunt it! Join the GOLD WING ROAD RIDERS
ASSOCIATION, the motorcycle gang for folks who care too much
to risk the very best.

The Gold Wing is a motorcycle made by Honda. Not just any
motorcycle, mind you: the most powerful (1200cc), gadget-
bedecked (even a trip computer), and expensive (figure $11,000)
touring cycle available. Introduced in 1975, the bike was targeted
to an older, richer audience that liked a bit of comfort with its
thrills. This easiest of riders has succeeded beyond Tokyo's wild-
est dreams.

Gold Wing owners love their machines so much that they never
resist an opportunity to get together to admire one another's good
taste. Some 34,000 of them, from 22 countries and all 50 states,
belong to the Gold Wing Road Riders Association. Most are
adults (average age: 38); many are married (couples welcome);
none is likely to be mistaken for a Hell's Angel.

Gold Wingers' rallies feature slow races (last one across the finish line wins), pie runs (five kinds in five different towns), sometimes scavenger hunts. It's not all Fun and Games, though; it's
also Show and Tell. There are customized paint jobs to be com-

pared, new accessories to be admired (CB radios, radar detectors, armrests, etc.), gossip to be shared.

Interested? Write to the Gold Wing Road Riders Association, PO Box 14350, Phoenix, AZ 85063; or call 602-269-1403. On second thought, better begin with a visit to a Honda dealer. Other than a sense of humor and an admiration for chrome, the only requirement for membership is ownership of a Gold Wing.

. . . .

Honda Gold Wing motorcycle (Courtesy of American Honda Motor Company)

THE BEST
Mutual Fund

· ·

S uppose you'd been wise enough to invest $10,000 in the Fidelity Magellan Fund on September 30, 1976, then hung onto the fund's shares until June 30, 1986. Even after paying hefty income taxes on the profits, you would have ended up with more than $150,000.

On the other hand, suppose you'd flown to Las Vegas, converted the $10,000 to chips, and bet it all on a few turns of the roulette wheel. If you'd picked the right color just five times in a row, you would have ended up with larger after-tax profit. And you wouldn't have been forced to wait 10 years for the loot.

No, this isn't a pitch for doing your investing at Caesar's Palace. The point—a touch heavy-handed—is that for most folks, investing is simply another form of gambling. And though it may be more difficult to lose all your money overnight in mutual funds, the next decade's version of Fidelity Magellan isn't likely to be any easier to pick than the winning color in roulette. Of the 289 mutual funds recently surveyed by *Consumer Reports*, only 63 outperformed a simple price index of stocks of large corporations. That's right: 226 funds would have made more money by selecting stocks randomly.

How could three-quarters of all those funds do worse than a chimpanzee equipped with *Wall Street Journal* and crayon? One reason is that real talent for picking stocks is a rare commodity. Another is that mutual funds spend a lot of their shareowners' money on research, lunch, advertising, cocaine, etc. Most funds, moreover, pay hefty commissions to salesmen, reducing the amount of cash available for investing by as much as 8.5 percent.

No problem, you say: Just pick the mutual funds with good track records, the ones that have proved over the years that they can do better than our proverbial chimpanzee. But all too often the funds that have performed exceptionally well when stocks were on a roll have done quite poorly when the market was falling. Of the 30 top performers from 1980 to 1984 on *Consumer Reports'* list of 289, only seven were among the top performers from 1975 to 1979.

Such calculations have led some business-school types to conclude that mutual funds are just another sucker's game. A successful fund, they sneer, is one that has been lucky, and nothing about past performance offers a clue to future performance. By their logic, only two strategies for picking funds make much sense:

Roll with the punches. If three out of four funds do worse than the average of all stocks, why not purchase all the stocks? There's no practical way for an individual to "buy the index." But one mutual fund available to individual investors, the Vanguard Index Fund (800-662-7447), does maintain a portfolio of stocks that tracks the ups (and downs) of the Standard and Poor's 500 index. An index fund has no need for a high-priced pack of MBAs—and it has no reason to pay salesmen to spin fantasies of big profits just around the corner. Expenses subtracted from shareowners' returns are minimal, allowing the fund to come within one half a percentage point of the return provided by the average portfolio of stocks.

Roll your own. Most mutual funds buy stocks from dozens of different industries, trying (and usually failing) to generate exceptional returns for investors. "Sector" funds buy stocks from a much smaller universe—precious metals or electric utilities or banks or whatever is trendy this year. They claim to exercise judgment in their choice of investments within an industry. But as a practical matter, they buy a sufficiently large number of companies to track the industry's general performance. Such funds can be smart buys for individual investors who think they have a good idea what will happen to, say, the price of gold, but don't want to guess which gold mining companies are well-managed and don't want to pay high commissions on the purchase of a small number of shares.

Some sector funds are independently managed. But a number of the big investment companies maintain a whole portfolio of sector funds, allowing individuals to mix and match without much fuss or expense. Fidelity (800-544-6666) offers the largest menu and deducts relatively small sales charges. But it's worth comparison-shopping with Vanguard (800-662-7447) and Dean Witter (800-221-2685).

Not all the experts are convinced that all mutual fund managers are really chimpanzees in J. Press suits. While this year's big winner is indeed likely to be next year's big loser, a handful of funds has beaten the market several times running—among them, the Nicholas Fund (414-272-6133), the Evergreen Fund (800-635-0003), the Janus Fund (800-525-3713), the Neuberger and Berman Partners Fund (800-367-0770), and Twentieth Century Select Investors (816-531-5575).

Our own favorite is the relatively small, virtually unadvertised **ACORN FUND** (312-621-0630). It can't boast of the highest return across the last decade. But Acorn has averaged a nifty annual rate of 21 percent, seven percentage points better than the Standard and Poor's index. And it has managed this feat with a strategy of buying and holding individual stocks, rather than looking for this year's fad.

This conservative strategy has made Acorn an outstanding performer in declining markets, as well as a pretty good one on the way up. It has also inhibited the fund from attracting enormous numbers of edgy investors, reducing the pressure on Acorn's managers to go for broke on every roll of the dice. Will Acorn's record hold up over the next decade? No one knows—but it's probably a better bet than roulette.

National Enquirer Headline

· ·

Remember this one: BIGFOOT THWARTS RED NUKE ATTACK. Or this one: MARILYN WAS MURDERED BY SLIME MAN FROM VENUS. How about AIDS LINKED TO ANCHOVY PIZZA or FETUS SURVIVES ELECTRIC CHAIR?

No? There's a good reason. None of them ever appeared in the *National Enquirer*—and nothing so bizarre is ever likely to. For in spite of its reputation among those who don't read it, "the largest circulation newspaper in America" has never been keen on the truly outrageous. The *Enquirer*'s sensibility is checkout-counter-innocent, a downscale blend of envy, hope, sloth, and gullibility.

Consider the (randomly chosen) issue of July 29, 1986. Boy George's problems with heroin receive top headline billing in MARKED FOR DEATH FOR SQUEALING (So says a "top police insider"). Then there's CONNIE STEVENS' AGONY: MY BELOVED PET DOGS MAULED ME—I CAN'T DECIDE WHAT TO DO WITH THEM (seems she intervened in a feud between her huskies). Down below, we discover that FURIOUS BATTLES THREATEN JOAN COLLINS' REAL-LIFE MARRIAGE AFTER ONLY EIGHT MONTHS (Joan and hubby Peter shout at each other a lot, in public). Top billing, the cover story complete with glowing color photo, is WHO LIVES AND WHO DIES IN DYNASTY CLIFF-HANGER (Alexis, Dominique, and Garrett survive; Claudia's contract wasn't renewed).

Wait; it doesn't get better. Interior features include CAN YOU BELIEVE HE ATE THE WHOLE THING, in which the *Enquirer* takes Fat Albert, the heaviest living man (891 pounds), to dinner at Bern's Steak House in Tampa. Moving right along, the consumer-

conscious *Enquirer* reports that CHEAP RUNNING SHOES LAST AS
LONG AS COSTLY ONES. On page 18, Ali MacGraw, Angie Dickin-
son, Audrey Hepburn, and Ursula Andress tell all in FOUR AGELESS
LOVELIES REVEAL THEIR BEAUTY SECRETS (Ali eats little and works
out lots; Angie fights hunger pangs by brushing her teeth). But
the best is saved for last in TASTY PORK DISHES YOUR FAMILY WILL
LOVE (Knockwurst and Beans: "Pour two 13-ounce cans into a 2½
quart casserole . . .").

The real stars of the issue are neither the headlines nor the sto-
ries. They're the ads. Window maid (a liquid cleaner, not a servant) is guaranteed to keep panes free of dirt, grime, insects, and
acid rain for one year. The Special Report Office of Fifth Ave.,
New York, sells a Lottery Disclosure Report which helped a certain Manuel Garcete win $13.7 million in the State Lottery. And
for only $23, plus $2 postage, the Federal Redemption Center of
Miami, Florida, will designate you a "Registered Coupon Supplier,"
allowing you to "Make Up to $300 Weekly" by clipping coupons
at home.

A plow through decades of back issues (yes, the Library of Congress collects them on microfilm) proves equally disappointing.
Three-headed babies, assassination plots against Liz Taylor, lost cities of Atlantis, and extraterrestrials that eat pickup trucks are nowhere to be found. Even mummies' curses and confessions of
abortionists-to-the-stars are few and far between.

Searing looks at show business (WHAT ED SULLIVAN IS REALLY
LIKE) have always been popular. Medical exposés figure heavily
(HEALTHY GIRLS PRETEND TO BE BLIND AND CRIPPLED . . . ELECTRIC
HOSPITAL BEDS KILL MANY PATIENTS . . .). Horatio Alger bits (AT
38 HE EARNED $67.50 A WEEK. AT 67 HE'S WORTH $150 MILLION)
have only recently been deposed by tales of lottery winners. And
when the *Enquirer* does go for the loony headline, one is left with
the impression that the writer's heart wasn't in it. (STRANGE MES-
SAGES FROM BEYOND THE GRAVE . . . TWO POLICE OFFICERS SIG-
NALLED BY HOVERING UFO . . .).

Where to find the great *National Enquirer* headlines that are never really there? The *New York Post* ("Khadafy is Daffy") provides daily morsels. Then, every seventh day, gorge on the sublime offerings from a sister publication of the *Enquirer* called the *Weekly World News*. Unlike the *Enquirer*, or clones like the *Star* and the *Globe*, this checkout-counter rag contains no color photos of Vanna White in short shorts, and no purloined secrets from the sets of soap operas. But the *Weekly World News* headlines are inspired.

The paper carries more than its share of shockers: TEEN GIRL KIDNAPPED BY A VAMPIRE . . . GENIE RISES FROM ANCIENT BOTTLE . . . POPE SNUBS FIFTY WIZARDS . . . MOM EXPECTING SECOND TWIN TWO YEARS AFTER BIRTH OF FIRST . . . TALKING ELEPHANT TELLS KEEPERS "I'VE GOT A CAVITY"* . . . But its true genius lies in absurd twists on the commonplace: TEENS ARE PETRIFIED OF GHOSTS, SAYS STUDY . . . PREGNANT MOM KNOCKS OUT KANGAROO AT CIRCUS SIDESHOW . . . TOT LOCKED IN A KENNEL KEPT ALIVE BY HIS FAITHFUL DOG . . . HOUSEWIFE DIES AFTER GULPING ROACH POWDER TO CURE THE HICCUPS . . . GAS STOVE MISHAP TURNS CHEF INTO HUMAN SHISH KEBAB . . .

The *Weekly World News* is, of course, available at supermarkets everywhere. Those who don't patronize supermarkets, or just can't wait until they run out of Doritos and Brillo, can order by mail. Subscriptions run $13.95 a year. Write: *Weekly World News*, 600 S. East Coast Ave., Lantana, FL 33462.

---

*"Animal experts have an explanation for the beast's amazing ability to talk. The elephant was rejected by his mom at birth and was raised by talkative humans."

Nude Beach

. . . .

*E*uropeans have almost forgotten that bikinis come with tops as well as bottoms. But those who want to take it all off face a conundrum. The countries most tolerant of public nudity—West Germany, Denmark, Sweden—lack warm water, sunny climates, and beaches free of undertow. One answer is to take a cruise out of Bremerhaven: The *Europa*, a gorgeous, German-run ship, features a nude "beach" on its uppermost deck. The more common solution is to go south.

France has dozens of beaches where clothes are optional. The Ile du Levant was the first and probably remains the best known. But, like most beaches on the Côte d'Azur, it is short on sand and long on crowds. Cap d'Agde, a beach colony farther to the west on the Mediterranean, is surely the only place in the world where you can open a bank account in the nude. But this rather unromantic, suburban-style planned resort is jammed in summer. Probably your best bet in France is on the Atlantic coast. Sauveterre, near the town of Olonne-sur-Mer, offers a broad, little-used expanse of white sand with nice surf and no sightseers.

Italy, Spain, and Greece remain ambivalent about nudity. On one hand, they think the clothes-off crowd will be a bad influence on the kiddies. On the other, they fear a prudish image will starve the tourist trade. Go for one of the Mediterranean islands where the locals have largely overcome their scruples. Formentera, in Spain's Balearic Islands, is ringed by calm, sunny, clothes-optional beaches. Sardinia has some nice spots, notably near Cagliari; unless you're partial to traffic jams, avoid July and August. Santorini and Ios, in Greece's Cyclades, offer the prettiest yet-to-be-spoiled beaches on the Mediterranean.

Yugoslavia doesn't share its neighbors' concern for the corruption of youth. It has been openly welcoming sun worshippers from the north for decades. Trouble is, most of the beaches are rocky, and most of the resorts are geared for high-density package tours. But the island of Hvar, and the smaller islands near it, do offer some sandy beaches without the built-yesterday feel.

American beaches can be frustrating because you hardly ever know where you stand. Public nudity is illegal virtually everywhere (exception: Vermont, which has an official use-a-little-discretion policy). But local laws are often unenforced. California offers a number of gorgeous beaches with no-hassle policies. Try More Mesa beach near Santa Barbara, Pirate's Cove near San Luis Obispo, Pfeiffer and Molera State Park beaches on the stunning Big Sur coast. The privately operated Red, White, and Blue beach north of Santa Cruz could hardly be prettier.

You'd think a free-spirited place like Hawaii would be tolerant of a little flesh, but the cops don't always see it that way. Honokohau Beach on the big island of Hawaii is a pleasant exception. So is out-of-the-way Kalalau Beach, on the empty, northwest shore of Kauai. Better yet, try the Seven Sacred Pools in Haleakala National Park on Maui. These postcard-perfect waterfalls and pools leading down to the sea get a lot of visitors, and the Park Service does insist on bathing suits where the crowds congregate. However, if you climb to the less-visited pools high up, the rangers will pretend not to notice.

See-no-evil, by the way, is now official policy in all of America's national parks and forests: If you are reasonably discreet, the rangers will ignore you. Lake Mead National Recreational Area, the eerily beautiful desert lake formed by Hoover Dam in southern Nevada, has dozens of out-of-the-way spots for skinny-dipping. The same goes for Cape Lookout National Seashore, on the Outer

Banks of North Carolina, and the Assateague Island National Seashore, on the eastern shore of Virginia.

Ready to brave jet lag for a place in the sun? Consider Phuket, a lightly developed resort island off the coast of Thailand. While the Thais are generally fussy about keeping their clothes on in public, they've made an exception of Kata Beach, an utterly perfect stretch of white sand complete with Club Med. Linda Ronstadt and Jerry Brown are said to have made the trip to the nude beach at Lamu, an island just off the coast of Kenya that is famous for its lovely ruins. Australia has lots of "free" beaches, most of them near the easygoing cities of Sydney and Perth. Probably the prettiest, though, is Granite Bay in the tropical Noosa National Park, a hundred miles north of Brisbane.

The Caribbean used to split cleanly between tight, no-nudity, English-speaking islands and the let-it-all-hang-out French islands. Guadaloupe's Plage Caravelle (near Ste. Anne) and St. Martin's Orient Bay Beach still fit the image. But the pressure of economic competition is making the former British colonies more accommodating. The gorgeously unspoiled Turks and Caicos Islands are now wide open. Many of the out islands of the Bahamas, including Eleuthera and Little Exuma, now welcome skinny-dippers. And don't forget St. John, in the U.S. Virgin Islands, Nudity is ignored in the fabulous Virgin Island National Park, which covers two-thirds of the island.

But the nicest nude beach in the Caribbean—or anywhere else—is tucked away in the Grenadine chain, north of Grenada. The 110-acre Palm Island is a delightful, easygoing place with handsome beaches, safe swimming, and a good coral reef for scuba diving. It is entirely owned by the **PALM ISLAND BEACH CLUB,** a string of comfy, breeze-conditioned cottages designed for privacy. Owners John and Mary Caldwell don't care what you do or do not wear. Oh yes—the food's pretty good, too.

Getting to Palm Island can be a nuisance. The standard way is through Barbados, with a charter hop to nearby Union Island.

For booking and transportation information contact Robert Reid Associates, 1270 Avenue of the Americas, New York, NY 10020, or phone 212-757-2449. Rates are fairly high, even by Caribbean standards. But Palm Island is worth it.

THE BEST
Way to Overcome
Stage Fright

. . . .

*D*oes your heart go thumpa-thumpa when the executive
vice-president solicits advice on the right color for the
stripe in the new tooth gel? Does your chest tighten and mind go
blank when you stand up to pitch crunchy granola with licorice
bits to the company's marketing committee? Does the idea of in-
troducing the young-computer-analyst-of-the-year at the Jaycee
lunch change you into a quivering mass of protoplasm? Believe it
or not, there's a pill to cure the condition. What's more, it has
few side effects of consequence and is easy to obtain.

The substance is propranolol hydrochloride, a common drug
prescribed for hypertension, heart pain, migraine headaches, and
thyroid disease. Sold under the brand name Inderal, it is, in fact,
the most frequently prescribed drug in America. Inderal is a beta-
blocker, working its magic by inhibiting the chemical reaction in
the nervous system that triggers the primitive "fight or flight" response in the face of danger.

Patients with life-threatening diseases take anywhere from 30 to
700 milligrams a day to slow heartbeat or reduce blood pressure.
Actors and musicians find that as little as 5 to 10 milligrams pre-
vents trembling and cold sweats in those awful moments before
the stage lights go up. And at such low dosage levels, the only
common side effect in otherwise healthy individuals is a sense of
emotional distance from events. That could prove a problem for a
harpsichordist interpreting The Goldberg Variations. But it might
even be an advantage for an executive outlining the reasons for
closing down the Philadelphia branch. Still, better safe than sorry:
Run it past your doctor before you let Inderal make you a star.

THE BEST
Painkiller

. . . .

S tart with the lightweights, the over-the-counter potions, where most of the money is. Aspirin leads the $1.7 billion hustle to sell nonprescription pain relievers. Acetominophen (Tylenol, Datril) is a healthy second; ibuprofen (Advil, Nuprin), the latest off the blocks, is a distant third.

As close as anyone can figure, the three are generally effective against many sources of mild pain. The big exceptions are arthritis and injuries—bruises, burns, backaches—where the hurt is linked to swelling. Here, aspirin and ibuprofen have a big edge because they inhibit the release of prostaglandins, chemicals that make nerve endings more responsive to pain by inducing inflammation. Acetominophen, by contrast, works directly on the brain, raising the threshold at which the pain registers in the mind.

All three drugs are capable of (though not very likely to produce) nasty side effects. Aspirin irritates the stomach lining and makes bleeding ulcers bleed more. It may also cause Reye's Syndrome (a devastating disorder of the nervous system) in flu-infected children. Ibuprofen isn't as tough on the tummy as aspirin, but it, too, has been linked to gastric bleeding. There's also some evidence that it can damage kidneys and exacerbate high blood pressure.

Acetominophen was long billed as the painkiller so user-friendly that three-year-olds could gulp a whole bottle and live to gulp again. It is pretty safe stuff—unless you happen to be a heavy drinker. According to one new study, as little as three grams a day (six extra-strength tablets) can cause damage to livers that are simultaneously stressed by alcohol.

The Rx: If the pain isn't related to swelling, stick with acetominophen and drink in moderation. If there is inflammation, use aspirin or ibuprofen, but tread with some care. Enteric-coated aspirin (Ecotrin, Encaprin), the kind that doesn't dissolve until it has passed through the stomach, may beat the gastric irritation problem. Before feeding either aspirin or ibuprofen to a child, ask a doctor. And be sure to buy the cheapest generic available; brand names are for suckers.

Suppose over-the-counter painkillers don't do the trick. What prescription drugs might?

Forget propoxyphene (Darvon), a distant, nonaddicting cousin to morphine that was once every family physician's favorite; it's no better a painkiller than aspirin or acetominophen. Codeine, another opiate with little addicting effect, is only slightly more effective than Darvon. But in combination with aspirin (or acetominophen) it is a big step up from the nonprescription pain pills.* Note that codeine infrequently causes nausea, and usually causes constipation.

Next in line are the heavyweight opiates that can be taken in pill form. Hydromorphone (Dilaudid), methadone (Dolophine), and Percodan (the opiate oxycodone, plus aspirin) are all excellent painkillers with similar, and fairly serious, drawbacks. They are likely to make you sleepy, perhaps lightheaded or nauseous. And they interact badly with a whole variety of drugs including alcohol, most sleeping pills, allergy remedies, and muscle relaxants. Another opiate, meperidine (Demerol) has equally problematic side effects, but doesn't deliver much pain relief.

The most effective painkillers by far are the injectable forms of

*The number attached to these combination products (Tylenol No. 3, Empirin No. 2, etc.) refers to the amount of codeine in the compound. No. 1 = 7.5 milligrams; No. 2 = 15 milligrams; No. 3 = 30 milligrams; No. 4 = 60 milligrams.

narcotics. Morphine, the granddaddy of opium derivatives, remains one of the best. Dilaudid-HP is an extremely potent form of hydromorphone usually reserved for patients who have used other narcotics to treat chronic pain, and have thus built high levels of tolerance.

Everyone, of course, is frightened by the prospect of addiction to the injectable narcotics. Taken long enough and in large enough doses, they inevitably produce physical dependence. But the danger of addiction from the opiates, injectable and oral, is vastly exaggerated. Narcotics rarely generate a sense of pleasure in people suffering from pain, so they are less likely to leave the patient emotionally dependent on continued doses after the pain goes away. Used to treat pain in serious burn cases, the rate of addiction from hospital-administered meperidine is just one case in a thousand!

Ironically, the real risk seems to be too little use, not too much. According to study after study, most patients in severe pain are under-dosed by physicians and nurses who are wary of addiction. That's a prudent strategy for someone who must learn to live with chronic pain and still function in the outside world. And it may be a bearable mistake for post-operative patients who are only in pain for a matter of hours. But an exaggerated fear of narcotics can be disastrous for the terminally ill, who have better things to worry about than addiction.

Mercifully, physicians sophisticated in combating pain have made important advances in recent years. Heroin has been added to the anti-pain arsenal in Britain and Canada, reportedly with excellent results. It remains out of favor in the United States. Dilaudid-HP is claimed to be equally effective, a view bitterly disputed by many pain specialists as well as the American Nurses Association.

Whatever its merits, heroin is no panacea. Like all narcotics, it depresses the other functions of the nervous system along with depressing the recognition of pain. So as tolerance grows with continuing use, patients are often forced to choose between pain relief and a clear head. A standard way around the problem is to counteract the depressant effect by mixing the narcotic with cocaine or amphetamines. Another is to combine narcotics with tranquilizers or antidepressant drugs; they often seem to increase the painkilling effect.

Better fixes, perhaps even the ideal painkiller, may be lurking on the technological horizon. Opiates work their wonders by plugging the receptors in the brain cells that process pain signals. But they fit the pain "plugs" imperfectly, inducing tolerance and creating the well-known side effects. It is now understood that the body produces its own chemical pain fighters, called endorphins, that neatly fit the receptors and are thus hundreds of times more potent than heroin. The hope is that one or more of them can be synthesized and used as a drug.

The other "big think" approach to pain fighting is to disable the pain response at the site of the damage. When cells are injured, they set off an alarm by releasing a chemical called bradykinin. The bradykinin, in turn, triggers a variety of defenses, bathing the injury in protective fluids and calling up white cells to fight bacterial invaders. It also plugs directly into the pain receptors on local nerve cells, notifying the brain that damage has been done. That's useful if evasive action is needed. But bradykinin just doesn't know when to quit—a burn hurts for hours after you've removed your finger from the frying pan.

Interrupting the production of bradykinin at the injury site might also interrupt the healing process. But researchers have isolated a chemical that does nothing more than block the pain response by filling up the local pain receptors. And one drug company, Nova Pharmaceutical of Baltimore, is working on a relatively cheap bradykinin blocker that could be taken orally. But don't hold your breath; the perfect painkiller is still years away.

Paper

· ·

*F*or most of us, paper is paper, handy stuff to have around
should you care to compose a sonnet or housebreak a
puppy. For Japan's nostalgic élite, it is also a link to a simpler
past, when the making of paper was craft, ritual, and art rolled
into one.

By the middle of the 19th century, paper was being mass-
produced in America and Europe. But Japan was still a medieval
island fortress, closed to modernizing influences. And paper was
made much the way it had been centuries earlier, with only the
simplest machines and without the benefit of steam power. An
astounding 100,000 home workshops turned out hundreds of varieties, many using raw materials found only in Japan.

Handmade paper is far more costly, of course, than the factory
kind. So once Japan opened its borders, imported technology
blew away traditional technique, and with it, the livelihood of
whole villages devoted to papercraft. Today, just 500 of the old
workshops survive, living museums to hopelessly impractical—and
fabulously beautiful—handicraft.

What makes traditional Japanese paper, or "washi," so special?
Modern paper is made from wood pulp. Rather than spend time
and money separating unwanted, naturally occurring impurities
from the cellulose fiber, the pulp is chemically treated to create a
uniform consistency and color. The finished product is fine for
most purposes. But, according to traditionalists, such technical
shortcuts make the paper less stable in heat and light. Most modern papers discolor and grow brittle over time.

The fiber in traditional Japanese paper comes from the inner layers of plant barks rather than the pulp of softwood trees. The raw material is repeatedly soaked and boiled with ash to remove impurities, then dried and bleached with sunlight. The finished product, say connoisseurs, is acid-neutral paper that is incredibly durable and unlikely to react to inks or dyes or lose strength over time.

Those may not be important qualities for paperback thrillers or memo pads. But they make for winners in the decoration department. Washi is still used for lampshades and room-dividing shoji screens. Vividly dyed sheets, either plain or patterned, make super-luxurious giftwrap. Actually, the paper itself can be the gift: Printed washi is used to decorate desk accessories, to fashion wallets, to make dolls.

Washi is dazzling in its variety of textures, colors, and print techniques. Probably the best place to be dazzled is a store called **MORITA WASHI,** located in a scruffy wholesale district near the Shijo's, Kyoto's main shopping drag. The glass cases in the front of the little store contain a nice selection of writing paper and washi-decorated baubles. But the real thrill is the back display rooms, where patrons in their stocking feet browse at leisure among thousands of paper samples.

Check out the thick, crepe-like chirimen-gami . . . repeating designs of chiyi-gami, originally used as patterns of kimonos . . . bold, modern stencil-dyed designs from Okinawa . . . elegant cream-colored papers for art reproductions, made from kozo plant fiber . . . silky, translucent gampi-fiber paper used for tracing . . . papers with artificial wood grains, created by rubbing the surface with the leaf of the camellia plant.

Washi-decorated fans and boxes and toys, the ritualized gifts so crucial to Japanese social life, run from $5 to $50. Individual, 16 × 22 inch sheets of washi will set you back as little as $2, or as much as $8. Morita Washi's address is Higashi-no-Toin, Bukkoji-agaru, Shimogyo-ku, Japan. Telephone 81-75-341-0121.

Pasta

. . . .

Remember the shmoo, the amiable little creature in Al
Capp's "Li'l Abner" comic strip? It tasted like sirloin
when broiled, chicken when fried. Eating shmoos was guilt-free:
eager to become dinner, they were ready to jump into a frying
pan at a single, hungry glance.

Pasta can't quite compete. But as assorted cookbook writers,
trendsetters, and Italophiles are eager to explain, it is as close to
the perfect food as you're likely to find outside the funny pages.
Pasta is cheap, relatively low in calories (100 per ounce), and a
snap to prepare. Everybody likes it, even the sort of five-year-old
who considers ketchup the only edible vegetable. The main
source of food value in pasta, the complex carbohydrate, is virtually the only nutrient that has yet to be linked to cancer or
heart disease. Why, if we forsook McDonald's' thin fries for lin-
guini in olive oil, we'd probably all live to 100. . . .

The ingredients listed on the pasta box are pretty much the
same, no matter what the brand. But don't be misled; the differences in the manufactured product are enormous.

Pasta is mostly flour. Good pasta, including all Italian brands
(by law) and most American, is made from semolina, the flour
milled from hard durum wheat. Pasta from softer wheat becomes
sticky as it cooks, losing resiliency before it is ready to serve. But
not all durum wheat is equal in hardness or in taste. Italian manufacturers generally use superior blends, which explains why virtually every imported brand of pasta is better than every
American.

Good wheat is just part of the story. The other key to fine pasta is the care taken to avoid exposing the dough to high temperatures during the kneading, cutting, and drying processes. Heat breaks down the protein chains in the semolina, preventing the pasta from achieving a pleasing *al dente* chewiness when boiled.

Among widely available Italian brands, Sigadoro and Barilla are good. De Cecco and Del Verde, slightly more expensive brands from the Abruzzi region, are even better. Fini, a big food company in Modena, makes a lovely, tender egg pasta that is now sold in specialty food stores in America. But the best pasta to be found anywhere—well, anywhere outside Italy—is from the **HOUSE OF MARTELLI.**

The two Martelli brothers run a tiny factory in Tuscany, producing just four shapes of pasta. Martelli pasta dough is kneaded for 40 minutes—about twice as long as the mass-produced kind—then forced through bronze dies rather than the more commonly used Teflon-coated machinery. Bronze cutters leave a dull, pitted surface that permits the cooked pasta to absorb more sauce. To avoid overheating, Martelli uses fans to dry the pasta over a 48-hour period; lesser brands may be in and out of drying tunnels in as little as six hours. As a mark of the company's special attention to craft, the finished spaghetti is packaged in the curls it forms on the drying racks.

In America, Martelli pasta can be found in the Williams-Sonoma kitchen supply stores. Or order it from the Dean and DeLuca food shop in New York (800-221-7714).

P.S. No pasta, no matter how élite the pedigree, will taste better than Spaghetti-O's if it is overcooked. Bring a big pot of water to boil—figure at least two gallons for a pound of the raw material. Add a teaspoon of salt per gallon unless you're avoiding the stuff for reasons of health. Then toss in all the pasta at once and keep it separated with a wooden spoon as the water comes back to a boil. Cook for about five minutes, or half that long if it's pasta made with eggs. Then check its progress every half minute or so. The "toss test" doesn't work: Pasta that sticks to the wall is already overdone. Nor is there any reliable visual test. You'll just have to do it the old-fashioned way: Fish out a strand with a fork, blow once or twice, and bite.

Pasta is ready to remove from the water when the dough barely tastes cooked; wait any longer and it will become soft as you drain it. Italian cooks usually remove pasta from the pot with tongs, rather than draining it in a collander. That way, the pasta retains the bit of water it needs to finish cooking on the table.

Toss in cheese first (only the mild, imported Parmigiano-Reggiano, and only if the recipe calls for it), then sauce and serve. Time is precious—don't linger over an artful arrangement.

Peanut Butter

. . . .

Wouldn't it be great if peanut butter were just that—
puréed peanuts—instead of a witch's brew of nuts,
dextrose, sucrose, salt, hydrogenated vegetable fat, and mono- and
diglycerides?

Not really. Pulverized peanut *au naturel* has a number of strikes
against it. The sweeteners (table sugar or corn-based dextrose)
and the salt are flavor enhancers; without at least a little bit, most
people think peanut butter tastes bland and boring. Hydrogenated
vegetable fat (in other words, Crisco) may sound unappetizing, and
it certainly isn't friendly to your arteries. But without the solid
fat to act as an emulsifier, the liquid oil from the peanuts floats to
the surface. Once the liquid is stirred back into the peanut
goop—a messy process, at best—the peanut butter turns slimy.
Worse, it takes on a sticky, choking texture so unpleasant that a
phobia has been named after it.*

Then there's the matter of the mono- and diglycerides: they add
the creaminess to creamy-style peanut butter. One could do
without the velvet texture, perhaps. But as food additives go,
mono- and diglycerides aren't high on anybody's hit list. They
certainly aren't worth much worry compared to, say, the natural
fat in peanut butter.

Among the major brands, Skippy's marketing strategists at CPC
International have positioned their product as the adult peanut
butter, the one for folks with sophisticated palates. Skippy con-

---

*Arachibutyrophobia: the fear of peanut butter sticking to the roof of your mouth.

tains dextrose rather than sucrose, which gives the peanut butter a somewhat subtler sweetness. And guessing from the slightly reduced calorie content, the recipe probably calls for less hydrogenated fat.

But for all of Skippy's virtuous attention to basics and its intensely nutty flavor, the overall effect is disappointing. It excels as an ingredient in sauces or desserts. Served straight on bread, however, it is grating to the tastebuds and very, very sticky. Skippy was probably the peanut butter your mother spread on the sandwich you took to school—the sandwich you were lucky to barter for baloney-on-white. That leaves Peter Pan (Beatrice) and Jif (Procter and Gamble).

Peter Pan, a sweet, delicately flavored peanut butter with a very thick, creamy consistency, has some respectable champions. In a taste-off sponsored by *The New York Times,* it rated number one. For our money, though, the edge goes to JIF, an equally sweet, somewhat less salty mixture with faint overtones of smoke and honey. Jif has a nonstick, ultrasmooth texture which succeeds in the chunky as well as the creamy version. True believers insist that PB with J is like sex without guilt, but we're partial to Jif straight, served Gerald Ford–style on toasted English muffins.

Polish Joke

· ·

No, not the ethnic slurs about changing light bulbs or driving garbage trucks in Chicago.* The political jokes Poles tell about themselves and their Russian friends—the sad, defiant jokes of proud people who insist that this, too, shall pass.

Good Joke

Man walks into an appliance store and, pointing to an object in the window, asks the clerk, "How much is that refrigerator?"

"It's 20,000 zlotys, Comrade Captain," the salesman replies.

The customer is astonished: "How did you know I was a policeman?"

"Because you are pointing at a stove."

Better Joke

A Pole is visiting Moscow for the first time. Approaching a man on the street carrying two heavy suitcases, he asks for the correct time.

"My pleasure," replies the gracious Russian, carefully putting down his bags. "It is 11:16 and 27 seconds. The date is October 12. We are standing 354 meters above sea level, and the express from Leningrad is due in 16 minutes."

---

*Actually, one of them has a certain goofy purity: "Did you hear they had to close the Warsaw zoo?" "The clam died. . . ."

The Pole is amazed. "Are you permitted to buy such watches from Japan?"

"This is a Russian watch," the owner proudly responds.

"Your technology is certainly full of wonders," says the Pole.

"Yes," grunts the Russian as he lifts the suitcases to leave, "but these batteries are still a little heavy."

Best Joke

Man goes into a pet shop, looking for a parrot. Pointing at one brightly plumed creature, he asks the price. "It's 40,000, but worth every zloty," the salesman replies. "This bird can say thank you in four languages and whistle 'The Internationale.'"

And what about the handsome blue and red bird in the corner? "Oh, he's 60,000 zlotys. You pay through the nose for a parrot that can do long division and recite the names of all the battles in the Second World War."

Depressed, the customer points to a drab brown bird with disheveled tailfeathers.

"Ah, he's 125,000 zlotys."

"Well, what are his talents?" asks the disgusted shopper.

"To tell the truth, he just squats there and dozes," the shopkeeper replies. "But the other birds address him as Comrade Secretary."

THE BEST
Portable Personal Computer

. . . .

*I*f the personal computer on your desk is a valuable tool, one that stowed under your airplane seat ought to be indispensable. Somehow, though, it has never quite worked out that way.

Light, inexpensive, battery-operated computers made by Radio Shack are small enough to go anywhere and adequate for composing memos or keeping simple records. But they are handicapped by tiny memories, hard-to-read screens and woefully inadequate number-crunching power. At the other end of the cost and performance scale, Compaq offers wonderful machines, equivalent in almost every way to deskbound IBMs. But these lunchbox-shaped computers are really "transportables," not portables: at 20 pounds and up, they're albatrosses for all but the most muscular travellers.

Happily, technology is marching on. The very latest generation of portable PCs aren't quite perfect substitutes for desktop models. But each of these machines offers fabulous features.

The Toshiba 1000 (about $1,000)

It isn't the fastest portable: the microprocessor brain runs at only a quarter the speed of the state-of-the-art 80386 chips. It sports just a single 3½-inch disc drive. The keyboard is a little cramped, and the screen is hard to read in low light. But at barely a foot square, two inches thick, and 6.3 pounds, the Toshiba 1000 is the first full-featured computer that fits comfortably in a briefcase. And at a price well under $1,500, complete with every accessory, it is also the first affordable road machine.

Actually, this model is even more cleverly designed than you might imagine. Toshiba offers an extra 768K memory chip with its own battery backup. That little piece of etched silicon is set up to work like a miniature, superfast hard disc drive, holding programs and data for instant access while the machine is on, and storing work-in-progress for up to a week when the machine is off. Highly recommended for word processing and other light-weight computer chores.

The Zenith 181 (about $1,400)

Zenith's 12-pound, battery-powered, attaché-sized portable has all the computing versatility you'd expect from a full-featured IBM XT-compatible: 640K random access memory, two 3½-inch drives that hold 720K memory on a single disk, a full-sized keyboard, and an optional 300/1200 baud modem for calling home.

What makes it a big winner, though, is the screen. It has the proper proportions to display graphics without squashing the images. Even more important, it's a snap to read from any angle and in any light. Like most other portables, the Zenith creates figures with liquid crystal diodes. But unlike most others, it is backlit with a layer of luminescent chemicals to produce sharp bright-blue images.

The Toshiba 1200 (about $2,500)

Looking for speed? The Toshiba 1200 has a lightning-fast 80C86 brain and has room to add a math coprocessor for heavy-duty number crunching. There's a 20-megabyte hard disk drive for slurping up data in a hurry. The 1200 even lets you segregate a piece of the internal memory for a so-called "RAM disk," provid-ing instant access to pieces of your program and cutting down on battery use.

Looking for versatility? The whole package weighs just 12 pounds and has a pop-out battery pack that makes it practical to carry on long airplane flights.   Oh, yes: the modem is built-in at the factory, the keyboard is a pleasure to use and the screen is better-than-average.   This is the cheapest, lightest laptop in the "serious computer" category.

The GRiDCase 1530 ($4,700)

The GRiDCase isn't for everyone.   But if you are looking for the Mercedes of laptops, it is the only way to travel.   With its elegant, black magnesium-alloy case and knife-sharp gas plasma display, the 1530 looks different.   And this time, looks don't deceive.   It runs with the 80386 microprocessor, the fastest available for personal computers.   It can be configured with a 40-megabyte hard disk drive and, if you like, a 2,400 bps modem, a math coprocessor, and up to 8 megabytes of internal memory. The whole rugged package weighs just 13 pounds.

The catch?   Same as a Mercedes: price.   With all the extras — and why bother with a GRiDCase, otherwise — the machine can easily run to $7,000.

THE BEST
Prep School

. . . .

*P*ublic schools that skim the cream from big cities—Boston
Latin and Bronx High School of Science, for example—offer
a superb education and an inside track to the most prestigious colleges. Selective private day schools like Fieldston in New York,
Sidwell Friends in Washington, John Burroughs in St. Louis, and
the University School in Cleveland deliver the same goods, and in
higher style: small classes, individual attention, exotic lab equipment, maybe even a squash court or two. The élite boarding prep
schools offer an ingredient that class-unconscious Americans prefer
to ignore: Like their British counterparts, they prepare their students for business, social, and political power.

A handful of schools in the west, such as Webb in California
and Fountain Valley in Colorado, can make a credible claim to the
category. So can a few Catholic prep schools: Portsmouth Abbey
in Rhode Island and perhaps Georgetown Prep in suburban Washington. But the heaviest hitters, sometimes called the "select 16,"
are all in the East and all Episcopalian or nondenominational.
Strikingly, all but four (Deerfield, Episcopal, Hill, Woodberry) are
now coed.

Choate School	Wallingford, Connecticut
Deerfield Academy	Deerfield, Massachusetts
Episcopal High School	Alexandria, Virginia
Groton School	Groton, Massachusetts
Hill School	Pottstown, Pennsylvania

Hotchkiss School	Lakeville, Connecticut
Kent School	Kent, Connecticut
Lawrenceville School	Lawrenceville, New Jersey
Middlesex School	Concord, Massachusetts
Phillips Academy	Andover, Massachusetts
Phillips Exeter Academy	Exeter, New Hampshire
St. George's School	Newport, Rhode Island
St. Mark's School	Southborough, Massachusetts
St. Paul's School	Concord, New Hampshire
Taft School	Watertown, Connecticut
Woodberry Forest School	Woodberry Forest, Virginia

Three of the sixteen—Episcopal, Hill, Woodberry Forest—are marginal candidates for the best, if only because they're training grounds for a regional rather than a national upper class. It's fine to attend Woodberry Forest if you plan to return to horse country to clip coupons and improve the breed. But it's probably not the appropriate first step to becoming a managing partner in Morgan Stanley, or president of the World Bank.

Now the deselection becomes a bit arbitrary. Choate, Deerfield, Kent, Lawrenceville, Taft, St. George's, and St. Mark's aren't selective enough academically to get a high percentage of their graduates into the very best colleges on pure merit, and don't have enough social clout to get them in on pull. Hotchkiss loses on the next cut: By the standards of the company remaining, it's nouveau, too closely associated with money made in this century. Mr. Hotchkiss, whose endowment built the first buildings, actually made his pile by inventing a better machine gun.

The four schools that are left fall into two camps. By no accident, Groton and St. Paul's look like English "public" schools. At Groton, the boys are even encouraged to play an obscure 19th-century English handball game called "fives." Both are Episcopal-tradition schools, with compulsory chapel. Both are small, conservative, academically demanding, and incredibly well endowed.

Both have made efforts to enroll a few blacks, offering huge scholarships to offset the $11,000-plus tuition and board. But make no mistake: These are places where social class is polished, not abolished. Franklin Roosevelt's Groton classmates never did forgive his treachery in running as a Democrat. Even today, some 40 percent of recent graduates come from families listed in the Social Register.

EXETER and **ANDOVER** were both founded by Samuel Phillips, revolutionary and purveyor of gunpowder to the army of George Washington. Andover was first, in 1778—Paul Revere designed the school seal and John Hancock signed its certificate of incorporation. Exeter came three years later, in Phillips's home town. And while, as a practical matter, Phillips's two academies are largely in the business of educating the children of the establishment, their enthusiasm for democratic ideals is more than window dressing.

Both schools started with close ties to local communities, enrolling local farm boys as well as gentry. Both have pushed hard to attract blacks and Jews and Catholics. Both identify with progressive trends in education, de-emphasizing religious training, experimenting with student-led seminars, broadening the curriculum to compensate for early specialization in colleges. Both have active exchange programs, opening the possibility of years abroad in Spain or France or even China.

How to choose? The British-model intimacy and social exclusivity of Groton and St. Paul's make them the best tickets to the old boy network of clubs and banks and law firms—providing you qualify by birth and race. But Exeter and Andover are almost as suitable in the snob department, and offer something very important and very American: a sense of how large and diverse the world is, and how it won't remain our oyster unless there is someone to work at it. The two schools spew out as diverse a set of graduates as can be imagined—George Bush, Frank Stella, William Coors, Victor Kiam, Joyce Maynard, J. D. Rockefeller IV, George Plimpton, and Gore Vidal, to name a few.

Neither Exeter nor Andover can guarantee to transform a pampered teenager from Grosse Pointe or Shaker Heights into a statesman, Supreme Court judge, or social critic. But they do offer an edge up.

Question in
Trivial Pursuit

· ·

*T*hough it's not always easy to tell from the game, the three Canadian inventors of Trivial Pursuit are bad boys at heart. The debut edition, which was first sold in Canadian stores in 1981, had to be censored to fit sensibilities down under. Among the questions missing from the American version put out by game conglomerate Selchow and Righter:

How many months pregnant was Nancy Davis when she walked down the aisle with Ronald Reagan?

Answer: 2½.

Radar Detector

. . . .

*B*ig Brother has a thing about speeding—and no compunc-
tion about using radar to look over your shoulder at the
speedometer. But this is democratic America, where underdogs
are almost always given a sporting chance. Radar detectors, eyes
for spying on the spymasters, are legal everywhere except Connecticut, Virginia, and the District of Columbia. And as frustra-
tion with the 55-mile-an-hour speed limit grew, so did sales of the
dashboard- and window visor-mounted gizmos. Six million detectors are now in use.

Do they work? Yes and no. Radar detectors are simply radio
receivers tuned to pick up signals on the two microwave frequencies (X and K band) used by police radar. All the brand-name
models are capable of picking up line-of-sight signals from three to
five miles; most can provide 500 to 1,000 feet of warning around a
corner or over the crest of a hill. Unless you're driving in kami-
kaze mode, that is often sufficient warning to slow down.

Unfortunately, caution is not always enough. Some cops have
instant-on, instant-measure radar guns that provide no advance
warning of their use. Others are using Vascar, a new electronic
system that measures speed by measuring the time it takes for a
vehicle to move from one predetermined spot to another. Since
Vascar doesn't employ radar waves, radar detectors are useless as a
defense.

Wait, there are more problems. The environment is littered
with microwave-frequency signals, emitted by everything from
long-distance telephone towers to airliners to other people's radar

detectors. Radar jammers,* in use on thousands of cars and trucks, muck up detectors even worse than they do police radar systems. So even where an old-fashioned, wide-beam radar betrays its presence, there's a chance your detector won't distinguish it from the electromagnetic garbage it is buried in.

Still, assuming you're planning to speed anyway, a radar detector does reduce the odds of getting caught.

What to care about:

Signal Discrimination

The more sensitive the detector, the more warning you'll have— and the fewer "false positives" to irritate you. All detectors let you shift from a country to a city mode, raising the warning threshold in places where the airwaves are thick with false signals. Better detectors also offer special (but far from foolproof) circuitry for rejecting harmless signals, as well as controls for tuning the sensitivity to your own wishes.

Alert Modes

All detectors warn of trouble with an audible chirp, click, or buzz, as well as a set of flashing lights. The better ones also give a clear indication of signal strengths. And some distinguish between K and X band frequency signals, possibly useful in determining the number of seconds you have to slow down.

---

*Yes, radar jammers that broadcast signals to fool police radar, much the way the electronic black boxes on Israeli fighter planes fool Syrian anti-aircraft missiles. According to *Car and Driver* magazine, two commercially available models (the $345 Envader from Automotive Outfitters, 96 Old West Country Road, Hicksville, NY 11801, and the $349 Judge Pulsar from Midland Instruments, PO Box 3052, Midland, TX 79702) are moderately effective against some police radar. Take heed, though: Unlike detectors, their use without a license is a federal offense, punishable by a $10,000 fine or—in theory—up to two years in Danbury.

The Micro Eye Quantum radar detector (Courtesy of B.E.L.-Tronics)
. . . .

Size and Portability

Small is beautiful: no need to let every passing smokey know you
have a detector. So is light: Heavier units don't fit on the sun
visor. So is portable: If you are caught, it's nice to be able to
unplug the unit and stow it in the glove compartment before the
trooper gets a look. A few of the more expensive models attach
under the dash, with an antenna concealed in the front grill. This
arrangement certainly looks better, and is less vulnerable to theft.
But it can't be detached quickly when the sirens go off.

For no-frills value, consider the Cobra model 3110 from the Dy-
nascan Corporation, discounted to about $125. At roughly 4 × 3
× 1.2 inches, it is relatively bulky. And its LED warning lights
aren't bright enough to be useful in sunshine. But the unit's sensitivity is more than adequate, and the filtering system for rejecting
false signals is excellent.

For state of the art, go for the PASSPORT from Cincinnati Microwave ($295, not discountable) or the MICRO EYE QUANTUM

from B.E.L.-Tronics ($330, probably discountable). The Passport is very compact (4.5 × 2.8 × 0.7 inches) and very light (6 ounces). The Micro Eye Quantum is even smaller (3.3 × 2.8 × 0.8 inches) and lighter (3.7 ounces). Both are exceptionally sensitive and have the best available systems for rejecting false signals. The Micro Eye even allows you to program a variable warning delay, in which you decide how many seconds the detector samples a signal source before making a decision on its danger.

Passports are available only by ordering from the manufacturer. Phone Cincinnati Microwave at 800-543-1608. B.E.L.-Tronics and Cobra units can be purchased at substantial discounts from the big auto supply houses that advertise in *Road and Track* and *Car and Driver* magazines.

THE BEST

Reason to Make K Mart
Your Saving Place

· ·

W
hen NBC was swallowed by General Electric, network
employees were consoled with an offer of discounts on
GE toasters, washers, and whatnot. The only catch: Appliances
purchased under the discount plan were solely for the use of NBC
employees and their dependents.

An unenforceable rule, you say? According to the GE memo,
"The form you sign authorizes the company to inspect, in your
home, any such product you purchase . . . abuse of this plan will
subject the employee to such discretionary action as the company
deems appropriate." There is not a shred of truth, though, to the
rumor that the GE Appliance Police also plan to spot-check pillows and upholstered furniture for content labels.

THE BEST
Undiscovered Resort

· ·

*I*t's six P.M. Dusk is settling over the river and the grassy savannah beyond. Gin and tonic in hand, you watch fish eagles diving
for prey. Just downstream, a single adult elephant and her baby linger in
the shallows after a long drink. Invisible but close by, a hippo bellows a
complaint . . .

There are other resorts in Africa where the game is as plentiful,
the accommodations as comfortable—the Aberdare Country Club,
for example, in Kenya's achingly beautiful Aberdare Mountains.
But animal-watching at its very best is a spiritual experience, easily
disrupted by clicking cameras and clacking tongues. And few, if
any, resorts can match the serenity and beauty of the **CHOBE
GAME LODGE,** tucked away in the northeast corner of Botswana.

The lodge, 49 rooms and suites hugging the southern bank of
the Chobe River, is the only real hotel in the Chobe National
Park. Actually, it is one of only a handful of places to sleep in
the park, a wilderness of bush and plain and desert roughly the
size of New Jersey.

Most of the common African animals can be found here: hippo,
cape buffalo, giraffe, warthog, baboon, impala, kudo. Birds, especially the big predators and scavengers, are abundant. But
Chobe's pride, and visitors' joy, are the elephant herds.

Some 25,000 elephants live in the park, with the greatest concentration near the river that marks the boundary between Botswana and Namibia. Extended families of 20 or more are a common sight, especially in the afternoons when they come to drink
and play and douse each other with mud. Viewing is done by

Land Rover provided by the lodge management. An even better way to witness the spectacle is to hire a motorboat and guide, then troll the shoreline for the thirsty beasts.

The lodge itself is an oasis of discreet luxury. The summery, handsomely furnished rooms are air-conditioned and have terraces facing the river. Four suites have their own swimming pools. Those less fortunate share one large pool surrounded by flowering bushes and shade trees. Sculpture and ivory carving from local tribes decorate the public rooms.

Dining is al fresco, a dozen yards from the water. The menu is eclectic, running from cruise-ship bountiful to nouvelle French. If the restaurant were in London or New York, the food would rate an A-minus. Served by candlelight, 800 miles from the nearest big city, it is a miracle. Since Botswana is part of a free trade zone with South Africa, the lodge is able to supply estate-bottled wines from the Capetown area that are rarely seen in America or Europe.

After a post-dinner cognac, there is (blissfully) little to do. One might stroll under the blanket of stars, listening to the distant roar of lions mating. Or one can tune in Radio Moscow's English-language service, the sole radio station that reaches this part of the world at night, and a bizarre counterpoint to the cultural dominance of South Africa in the region.

Chobe's only drawback, as well as its saving grace, is isolation. It was built in the mid-1970s on the optimistic assumption that a lot of people would be willing to come a long way in search of perfection. However, the only practical access to Chobe is by road from Victoria Falls, in western Zimbabwe. And when civil war made travel in Zimbabwe dangerous, the lodge was forced to close. Recently reopened (and safe for visitors), it is beginning to serve a trickle of European and American travellers.

To get there, you take the one-hour flight from Harare, the capital of Zimbabwe, to Victoria Falls. Air Zimbabwe's Boeing 720s and 737s are well maintained and often on time. The Game Lodge can arrange transportation from the airport by minibus.

Hardier travellers have the option of renting cars from one of the major rental agencies located at the airport. From Vic Falls (worth a look) there is a good paved road to the Botswana border, some 50 miles away. Chobe is just 15 minutes' border formalities and another 10-mile drive beyond.

The Game Lodge is not cheap—everything from light bulbs to Amstel Lager must be trucked in from Francistown, the closest market town, some 300 miles beyond. Daily rates run about $150 per person, including meals. Reservations can be made direct by telex: 2765 BD, Kasane, Botswana. The easier way is to contact the offices of Sun International, the hotel chain that manages the lodge. In America, phone 800-421-8905. In London, 01-580-6133. In Canada, 416-967-3442. In Germany, 06084-568.

THE BEST
Resort in the Caribbean
· ·

*F*or diversion, there's the 7,000-acre Casa de Campo, designed by Oscar de la Renta and located in the Dominican Republic. At last count, there were 17 tennis courts (eight lit for night play), seven swimming pools, two polo fields (lessons available), horseback riding, squash, and racquetball. Oh yes: Casa de Campo is a beach resort, so there are all the usual water sports. Not to mention restaurants, bars, discos, well-proportioned men and women wearing very little clothing . . . you get the picture.

For gambling, Aruba is the choice—though, in truth, no Caribbean island can match the trashy mega-glitz of Las Vegas or Sun City, the romance of Macao, or the elegance of Monte Carlo. Stay at the Playa Linda Beach Resort, and try any of the five casinos that line the Palm Beach Strip.

For a subdued blast from the colonial past there's Barbados, an island that remains sentimentally and economically attached to Britain. Sandy Lane is the hotel of choice; the decor is Anonymous Continental Posh, but the feel is Authentic Old World.

For diving, there's the Caribbean Club on Grand Cayman, the best hotel on the best island for scuba and snorkling. Eighteen two-bedroom villas on a glorious beach, a skip and a jump from the great reef. Or really get away to Pine Cay, in the Turks and Caicos islands. The delightfully isolated Meridian Club has two miles of beach for its guests. Meridian Divers provides lessons, equipment, and transport to some of the nicest shallow-water coral anywhere.

For chic, follow what is left of the jet set to Mustique, a few square miles of very privately owned sand in the Grenadines. You may not rate guest privileges at Mick Jagger's villa, or Raquel Welch's. But you can still get a feel of how the other .0001 percent lives at the Cotton House, a collection of handsome, clubby cottages attached to a renovated sugar mill.

But for our money (much money), the Caribbean is about doing as little as possible in sunshine, privacy, and unpretentious luxury. And here the competition is quietly fierce. Little Dix Bay, Laurance Rockefeller's place in the British Virgins, consists of 84 cottages, 300 beachfront acres, and 220 servants to pamper you. La Samanna, on the French side of St. Martin, is the one refuge of comfort and calm on this overdeveloped island. The Biras Creek Hotel also has its fans. And why not: Situated on an isolated peninsula of Virgin Gorda, the few dozen guests all have spectacular views, plus a fine restaurant to repair to when they tire of looking.

Our favorite luxury resort is one of the newest: **MALLIOUHANA,** on Maid's Bay, Anguilla. The little hotel is the recent creation of a British couple, Robin and Sue Ricketts. After stints at The Dorchester Hotel in London, The Meurice in Paris, and The Mandarin in Hong Kong, the Rickettses purchased 25 acres on the tip of this speck of an island 10 miles from St. Martin, and built their dream. Malliouhana (reportedly, the Arawak Indian name for Anguilla) is dedicated to tranquil luxury.

The two-story main lodge, whose architectural style is best described as Moorish Beachfront, contains 20 huge, airy rooms, all with balconies overlooking the sea. The furniture is plumply cushioned rattan, the floors white tile, the bathrooms marble. Uncommon touches include Haitian primitive paintings, king-sized tubs, bidets, separate showers, and wet bars. For those who need more space, the seven outlying villas offer three-bedroom suites.

Breakfast (real croissants, Caribbean fruit, and café filtre) on your balcony. Then repair to the pool—actually, three freshwater pools connected by waterfalls with a view of St. Martin in the dis-

tance. Or work off the croissants with a long swim in the shel-
tered water of the bay.

More activity? Borrow a sailboat from the hotel's water sports
center. Play tennis on one of three Laykold artificial surface
courts. Drop a wad of American Express checks in the hotel's
tiny shop, generously stocked by Armani, Hublot, Ferre, Porsche,
and Bottega Veneta. Or give some serious thought to dinner.

Should mood or romance require, any meal can be had in your
room. If you are feeling sociable, the shaded, open-air restaurant
will do nicely. The menu is ambitious French, created and over-
seen at long distance by Jo Rostang of the two-star Bonne Au-
berge in Antibes. The silverware is Christofle, the china Limoges.
Critical provisions are imported from Europe and the States. Try
a simple roast chicken, from Bresse. Or local crayfish, perfectly
grilled. Forgive the occasional slips—this is the British West In-
dies, after all, not la Côte d'Azur.

The wine list is extensive. And pricey.

After dinner, watch a Bogart movie on the hotel's projection
television, stroll the mile of deserted beach in the moonlight, or
do what any sensible couple would want to do in this paradise.

The best way to Anguilla is by air from the Dutch side of Sint
Maarten or by water shuttle from the French side. Reserve a
room far in advance for the winter season. Travel agents will do
it, of course. Or, for last-minute booking, telex 9316 Malhana or
phone 809-497-6111 and pray there's been a cancellation. Rates
start at about $350 a day.

THE BEST
Remedy for Jet Lag

· ·

*I*t's six P.M. Paris time, eight hours since your 747 touched the tarmac at de Gaulle Airport and 18 since you left Toledo. You're standing at the summit of Montmartre, at Sacre Coeur. The sky is clear, the crowds in front of the sprawling Romanesque church have long since dispersed. Below, the sun is changing the city from monochromatic grays to sunset-gold. In the distance, the Eiffel Tower glows in its new suit of floodlights. It is one of the most beautiful urban vistas on earth—yet you couldn't care less.

No, your malaise isn't the hangover from the long, claustrophobic twilight of Cutty's-on-the-rocks, littered aisles, and whimpering infants. It isn't the memory of the death-defying taxi ride from the airport or the hotel clerk who treated you like a drooling retard because you couldn't speak French. It may not even have much to do with the truncated night of sleep, sitting virtually upright. The villain is the asynchronization of the biological clocks in your brain. In plain English: jet lag.

Put a person in a windowless environment without a timepiece and let him choose his own bed and meal times for a few days. Stripped of external cues, his internal rhythms of sleep, hunger, and alertness will create a "natural" day about 25 hours long. Bring him back to the real world of sunrise and sunset, exercise, work, and sex, and he will quickly readjust to the 24-hour rhythm.

The body, it seems, routinely sets back its internal clocks about an hour each day. But ask it to shorten the day by more than an hour (or lengthen it by more than two hours) and you're asking for trouble. Coordination and powers of concentration are diminished. You become moody, ever-ready to slip into apathy. Depression and fatigue, far more disruptive than simple sleeplessness, consume the soul.

What to do? The standard remedy is to grin and bear it, avoiding stressful situations until the internal clocks adjust. Symptoms disappear more quickly on westbound trips with an artificially lengthened day, presumably because the natural, "free running" body cycle exceeds 24 hours. But for days after you think you've returned to normal, there'll be an occasional unhappy reminder—a brief bout of fatigue or indigestion or depression. For those who have only a week or two for a jaunt to Europe or the Far East, the trip may not even be worth the hassle.

Happily, stoicism isn't the only answer. There are relatively simple ways to speed the adjustment, and one not-so-simple remedy that may work even better.

The body clocks use external cues (the jargon is "zeitgeber," German for time-giver) including light, food, and physical activity to reset. By manipulating and exaggerating the cues, the clocks can apparently be made to reset faster. One obvious remedy is to get a headstart on the time change, going to bed and getting up an hour early for an eastbound flight. Dr. Alfred Lewy of the Oregon Health Services University goes a step further. He found evidence that outdoor light is a more efficient cue than artificial light. So if you're travelling east, go outside early in the morning for a few hours. Westbound travellers should stay inside in the late afternoon to avoid reinforcement of the old clock schedule. Once you reach your destination, the more time spent outdoors in the sunshine, the better.

Sleep during travel, even a few hours' snooze, is important. Less because it is refreshing—even a week of total sleep deprivation can be made up with a single ten-hour respite—than because it helps to wipe the slate clean of the old cues and increases the effect of new light, food, and activity cues on the body rhythms. The problem, of course, is tricking your body into sleep when it is tense, or uncomfortably sandwiched into an airline seat.

Any number of sleeping pills are likely to put you out, but most create a hangover, compounding your problems on the first day of jet lag. The solution, according to a study at the Stanford University Medical School, is to use a very short-acting pill from the relatively safe family of chemicals called benzodiazepines. Valium, the most commonly prescribed benzodiazepine, takes too long to be flushed out of the blood. It is far better to use triazolam, sold in the United States as Halcion (see "The Best Sleeping Pill").

Dr. Charles Ehret at the Argonne National Laboratory offers a more complicated, pill-free plan that has apparently been used by President Reagan and the U.S. Army's Rapid Deployment Force. Ehret is also a believer in the zeitgebers, but refines their use. High-protein foods, he notes, stimulate the pathways of the brain that set the clock to daytime and keep you active and alert. High-carbohydrate foods may give you a brief burst of energy, but they perversely stimulate the production of sleep-inducing chemicals. A multi-time-zone traveller can make use of the difference by eating high-protein foods (meat, fish, dairy products) for breakfast and lunch, high-carbo foods (starches and sugars) for dinner.

He also believes that caffeine, as well as the related chemicals theophylline and theobromine (found, respectively, in tea and chocolate), exert a powerful influence on the body clocks. Consume them in the morning, early in the waking phase, and they set the clocks back, lengthening the body's day. Consume them at night, and the day is shortened.

Now for the catch. The body is far more sensitive to the effects of the protein and carbo cues if they are used after a sequence of fasts and feasts. Similarly, the caffeine-family chemicals work better if you avoid them for several days prior to the trip. So to get the maximum effect, Dr. Ehret advises a regimen beginning two or three days before departure, and ending only the day after your arrival.

That makes the whole thing a bit of a bore. Going east across the Atlantic, for example, you eat heavy meals (protein in the morning, carbos at night) three days before the time change. The next day, you follow the same diet, but eat very lightly. The day before the flight, you feast again. On the departure day, you eat lightly. Early in the evening (that's right, the evening), you drink three cups of strong coffee or tea in order to set your clock forward. Then you try to sleep, using a mask to eliminate the effects of other travellers' reading lights. Once you've arrived, slurp up the daylight and stay busy as long as the sun is up. No naps, please. And follow the feast routine, avoiding caffeine.

Is it worth it? Much depends on how important it is to get back to your best quickly, and how successful you find the less disruptive alternatives. If a short-acting sleeping pill combined with a determined attempt to follow the new day-night pattern on arrival works for you, why hassle with the fast-feast bit? On the other hand, if you're particularly sensitive to jet lag and must get back in shape pronto, Ehret does seem to work.

For details on using the Ehret method going east or west, buy his (heavily padded) paperback *Overcoming Jet Lag,* published by Berkley Books.

Restaurant in New York

· ·

*I*nspired by wave after wave of clever, creative chefs yearning
to become rich, bankrolled by a vast army of gourmands who
think nothing of dropping $50 for properly grilled swordfish, rad-
icchio salad, and goblet of Perrier, this is the golden age of New
York restaurants. Where to begin? With less trendy establishments that still deliver fine value as well as fine food.

HSF (46 Bowery)

The action here is dim sum, a hundred variations on the Chinese
dumpling. Stylelessly shovelled from rolling carts to an orderly
mob of second-generation Chinese-Americans, uptown round-eyes,
and European tourists, they make for a heavenly lunch under $10.

Cabana Carioca (123 West 45th St.)

New York's best cheap Brazilian restaurant, and perhaps the ultimate nightmare for weight watchers. Start with cherrystone clams
in broth, or the deadly fried sausage on grease-wilted lettuce.
Move on to giant shrimp, grilled in garlic and oil with a side of
black beans, rice, and crisp cottage fries. Or be daring: Order ba-
calhau a braz, a mountain of salted cod with black olives, sauteed
onions, and eggs. Don't even consider the desserts. . . .

Omen (113 Thompson St.)

Informal Japanese, served in an atmosphere suspended somewhere
between 19th-century Kyoto and 21st-century SoHo. Make an en-

tire dinner from the gorgeously presented appetizers: scallops with peanut creme, squid with green pepper, salmon broiled in salt, spinach with sesame, tuna sashimi, and whatever else inspires. But don't forget to finish with omen, the restaurant's namesake dish of noodles in hot broth. You add the lightly cooked veggies and toasted sesame seeds.

Quatorze (240 West 14th St.)

The closest thing in New York to a great upscale Paris bistro—Brasserie Lipp, say, but with better service. Every dish on the small, rarely changing menu is a memory of good times in the City of Light: chicory with croutons and bacon in a vinaigrette, grilled chicken with a mass of pommes frites, grilled salmon in a pink choron sauce. And dessert! Pear tart with marzipan cream, crème caramel, paper-thin apple tart. Enough said.

But as good as these places can be, they suffer from human scale. The real sex appeal is in the expense-account palaces, where food is religion and price is virtually irrelevant.

Lutèce (249 East 50th St.)

The grande dame of New York French. Housed in an unpretentious brownstone, serving pleasantly (but not spectacularly) plated dishes, Lutèce lies on the unpretentious edge of haute cuisine. But its reputation as the most dependable of good French restaurants is largely deserved. Fine, fresh ingredients are used in simple variations on a classic repertoire: roast chicken with morels; sweetbreads with capers; turbot in a beurre blanc; salmon in puff pastry. But be warned: Those accustomed to excellent bourgeois cuisine in comfortable settings will wonder what the fuss is about.

The Quilted Giraffe (550 Madison Ave.)

A place of fabulous excess, from the stunning "beggar's purse" appetizer (tiny crepes filled with beluga caviar and crême fraiche) to

Le Bernardin restaurant (New York City) (Courtesy of Le Bernardin)

Le Grand Dessert (a dinner plate of ice creams, sorbets, tarts, custards, and pastries) to the wine list (computerized and reprinted daily) to the powder rooms (space-age stainless steel with piped-in opera) to the check. Oh, the check! Bring money; bring more money.

The Four Seasons (99 East 52nd St.)

The first New York restaurant to marry fine food with fine show. The decor is no longer changed with the seasons. But the Pool Room still offers lush atmosphere, attentive service, and an excellent version of whatever food style is in fad. The Bar Room, by contrast, specializes in essence of Fortune 500: leather banquettes, grilled bass, and raw corporate power. The wine list may be the best in New York—not that anyone drinks anymore, mind you, but it's fun to browse.

La Côte Basque (5 East 55th St.)

What most people think of when they think of haute cuisine. La Côte Basque was in a long, apparently terminal decline into snob tourist French when it was sold and spruced up. Back in form, the room is comfortable and inviting, the food complicated, beautiful to look at, and usually tasty. The service is considerate, especially if they recognize you.

The list of candidates could go on. Maurice . . . Chanterelle . . . Montrachet . . . Lafayette . . . Argenteuil . . . Brive . . . Il Nido . . . La Tulipe . . . Jams . . . Prunelle . . . Palio. . . . But why tease?

Le Bernardin

One restaurant stands well above even this exalted crowd: LE BERNARDIN.

Twin of the now-defunct Parisian fish restaurant of the same name, Le Bernardin is an understated oasis of comfort and serious eating in a city hooked on glitz. The teak-ceilinged room, decorated with huge oil paintings of fishing scenes, has the feel of a luxurious, not-too-stuffy business club. Widely spaced tables, thick carpeting, and a friendly, utterly competent staff create a sense of serenity in which no one is tempted to raise his voice above conversational level.

This is seafood paradise, where seasonings are delicate and cooking time is held to a minimum to emphasize the quality and freshness of the fish. Ready for raw? Start with a variety of oysters—bluepoints, belons, cotuits; or the carpaccio of tuna, pounded thin and dressed with a ginger sauce; or slivers of black bass in olive oil, coriander, and basil; or tiny samplings of chopped and dressed tuna, salmon, and snapper. This is also a great (perhaps the only) place to try sea urchins baked in butter. Or, the winner among winners: a fricassee of shellfish in a light cream sauce.

Main courses include amazing scallops with asparagus and curry, sautéed grouper fillet over melted leeks, barely cooked salmon with sorrel sauce (attributed to the great Troisgros), poached halibut in a warm vinaigrette, roasted monkfish on shredded cabbage and salt pork.

Le Bernardin offers a nice list of expensive, familiar white burgundies and champagnes. Go crazy on the Bâtard-Montrachet or the vintage Dom Ruinart rosé. Bargain hunters might try a lesser-know burgundy called St. Aubin.

Dessert? The owners, Gilbert Le Coze and his sister Maguy, never paid much attention to sweets before they came to New York, but they have made up for lost time with some lovely choices that won't leave you stuffed. Try a caramel sampler (tiny portions of caramel ice cream, mousse, flan, oeuf à la neige). Or a chocolate millefeuille: thin layers of crisp chocolate cookie filled with pistachio cream, floating in a puddle of chocolate sauce. Then there is the passion fruit mousse with sugar crunch, or the Zen arrangement of pear tart, pear sorbet, and poached pear. The pear bit is also done in a slightly less successful raspberry version. Save a little room for the fresh chocolate truffles that come with coffee.

Le Bernardin is located in the Equitable Life Building, 51st Street at Seventh Avenue, and is open for lunch and dinner every day but Sunday. Reservations are absolutely, positively necessary: 212-489-1515.

THE BEST

Restaurant in Paris

. . . .

New York restaurants can't be topped for variety or show—where else can you sample everything from sea urchin sushi to Mississippi mud pie, and perhaps in the same establishment? Hong Kong offers the most sophisticated forms of the ten or fifteen distinct cuisines too often lumped together as "Chinese." Rome is where the world goes to eat, a refuge of soothing noodles, sparkling vegetables, fresh mozzarella dripping with milk, and uncomplicated country wines. Singapore is the Asian crossroad, celebrating ethnicity in an explosion of tastes. Marrakesh is a shocker for people who think Arab food is little more than grilled lamb and baklava.

But for true foodies, Paris is still It. Start with "honorable mention," restaurants that would be the best almost anywhere else:

L'Ami Louis

The critics are bored by the menu, which was carved in stone 50 years ago. Health-conscious Parisians complain of calorie overkill and indifferent sanitation. Foreigners not fluent in the world's only civilized tongue occasionally grump about the frosty welcome. But none of this fazes owner-chef-octogenarian Antoine Magnin, whose astounding bistro food (at astoundingly high prices) continues to draw the crowds.

The attractions: slabs of fresh foie gras, the plumpest snails in the Republic, roast chicken with crackling-crisp skin, great tranches of juicy beef rib, perfect thin-cut fries. In winter, Monsiour Magnin works peasant magic with wild pheasant and duck. Forget dessert. (32 rue du Vertbois, 3rd arr.; phone: 887-77-48)

Ambassade d'Auvergne

To enter this handsome old restaurant is to trade the chill of modern Paris for the time-stop warmth of remote south-central France. Auvergnian cuisine leans toward the lusciously leaden— cassoulet, country sausage, pot-au-feu, duck stew. However, chef Emmanuel Moulier, has succeeded in lightening the traditional overstuff with lovely salads and vegetables.

Be sure to start with the grilled goat cheese on greens. And don't miss the chance to taste aligot, an amazing combination of potato and melted mozzarella-like cheese called tomme. Accompany it all with one or two of the striking local wines, rarely found outside the Auvergne. (22 rue du Grenier-St. Lazare; 3rd arr.; phone: 272-31-22)

Le Divellac

Less elegant than La Marée, less subtle than Le Bernardin,* this four-year-old establishment has won the hearts of Parisians with the utter freshness and simplicity of its seafood. The family Divellac used to run the great La Pacha restaurant in the town of La Rochelle. Now they've moved operations to handsome blue-and-white digs in a city where they can be properly appreciated.

Dine on oysters barely simmered with seaweed, turbot on a bed of black, squid-ink flavored pasta, and perhaps a braised sea bream with fennel. Things can get out of hand when the chef tries to placate the nouvelle cuisine mafia—avoid the herb sherbets, the duck livers with frog's legs, the candied cucumbers. But the bitter chocolate soufflé works very well. (107 rue de l'Université, 7th arr.; phone: 551-91-96)

*See "The Best Restaurant in New York."

Le Récamier

Hidden deep in an haut bourgeois neighborhood of the Left Bank, this bastion of fine food and wine generally escapes the notice of the guidebooks. That's fine with the management, which operates the place almost as a club for writers and publishers who can afford the $40 lunch tab. But strangers who seek out Le Récamier are welcome to share its lovely eclectic menu.

Try the salmon tartare, the fricassee of wild mushrooms, the lobster à la nage, the heavily caramelized apple tart. The wine list is rich with burgundies, but the house wines are a special delight. In summer, multiply your pleasure by reserving a table outside. (4 rue Récamier, 7th arr.; phone: 548-86-58)

A Sousceyrac

If you had to choose one Parisian restaurant to take back home, this is likely it. A Sousceyrac is the quintessential neighborhood place—friendly, comfortable, and reasonably priced, with a great variety of simple, delicious dishes. Begin with a terrine of goose liver, or the hot sausage in cream and morel mushrooms. Move on to the famous wild hare stew (Friday nights in fall only), or scallops in sorrel sauce, or the cassoulet. There are bargain wines, many of them real finds. (35 rue Faidherbe, 11th arr.; phone: 371-65-30)

La Tour d'Argent

Like Maxim's, Lasserre, and Ledoyen, this famous luxury restaurant long suffered from the uncritical adulation of tourists. But unlike the others, La Tour d'Argent has recovered. The show's still intact: the moonlight view of Nôtre Dame, the walk-through 140,000-bottle wine cellar, the red velvet everything. So, too, is the duck cooked every which way, long the menu's trademark. But the owner, Claude Terrail, has spiffed up what could euphemistically be called his classic repertoire to include shrimp and artichoke sautéed in walnut oil, lobster with wild asparagus, and rhubarb puff pastry with apricot sauce. Bring deep pockets: La Tour d'Argent is still the most expensive restaurant in Paris. (17 quai de la Tournelle, 5th arr.; phone: 354-23-21)

And the best? Not yet; this is too much fun. Consider two runners-up:

Lucas-Carton/Alain Senderens

Take one of the most beautiful Belle Epoque rooms in France, freshly restored with no concession to cost. Add one of the great entrepreneurial chefs of the age. *Et voilà*: an instant three stars. Alain Senderens, formerly the owner of L'Archestrate, was first off the mark with nouvelle cuisine. But don't hold the excesses of the underdone-pig's-liver-with-chocolate-syrup crowd against him. His version sometimes shocks, but hardly ever fails. Revel in smoked salmon, served warm with caviar and a beurre blanc sauce, duck liver layered with celery and apples, cabbage stuffed with foie gras, breast of duck in honey and peppercorns, scallop ravioli, fig tart, puff pastry with raspberries. Very expensive, and worth it. (9 place de la Madeleine, 8th arr.; phone: 265-22-90)

Taillevent

The service is efficient, the room handsome, the cuisine delicate and imaginative, the wine list simply staggering. And, considering the relentless attention to detail—dessert chocolates are made fresh each day—the prices are reasonable. There is probably not a critic who wouldn't include Taillevent among the three or four best restaurants in the world, let alone Paris.

Start with a salad of scallops with green vegetables, or a sausage of lobster and pike, or oysters warmed with truffles. Then a casserole of lobster with tarragon, or a lightly sauced sea bass, or a simple grilled turbot. Dessert might be chocolate mousse cake with pistachio cream, or a medley of intensely flavored fruit sherbets. Book early, and with a good accent: Like other Parisian restaurants that could fill every seating three times over, Taillevent has an informal quota on foreign guests. (15 rue Lamennais; 8th arr.; phone: 563-39-94)

Jamin/Robuchon

What could be better than the fireworks at Lucas-Carton or the understated perfection of Taillevent? Only the best: JAMIN/ROBUCHON. As food palaces go, this seems to have come from nowhere. Having done his training rounds in a series of hotel kitchens, Joël Robuchon bought a slipping luxury restaurant called Jamin in December 1981. Months later, the Michelin guide awarded him a first star; in 1983, a second. And in 1984, a third star, one of just 20 in France.

Michelin is out on a limb with plenty of company. Gault and Millau, the wise guys of the French food scene, rate Robuchon a 19.5 out of 20. And Patricia Wells, the most trustworthy of critics, calls him "one of the top chefs working in France today."

What makes Robuchon so special? Partly it is the utter professionalism needed to manage a cheerful, seemingly easygoing restaurant that virtually never makes a mistake. Mostly, it is the rare talent to create dishes as tasty as they are unusual. The list is long and growing: rack of lamb in a coat of truffle crumbles, sweetbreads and kidneys with wild girolle mushrooms, rabbit with bacon, ravioli stuffed with shrimp and cabbage, lobster and spinach in a red wine sauce, lamb roasted in a salt crust, rouget in saffron sauce topped with fried thyme.

For those who have trouble choosing, Robuchon makes it easy. His tasting menu offers five little courses, plus a medley of desserts. Pinching pennies? Robuchon also has a gorgeous lunch menu with meals priced under $40, which is one of the great food bargains of life. (32 rue de Longchamp, 16th arr.; phone: 727-12-27)

THE BEST
Road Food

. . . .

*T*he blacktop is smooth and dry, the view marred only by an occasional invitation to save money at Motel Six, or to shower free with a 20-gallon purchase of diesel fuel. There's little traffic, and nary a benzedrine-crazed trucker or spoilsport trooper in sight. All would be well, save for one fact: You're hungry, and can't bear the thought of masticating yet another flame-dried McDouble Whopper Nugget Deluxe. What's the alternative?

Good road food is down, but not entirely out. If, for example, the highway travelled happens to be in north central New Hampshire and you're in the mood for breakfast, head for Polly's Pancake Parlour, on Route 117 in the town of Sugar Hill. This is maple heaven, land of the perfect blueberry buckwheat pancake served with fancy-grade syrup and cob-smoked bacon. Iconoclasts may opt for the French toast. Either way, the point is to sample the fabulous syrup, product of the maple sugar farm next door.

Perhaps you're on I-95, in southern Georgia. Just seconds from Exit 6 (Brunswick) stands the GA Pig, a shack in a pine grove that happens to serve a great pork barbecue. GA's style is tangy tomato-sweet, with an emphasis on smoke. Take it straight, all crunchy and moist with a side of molasses beans. Don't spoil the effect with the Wonder Bread–like sandwich buns.

Or maybe you are on Route 130 near Collingwood, New Jersey, in the heart of the Philadelphia sprawl. Brown's Stop In makes a fine version of the legendary Philadelphia cheese steak: microthin slices of beef, fried up with lots of onions and served with melted American white on a warm (not toasted) Italian roll. If the traditional accompaniment, a milkshake made with real milk, smacks of cholesterol overkill, try the root beer in a frosted mug.

On Oregon's Route 30 near the town of Troutdale, there's Tad's Chicken 'N' Dumplings, source of the regional specialty of the same name. Big chunks of white meat in cream gravy, topped with spongy-doughy dumplings—plain, satisfying food invented by people blissfully ignorant of the caloric theory of body weight. The bland stew might be too much, were it not for the salty counterpoint of a side of mushy, bacon-flavored string beans.

The southern end of Maine's Route 1—tourist-choked in summer, deserted in winter—is a promised land for road foodicts. Among the most pleasing spots for a fix is the Maine Diner in Wells, south of Kennebunkport. The fried clams are first-rate. But lobster is the edible of choice, preferably in the form of the lobster roll. Nothing arty, here; just buttered chunks of lobster heaped onto a grilled bun. Top off lunch with homemade pie. Red raspberry, if it's in season; banana cream, if not.

However, if you're very lucky, the first spasms of hunger will hit somewhere in northwestern Connecticut, within detouring distance of **MARY DUGAN'S DEPENDABLE HOME COOKING** on Route 202, four miles east of New Milford.

According to the restaurant's place mat, Mary Dugan was born in Boston in 1923, the daughter of Teddy Roosevelt's personal cook at the battle of San Juan Hill. Mary served our boys as an army cook in World War II, then spent 10 years leading a fruitless campaign to make Mah Jongg the national pastime. Returning to her first love, she became an itinerant baker, touring the nation in her salmon-and-gray two-door Belair while fighting a one-woman war to "stem the tide of McDonaldization." It was during this period that her cookbook-memoir, "Creamed Chipped Beef . . . Servicing the Armed Forces," was published.

On one of her pie-baking forays to Litchfield County (a WASP bastion of chicken salad on toast and tuna surprise), she came upon the ideal site for a roadside restaurant: a white clapboard Victorian house just down the road from the A-Bar-A Riding Sta-

IN MEMORIAM
1923–1986

Mary Dugan was born in Boston in 1923. Her father came over from an old country in the mid part of the 19th century. He was Teddy Roosevelt's personal cook of San Juan Hill and was made an honorary Rough Rider.

Mary had a normal childhood growing up in Boston until she was forced into the Chelsea High School Fresh Air Program due to her ill health. There she was forced to spend early winter mornings bundled in blankets, resting on cots on the roof of the school building, eating boiled potatoes. She ran away from home and joined the army in 1941. After 4 years of undistinguished service, excepting the accidental burning of two mess halls, she received an honorable discharge.

In the late 40's and early 50's, she tried to make it big with the new national pastime to replace baseball. She reasoned that it was much less expensive, as a smart business woman, to travel out east for better East / West relations. This attempt failed.

In 1960's she became an itinerant baster, traveling throughout the southwest, New England, and New Jersey in the new salmon and grey 2-door Bel Air. It was her hope that her homemade pies could help stem the tide of "MacDonaldization" by keeping the small, homecooking establishments viable. This attempt failed. Her first, and thus far only published work, was a cookbook entitled *Creamed Chipped Beef: Servicing the Armed Forces*. It was later turned into a novel by Grove Press.

On one of her pie-baking trips through Litchfield County, Connecticut, she spotted the site of the existing Mary Dugan's Dependable Homecooking at U.S. Highway 202 in New Milford. It was her fervent hope that she could one day open her own restaurant where the motto could truly be, "If we don't serve it, we won't serve it." Mary Dugan died in her sleep, January 15, 1986, one day before her dream was realized.

Mary Dugan's Dependable Home Cooking, an institution since 1986, U.S. Highway 202, New Milford, Ct. Tel. 203-354-3412

ble and cheek by jowl with the Northville Hardware Store. She never realized her dream, alas, passing away just one day before the restaurant opened. But her name and dedication to the eradication of frozen flounder fillets live on.

Now, some believe Mary is a figment of the management's imagination. But co-owner Sam Cardonsky, formerly a New York art magazine publisher, swears every word is true. And once you dip into a bowl of Sam's New England–style clam chowder, overflowing with tender, barely cooked shellfish and chunks of potato in bacon-scented cream, you won't quibble.

Actually, Mary Dugan's is two restaurants in one. By day, it serves an upscale version of classic diner food. For breakfast, start with fresh-squeezed O.J. Then move on to a cheddar cheese omelet made with eggs laid that morning at the nearby Centerbrook Farm. Great hash browns. A side of country sausage, cured without nitrites by Nodine's Smokehouse in Goshen, Connecticut, would go nicely. If there's a chill in the air, you might want to add a bowl of McCann's Irish Oatmeal with warm milk and good maple syrup. Wash it all down with coffee brewed from freshly ground Colombian beans.

For lunch, there are burgers beyond belief—juicy, thick halfpounders (cheese and nitrite-free bacon optional) with buns baked daily on the premises. Or grilled cheese and ham on toasted homemade bread. Perhaps steak and eggs. The fries are thin-cut, with the skins left on. Onion rings come in a sizzling tangle. Desserts vary (in form, not quality) with the mood of the baker. Only the very lucky get a chance at the chocolate prune daquoise, a multilayered extravaganza of meringue, prune crunch, and chocolate fudge. But the selection almost always includes an oversized chewy brownie, rice pudding dusted with cinnamon, a lovely lardcrust pie, and a layer cake with butter cream frosting. The "à la mode" is courtesy of Ben and Jerry's Vermont Ice Cream.

But for weekend dinner, the mood changes from platonic shortorder to post-nouvelle eclectic: grilled skewers of swordfish and shrimp, paella with squid ink, scallops in vermouth, pancakes stuffed with mushrooms and ham, spaghetti with tomato and black olives baked in parchment, salads of arugula, radicchio, and goat cheese. Guest chefs, gifted amateurs like writer William Kinsolving (French peasant chicken), show off on occasion. But it is hard to beat the regular cooking, particularly the California creations of Linnea Millium, who trained at Chez Panisse in Berkeley. Very nice wine list at bargain prices. To avoid the weekend crush, call ahead for a table: 203-354-3412.

Rock Band

. . . .

Rock and roll began as a blend of musical opposites—gospel and honky-tonk, blues and country, black and white. Elvis Presley wasn't the only teenager in the early fifties to enjoy both the Grand Ole Opry and The Ink Spots; he just enjoyed the contradiction more than most. When Sun Records released his version of "That's All Right" (an Arthur Crudup blues number) backed with "Blue Moon of Kentucky" (a Bill Monroe bluegrass tune), Sun's president, Sam Phillips, knew he had what he'd been looking for: a white man with "the Negro sound." In the 30-odd years since, rock and roll has absorbed an even greater diversity of influences, from Indian ragas to Gregorian chants. The mutations have multiplied accordingly.

One of the most significant occurred in the mid-'6os, when The Velvet Underground—a New York quartet known earlier as The Warlocks—hooked up with Andy Warhol and became part of his Exploding Plastic Inevitable, a multimedia happening that was a prototype for disco.

At the time, rock was making a bid for acceptance as an art form; The Beatles were about to release *Sgt. Pepper,* and it wouldn't be long before The London Symphony Orchestra would deign to record with The Moody Blues. The Velvet Underground offered a reminder that art was not the same thing as mass-culture respectability. Raw and dissonant, they combined a deliberately primitive sound with an avant-garde sensibility. The group may not have sold many records, but in retrospect, their emergence from the pop art demi-monde stands as a seminal event in rock history.

By the mid-'70s, when their seed was bearing fruit in the form of punk bands with names like Richard Hell and the Voidoids, rock had become a broad-based entertainment form as easily consumable as network sitcoms. The ultimate expression of this was disco: depersonalized, yet highly erotic, party music that reached its apotheosis with The Bee Gees' soundtrack for *Saturday Night Fever*. Disco broke every rule of rock and roll but one: It had a beat you could dance to. Punk rock, which beneath its violent exterior combined an art-school sensibility with a purist's conception of what rock was all about, was exactly the opposite. Some sort of blend was almost inevitable.

It happened with New Wave, which combined the nihilism of punk with the revelry of disco. In America, the band that led this transition was Talking Heads, a bunch of art-school dropouts who got their start on the Bowery. They were soon exploring the possibilities of African polyrhythms under the tutelage of Brian Eno, the leading British art-rock experimentalist of the '70s.

In England, the New Wave came with a Manchester band called **NEW ORDER.** Years earlier, under the name Joy Division, members of New Order made exquisitely lugubrious music that betrayed a fascination with death which was extreme even for the stay pretty/die young world of rock and roll.* When lead singer Ian Curtis committed suicide shortly before Joy Division's second album was to be released, the other members reformed as New Order and started recording on their own. What's resulted, on a trio of albums called *Power, Corruption and Lies; Low Life;* and *Brother-*

---

*Joy Division, incidentally, was the name the Nazis gave to prostitutes who serviced the soldiers of the Reich. And the New Order was Hitler's dream of a purified Europe under German rule. Nobody ever said you had to have good taste to play good music....

hood, is music that's irresistibly kinetic, densely textured, and authoritative in a way few pop groups have managed. More than any other band, New Order represents what rock has become three decades after Elvis: serious, fun, and not for kids.

THE BEST
Running Shoe
. . . .

Aching for a quad-density midsole with Anatomical Cradle? Perhaps you'd prefer an ASICS GELpad layered on a plain old EVA midsole? Don't jump too quickly, though; to get either, you might have to forgo the subtler pleasures of a thermoplastic motion control collar. . . .

Why all the techno-babble? The shoemakers are desperate. With lunch-hour athletes distracted by aerobics, jazzercise, and whatnot, running-shoe manufacturers have taken to flogging high-tech fantasies the way Detroit used to peddle horsepower. But happily for runners, it's not entirely hype. Most of the new shoes are far easier on the feet than first-generation Adidas, Pumas, and Nikes. The trick is to match their strengths to your weaknesses.

If all you really want is a pretty face, go for Reebok LX8500's ($85). It is one of the few running shoes made from glove leather; most of the others are crafted from pigskin or synthetics, and it shows. The LX8500 is trimmed in a busy, '50s high-style look as well suited to the disco floor as the track. One other idea: the Diadora Impact 3000 ($97), a snazzy white shoe with gray and red trim. This model, by the way, is made from kangaroo leather coated with Gore-Tex to let air in and keep water out.

If price is the object, look no further than the Turntec Quixote Plus, a steal at $40. The secret to keeping the cost down is the single-piece, lightweight midsole that works as well as fancier designs.

Almost all running shoes come in both men's and women's versions. But some manufacturers cheat, changing the cosmetics without changing the shape on their women's models. Women who have trouble with fit might try the New Balance W690 ($70) or the Saucony Lady Shadow ($55), good all-around shoes that are definitely made on women's lasts.

If you run cross-country or venture frequently onto poorly maintained trails, traction and ankle-support are priorities. The Adidas Marathon Trainer ($50) has an outer sole that looks like the tread of an M-1 tank; unbeatable in mud or sand. Those who don't count their pennies, though, may find the ankle-protecting Hersey High-Top ($185) hard to resist. Like all Hersey shoes, the High Top is custom-fitted to the idiosyncrasies of your foot. For a brochure, write Hersey Shoes, RFD No. 3, Box 7390, Farmington, ME 04938, or phone 207-645-3015.

If you happen to be an electronics nut as well as a serious runner, consider the Puma RS Computer ($200). The shoe itself is good, but nothing to run home about. What makes it special are the sensors and microchips in the sole that measure and record your performance. After a workout you plug the shoe into a personal computer, then analyze the data with Puma's shockingly sophisticated and much-too-complicated software.

Runners whose feet roll sharply to the side as they stride—the same folks whose street shoes wear quickly on one side—need extra motion control to prevent a variety of aches and pains. Alas, no single design aimed at stability seems to suit every runner. Two interesting candidates that are both light and flexible: the Turntec Flexlite ($70) and the Brooks Argent ($75). Their extraordinary stability, by the way, makes them excellent walking shoes for the urban commuter. Those who don't get the control they need with conventional shoes might shell out for the custom-fitted Hersey DPS II ($165). See above for the address and phone.

Are you the lucky sort whose feet and legs were built for running? Forget about motion control and buy for cushioning alone. Here, the shoe of choice is the radically designed Nike Sock Trainer ($60). Resembling a cross between a beanbag and a bedroom slipper, the sock trainer is hard to take seriously. But once

New Balance 1300 Training Shoe (Courtesy of New Balance Athletic Shoe, Inc.)

. . . .

you strap on a pair—the elastic mesh uppers need no laces—you'll understand why Nike is risking its reputation on The Wimp Look. Pure comfort.

Ordinary mortals need both motion control and cushioning, and most would be pleased if the package were also light and durable. Consider three new shoes in the less-than-their-weight-in-gold category: the Avia 600 ($66), with its widetrack, cantilever sole for stability and B-plus shock absorption; the Kangaroos Omnicoil ($70), cleverly engineered for light weight and flexibility, as well as control; and the Nike Air Support ($75), with its fabulously squishy airsole.

But the conservative choice for best all-round shoe is a three-year-old design from NEW BALANCE. The model 1300 ($130) is the Honda Accord of running shoes, machines that do everything well without much fuss or flash. They rate an A for stability, an A-minus for shock absorption, and are built to last considerably longer than most of the competition. The heel sits a full inch above the toe inside the shoe—a fraction more than other models—reducing strain on sore Achilles' tendons.

The only real complaints about the 1300 (apart from price) are higher-than-average weight and a sense of distance from the road. The latter follows from the 1300's exceptionally bouncy shock absorption materials. Bounce a pair before you buy. Like all New Balance shoes, they are available to fit very wide (men's EEE, women's D) and very narrow (men's B, women's AA) feet.

P.S. Never, never, never buy a running shoe that doesn't feel great in the store. Running shoes don't become more flexible with wear, and don't stretch to fit the foot. What you feel the first time is what you get.

THE BEST
Scotch

. . . .

Whiskey drinkers are brand-loyal. Dewar's partisans never touch Cutty Sark. J & B fans turn up their noses at Johnnie Walker Red. And virtually every member of the clan considers "bar" scotch—you know, Glen MacBews, the one with the plaid label—beneath contempt.

Sip them straight, side by side, and you'll find there are indeed differences. Ballantine has a bite; J & B a slightly oily, perfumy aftertaste; Cutty Sark a pleasant mellowness edging toward Canadian whiskey. Premium brands, like Chivas Regal and Johnnie Walker Black, are a bit richer and smoother, reflecting longer aging and perhaps the superior pedigrees of the component whiskies. But once chilled and diluted by water or soda, these differences aren't easy to detect.

Name-brand scotches are all blends, typically from dozens of different whiskies. There is nothing inherently wrong with blending; many great wines and all sherries are blends. But with scotch, the whole point of blending is to create a bland brew with mass appeal, and at minimum cost. The blenders use distinctive (and expensive) barley malt whiskies as a base; add cheaper, generic malt whiskies; then fill up to 70 percent of the bottle with still cheaper rye- or wheat-based whiskies. The result is fine for mixed drinks, but has little of the complexity drinkers expect from good wine or cognac.

There's no way to unblend scotch, removing, say, the élite Laphroaig malt whiskey from White Horse, or the Glendronach from Teacher's. But, happily, the first-rate distilleries save a bit of their output for bottling as unblended "single malt" scotches.

Single malts are all made with similar ingredients and similar processes. Barley (typically from East Anglia in England) is soaked in warm water to start germination. The resulting "malt" is then dried over a smokey peat fire, ground up, mixed with water and yeast, and permitted to ferment. This alcoholic brew is distilled twice to yield a clear, 140-proof (70 percent alcohol) whiskey. Once cut with water, it is set aside to age in oak barrels flavored with traces of sherry or bourbon.

Distillers make a fuss about the water, often using only a single stream near the distillery to meet their requirements. But the really important differences are the source of the peat and the drying technique. Single malts from Islay generally reflect the higher iodine content of the local peat and a preference for smokier-tasting whiskies. Single malts from the Highlands, often cited as the best, are more delicate.

By law, all scotches must be aged at least three years. Single malts usually spend 10 or 12 years in wood. Some really amazing ones are aged for 25 years or more, usually in old sherry barrels.

The best place to start a quick tasting tour of single malts is with the Glenlivet, a model of Highland delicacy. No ice please, but a dash of water at room temperature is acceptable. Strike a contrast with Laphroaig, an Islay malt reeking with peat smoke. Then check out a variety of Highland malts: Cardhu, Glenfiddich, Glenmorangie, Glenfarclas, Talisker. Each is lightly peated and complex, yet quite distinct in flavor. End the tour with the scotch that many single-malt drinkers acknowledge as the best: MACALLAN, a smooth, delicate whiskey that surely ranks with the great cognacs.

Actually, the pleasure of single malts is the seemingly infinite variety. Macallan, for example, can be found in 12-, 18- and 25-year-old ages and in a number of bottling years. While they all belong to the same taste family, they are no more alike than different vintages of the same red wine, and no easier to rank in quality.

Many of the distilleries welcome visitors and willingly dispense samples. The more practical way to explore the terrain, though, is at a bar that carries a large selection. The Potstill, on Hope Street in Glasgow, stocks over 100. The bar at the Athenaeum Hotel, 116 Piccadilly, London, stocks 54. And Keens Chop House, West 36th Street, New York City, manages at least 40.

Most upscale liquor merchants in America and continental Europe carry a half-dozen single malts. Figure on spending $18 to $25 a bottle, or roughly the same price as 12-year-old blended scotches. But the best source is the Soho Wine Market, 3 Greek Street, London, which carries 150 different bottlings from dozens of distilleries. Its namesake on the other side of the Atlantic, Soho Wine and Spirits, 461 West Broadway, New York City, comes through with more than 30. A & A Wines and Spirits in Washington also carries an impressive list.

Screwdriver

. . . .

S o you think a screwdriver is a screwdriver? Join the throngs of penny-foolish amateurs who risk stripped screwheads and scraped knuckles every time they hang curtains or tighten a bicycle fitting.

Super-cheapo, six-for-$5 screwdrivers are typically made of low-strength steel alloys, poised to self-destruct the first time you put any real muscle into them. General purpose, hardware store-grade screwdrivers are made from tougher stuff, but are poorly designed.

Their tapered tips fit a variety of screw slots. But the taper guarantees that the only contact between driver and screw will be at the very top of the slot. This maximizes the stress on the metal, increasing the chance of damaging the screw as you apply torque. Worse, the taper acts as a cam, pushing the tool out of the slot as you twist. That's why the single most important feature of a good screwdriver is a parallel-cut tip.

The best available are the **PARAGON WORKED OVAL** screwdrivers, made in England for the Garrett Wade Company. Their blades have a broad, flattened-out portion on the shank, allowing a hold for a wrench to apply extra force. And the shanks are attached to the handles with a grooved, solid brass ferrule that makes it close to impossible for the parts to work loose. The handles themselves are made from beechwood in a bulbous oval shape that allows an excellent grip.

Garrett Wade Worked Oval screwdrivers come in 3- , 4- , 5- , 6- , 7- , and 8-inch lengths. Buy two or three to assure the right fit. Better still, buy the set. It runs a rich $50, but will probably last longer than you do. Phone: 800-221-2942, or 212-807-1757.

Shotgun

· ·

*I*f your aim is a well-designed weapon for shooting skeet or
water fowl, there's no need to spend a fortune. A classic,
double-barreled, double-trigger Savage-Stevens 311 costs $300.
The more modern, pump-action Mossberg Model 500, with interchangeable barrels, runs about the same amount. Or for $500,
you could have the gas-powered, autoloading Remington Model
1100, favored for its low recoil and utter reliability.

But cognoscenti are searching for something beyond function.
They seek a link with a mythic, gentler past, when devoted craftsmen made double-barreled shotguns by hand for an appreciative
leisure class. Such perfection is still available, but doesn't come
cheap.

Until World War II, several small factories catered to America's
would-be gentry with some of the finest shotguns in the world.
But the market for handmade guns declined as the price gap wid-
ened between superb and the merely good. Today, the only way
to buy a mint-condition L. C. Smith or Parker or A. H. Fox is at
an auction, or from a specialized dealer. The value of such antiques is determined more by scarcity than quality. A fairly common, utilitarian model can be had for a few thousand dollars. The
rarest, custom-engraved Parker will fetch well over $100,000. If
you're still game, pay a visit to the firm of Griffin and Howe in
New York City (589 Broadway, New York, NY 10012; phone: 212-
966-5323).

The only American manufacturer upholding an élite tradition is

U.S. Repeating Arms Corporation in New Haven. USRAC makes the Winchester Model 21 under license, from a design first sold in the 1930s. The basic "Standard Custom" weapon takes about 600 hours of labor to produce and costs about $8,000. A heavily embellished version, "The Grand American," runs over $21,000. If that seems steep, consider the extremely accurate replica of the Parker DHE shotgun, made in Japan by Ohlin-Winchester for about $3,000. Most, reportedly, are being purchased by collectors of real Parkers who dare not fire—or even display—their museum-grade originals.

Among European makers, the Italian firm of Armi Famars crafts a beautiful line of shotguns, sold in America by Griffin and Howe. Exel Arms of America (14 Main St., Gardner, MA 01440; phone: 617-632-5008) imports fine Spanish replicas of classic European guns at less than outrageous prices. Boss and Company and Holland & Holland of London maintain very high standards. Holland & Holland, incidentally, operates a superb school in shotgun use outside London. For information, write the company at 33 Bruton St., London W1X 8JS, England.

But for the absolute best, the real gentleman's shotgun, there is only one choice: the British-made **PURDEY.** James Purdey opened his first shop in London in 1814. By the 1850s the firm of Purdey and Sons was well established as custom gunmaker to the rich and famous—among them Prince Albert, Czar Nicholas I, and the King of Italy. The hammerless, double-barreled shotgun now sold at Purdey's South Audley Street store is an 1884 design, slightly modified to incorporate modern safety features and higher-strength steel alloys. A showroom display, still used to demonstrate its working parts to inquisitive visitors, is almost 70 years old.

Altogether, about 18,000 Purdey shotguns have been made, including a pair of one-sixth-scale miniatures for King George V's Silver Jubilee. Guns now trickle out of the factory at a rate of 100 a year. Bing Crosby, Charles Darwin, Leonid Brezhnev, the Duke of Windsor, and Queen Elizabeth II have been customers.

Nikita Khrushchev bought four to shoot ducks. General Franco blew part of his thumb off with a Purdey.* Prices currently start at about $20,000.

What you get for the money is an understated work of art. Parts are mostly handmade, then modified until they have the desired balance and feel for the individual customer. Stocks are handcarved from wood chosen for both strength and appearance. Once assembled, the polished wood and metal parts blend together, as if without seams. Buyers may specify custom engraving. But true believers—and why buy a Purdey if you aren't?—prefer Purdey's own traditional "Fine Rose and Scroll" pattern. Orders usually take about two years to complete.

For more information, write James Purdey and Sons, 57-58 South Audley St., London W1Y 6ED, England.

---

*The accident occurred in 1962, when the Spanish dictator was hunting birds with a gun manufactured in 1923. Purdey's sent an investigator to the scene, who concluded that the General's loader inadvertently added a second charge to the barrel. Franco apparently forgave the gunmaker: He subsequently ordered another pair of shotguns from Purdey. No one remembers what happened to the loader.

Sitcom

· ·

A horse is a horse, of course, of course. And a sitcom's a sitcom, right? Not quite. But good or bad—and we all know how bad they can be—the successful situation comedy is the ultimate mass entertainment.

Sitcoms are enshrined in the Museum of Broadcasting, the Library of Congress, and even the Smithsonian, where Archie and Edith Bunker's chairs have been added to the Archive of National Treasures. Classics like "The Honeymooners" offer shared reference points for a nostalgia-hungry culture ("One of these days, Alice . . ."). Some even cannibalize other shows to create a sense of continuity: "Diff'rent Strokes" 's Gary Coleman, playing a Harlem waif adopted by a Park Avenue millionaire, eyeballs his swank new home and exclaims, "This beats anything I ever saw on 'The Brady Bunch'!"

An excursion through the landmarks of sitcomania should start with "I Love Lucy," the first sitcom to demonstrate the creative potential of the medium, not to mention the incredible value of syndication rights. Make a brief detour to the surreal world of "Burns and Allen," where George observes the zany doings of Gracie et al. from a "television" in his garage office. Then laugh and cry (and try not to feel self-conscious) with the gentle country folk of "The Andy Griffith Show." Rediscover the wry wit of "The Adventures of Dobie Gillis." Time-trip back to the I-Like-Ike humor of "Ozzie and Harriet," "Leave It to Beaver," and "The Dick Van Dyke Show."

Most of the giants are of pre-'60s sensibility, before television began its transformation to polyester. But don't overlook more recent offerings such as "All in the Family," "Maude," "Cheers," "M*A*S*H," and the underrated "Taxi."

Still, compared to all that came before and all that have followed, there's no question that "**THE MARY TYLER MOORE SHOW**" is the apotheosis of the genre. It set the standard for the articulate television comedy that flowered briefly in the '70s. Mary Richards is witty, intelligent, moving—and, most important, a real person. There are no genies or Martians in her world. She is neither spacey mom nor wacky wife, but an adult with the hint of a Past. References are made to the medical student Mary apparently lived with before moving to Minneapolis to seek her fortune.

While Marlo Thomas broke new ground in "That Girl" in 1966 by showing that a healthy American woman could live on her own, the character she played—decidedly a girl—was mainly interested in her man. Mary, on the other hand, put career first. She knew what she wanted (or at least what she was supposed to want) but didn't always have the nerve to get it. On her first day of job-hunting she is interviewed by WJM-TV producer Lou Grant, who asks her if she wants a drink as he pulls a pint from his desk drawer . . .

MARY: No thanks.
LOU: Oh, come on.
MARY Well, all right, I'll have a brandy alexander.
LOU: How old are you?
MARY: Thirty.
LOU: What religion are you?
MARY (HESITATING): Mr. Grant . . . I don't know how to say this . . . but you're not allowed to ask that when someone's applying for a job. It's against the law.
LOU: Wanna call a cop? Are you married?
MARY: Presbyterian.

Lou might have been gruff, but he was a sucker for Mary. He and the rest of her TV family—Ted, Murray, Rhoda, Phyllis,

Georgette, and Sue Ann Nivens*—formed an exquisite comic ensemble. Probably most important, "Mary" knew what most other sitcoms didn't: Life could be cruel as well as zany, and sometimes simultaneously. In the show's most famous episode, Lou breaks the news that WJM's resident kiddie-show clown is the victim of a freak accident:

"Chuckles the Clown is dead," he sadly informs his staff. "He went to the parade dressed as Peter Peanut, and a rogue elephant tried to shell him." To break the ensuing stunned silence, Lou muses, "Lucky more people weren't hurt . . . lucky that elephant didn't go after anyone else." To which Murray replies, "That's right. After all, you know how hard it is to stop after just one peanut."

Laughter was also a rueful afterthought when Ted falsely spread the word that Mary was having an affair with him. "Why are you doing this?" she asks. "I've always wanted to have an affair with a class girl, an uptown chick," he replies. "But Ted," she protests, "I'm not uptown." His reply: "I know, but you're the nearest I can get. Most of the girls I've known chew four sticks of gum at one time."

To find "Mary" and other oldies-but-goodies, you have to keep your VCR primed for oddball time slots. For years NBC's New York station tirelessly recycled "The Mary Hour" in the one-to-two P.M. graveyard. The station received over a thousand protest calls when it finally discontinued the package in 1985.

---

*WJM's toxic-tongued Happy Homemaker, whose shows included "What's All This Fuss About Famine?" and "A Salute to Fruit."

Ski

· ·

*T*en years ago, it wouldn't have made much sense to talk about a best ski. Too much depended on where you skied and how. Skis that worked like wings on the dry powder of Alta would have been a bear to control on the crushed ice of Killington. Skis designed for World Cup slalom racing would have sent the one-week-a-year-at-Aspen crowd reeling back to Westwood.

It's still true that the edge of performance comes at the expense of versatility. But thanks to new materials and very clever engineering, skis can now be made that are fun for almost everyone on almost every surface. Cynics who run the upscale ski shops in suburban malls call them "doctor" skis—models good enough for experts, forgiving enough for weekenders, and pricey enough for social-climbing heart surgeons. We'll settle for the Madison Avenue euphemism: luxury cruisers.

Some possibilities:

Ohlin Ultra (about $700)

Ohlin specializes in the less-is-more look. No radical shapes, no pastel paint. Just beautifully finished machinery known for its quiet competence and predictability. The Ultra, Ohlin's most expensive ski, certainly fits the image. It is relatively soft and virtually vibration-free, as you would expect in a glass and carbon fiber ski with edges "segmented" for flexibility. The result is a very stable, surprisingly quick-turning ski that will please everyone except very demanding skiers who spend a lot of time on hardpack snow.

Rossignol Quantum 909 (about $330)

Never subtle, the world's largest ski company makes excellent products bristling with interesting gadgets. This new model has both internal and external vibration-damping systems for maximum hold on ice, plus a unique, flexible plastic shovel to reduce weight and speed the ski into turns. A bit on the quick side for timid intermediates, but a fine, all-around ski. Among the better values in the category.

LaCroix Espace Nidaramide (about $700)

LaCroix was the first of the boutique ski makers, small manufacturers who specialize in fine technology, beautiful finish, and more than a whiff of snobbery. This model is a real space-age wonderworks, an incredibly complicated combo of Nomex fiber (used in *Voyager*, the round-the-world airplane), fiberglass, carbon fiber, Kevlar, and plastic foam. The package is very light and quick, yet stable at high speed. Perhaps the most versatile ski ever made for experts.

K2 VO Unlimited (about $350)

The skis at the top end of most lines are generally designed with men in mind. The K2 VO Unlimited is an exception, a low-vibration, smooth-riding ski for intermediates and experts who are 10 to 20 pounds lighter and a bit less muscular. Construction is fiberglass and Kevlar for maximum strength, with a layer of rubber to prevent chatter on ice. Excellent price/performance ratio.

Atomic Avantgarde Trionic (about $375)

This ski is highly damped and very stable at high speeds, qualities that usually make a ski hard to turn. But with the Trionic, a soft-flexing laminate of aluminum and fiberglass with carbon fiber reinforcement, you get it both ways. It also features an exceptionally hard, state-of-the-art "sintered" base, which keeps the skis slippery in a variety of snow conditions.

Vielhaber Black Fusion (about $575)

Another gorgeously finished boutique ski, this one from a Norwegian company. But don't let the pretty face fool you. It is very strong and exceptionally stable on ice—the perfect ski for chewed-up New England snow, and a very good one in friendlier climes. Made from the usual stuff: lots of fiberglass toughened with carbon and Kevlar.

Nishizawa Demonstrator Formula Boron

And the best? We'd opt for the awkwardly named Demonstrator Formula Boron (about $565) from a Japanese manufacturer. Japanese skis have yet to make much impact in a market dominated by European and American companies. But thanks to Nishizawa (and Kazama, another innovator), the world is about to discover another product made very, very well in the land of the rising sun. This model was originally designed for instructors who might be demonstrating turns to beginners at 10 AM, and grand slalom techniques to hot-shots at 11. Such range is just what the doctor ordered for a luxury cruiser.

The Demonstrator Formula Boron is exceptionally flexible, which goes a long way toward explaining its tame behavior and easy turning at slow speeds. The surprise is at high speeds, where it remains stable and predictable. Just how Nishizawa manages this is unclear. Perhaps it has something to do with the fiberglass-aluminum laminate design and wood core. Perhaps it is the addition of ultrastrong, ultralight boron fiber as reinforcement. Whatever the explanation, affluent skiers in the intermediate class and beyond are in for a treat.

Nishizawa skis aren't easy to find in America; this year, only a few hundred pairs of the Demonstrator model will be imported. To locate a retailer call the distributor, Vail Alpine Specialists, in Denver. Phone (800) 873-3050.

THE BEST
Sleeping Pill

. . . .

*T*onight, 25 million Americans will lie awake long into the
wee hours wondering why they are cursed by consciousness.
Most insomniacs are eventually driven to pills. Those who don't
play it very cautiously almost always end up sorry.

First, the bad news. The most popular (and initially most effective) medications become useless within two weeks because they
interfere with the normal stages of sleep. Increased doses do
bring temporary relief. But, with the exception of chloral hydrate
(brand name: Noctec, Orodrate), high doses also bring nasty hangovers. And once the body's tolerance has grown to very high levels of a sedative, users face an additional set of risks. Most are
physically addicting: Rapid withdrawal can produce unpleasant side
effects ranging from sweaty palms to heart attacks. All are potent
central nervous system depressants that mix poorly with alcohol:
Chug down your Nembutal or Placidyl (Supreme Court Chief Jus-
tice Rehnquist's folly) with a snifter of cognac, and the next stop
may be the morgue.

So much for the label warning. Some sleeping pills do work
better than others. Used infrequently and in small doses, the best
ones work very well.

All the good sedatives belong to a chemical group known as
benzodiazepines, of which the most familiar are diazepam (Valium)
and chlordiazepoxide (Librium). Benzodiazepines create the same
risks as other sedatives—rebound effects, hangovers, addiction,
dangerously high potency when mixed with alcohol. But physicians generally prefer them because they are more forgiving and

less likely to lead to trouble. The one most commonly prescribed for sleeping is flurazepam (Dalmane), and with some reason. In clinical tests of severe insomniacs, flurazepam remained effective for about four weeks, far longer than other, traditionally prescribed sedatives. But two newer benzodiazepines are rapidly replacing Dalmane as sleeping pills of choice. Taken at bedtime, temazepam (Restoril) seems to be particularly effective in preventing frequent nighttime awakening, or waking very early in the morning. The drawback is occasional morning drowsiness. Triazolem (Halcion), doesn't quite live up to the promise of the brand name. But Halcion is distinguished from other members of the benzodiazepine family by its very short duration of action. Most of the dose is gone from the bloodstream by morning, making a hangover much less likely.

P.S. The Non-Pill Pill. There is one nonaddicting and probably harmless chemical that often induces sleep. Tryptophan, one of the amino acid components of ordinary proteins found in meat and milk, seems to have a mild sedative effect. According to Cheryl Spinweber, a psychologist who tested tryptophan on Marines at the Naval Research Center in San Diego, there isn't enough tryptophan in a glass or two of milk to make a difference—so much for Grandma's advice. However, since tryptophan is classified by Uncle Sam as a "nutrition supplement" rather than a drug, pure tryptophan pills can be purchased without prescription.

The recommended dosage: between two and four thousand milligrams nightly. It doesn't always work. But since it seems to be a benign chemical, it may be worth a try.

Soap Opera

· ·

MARSHA: (tenderly) John . . .

JOHN: (more tenderly) Marsha . . .

MARSHA: (wistfully) John. John. John.

JOHN: (more wistfully) Marsha. Marsha. Marsha.

MARSHA: (somewhat shocked) John!

JOHN: (taken aback) Marsha!!

MARSHA: (angry) John!

JOHN: (furious) Marsha!!

MARSHA: (crying) John . . . John . . .

JOHN: (voice breaking) Marsha . . . Marsha . . .

MARSHA: (tenderly) John . . .

JOHN: (more tenderly) Marsha . . .

*I*t does lose something in the retelling. There was a time, though, when Stan Freberg's send-up on the soaps said all there was to say about the medium. Today's daytime serials remain in tune with the sensibilities of the Tupperware set. But the form, if not the content, has come a long way since radio's "Our Gal Sunday" could wonder whether "a girl from a small mining town in the west [could] find happiness with a rich and titled Englishman."

When they first made the transition to the boob tube in the mid-'50s, soaps were broadcast live from cardboard sets, supported only by a hyperthyroid organist and a handful of actors reading cue cards for the union minimum. Occasionally, you still catch a glimpse of John or Marsha in search of an errant TelePrompTer.

And time warps are still used to cover a multitude of plot sins: A petty mystery—who stole the keys to John's BMW?—may take 20 shows to sort out, while, during the same month, some Barbie lookalike may be packed off to school and return as a coked-up, knocked-up degenerate.

But despite the idiosyncrasies, dimestore-gothic has proved the most durable format on television. The audiences have expanded to include college kids and career women with video recorders. And somewhere along the way, soaps became a big bu$iness, served by armies of brand-name writers, actors, and hairdressers.

The hottest show with the upwardly mobile crowd is "The Young and the Restless," which has a glossier feel than the competition. "Y & R" is set in the fictional midwestern community of Genoa City, but everybody knows it's really Los Angeles. Starlets abound; story lines mingle the sexy with the sinister. However, the show's special resonance for the YoPro is its preoccupation with careers and corporate intrigue. Dressed-for-success heroines agonized endlessly over the balance between work and marriage and the It word: children.

"Capitol," another soap on the upswing, specializes in the jet-set intrigue once reserved for prime-time soaps. And "General Hospital" takes top honors in both sexual and medical bathos. But for an era of two-earner families and weekend daddies—an era in which the focus of casual social life has migrated from kitchen to shopping mall—the best soap is the one that best captures the togetherness myth of Small Town, U.S.A. And for the last 31 years, no one has been doing that better than "As the World Turns."

"ATWT," the first network soap, is all about continuity. Whereas most of "Restless" 's original characters were long ago consigned to the ether, "World" 's founding couple, Nancy and Chris Hughes, are still at the center of a vast, extended family of children, in-laws, ex-in-laws, grandchildren, neighbors, etc. Cast veterans, including Barnard Hughes, Henderson Forsyth, and Tom Hastings, have the special poise that comes from long experience on the New York stage. Ruth Warrick made her film debut as Orson Welles's wife in *Citizen Kane*. Glamour has made some inroads, of course: Like the inhabitants of other fictional soap towns, most of the folks in Oakdale look like they've been dressed by Bob Mackie. "World" has even got its own Alexis-clone in the character of Lucinda, a chillingly cold manipulator of money, men, and cosmetics.

The show, incidentally, always did its bit in the Department of Redeeming Social Significance. CBS refused to let Mary Tyler Moore play a divorced woman in 1970. A decade earlier, "ATWT" had its own divorced, sexually active protagonist in Edie Hughes. Penny, Edie's daughter, managed to get herself pregnant by a young, married physician way back in 1957.* And, long before Alexis or Dominique was a gleam in the scriptwriter's eye, "ATWT" had Lisa (played by Eileen Fulton), the soap's first all-out bitch.

Granted, it's not as cleverly written or as well-acted as, say, "L.A. Law." But no matter what's right or wrong in your life, you can be sure that "ATWT" will remain just where you left it. A few weeks with the show is the next best thing to a trip back home. On second thought: much better.

---

*She lost the baby, of course. These days, she'd have it.

Soho Natural Soda (Courtesy of Soho Natural Soda)

. . . .

Soft Drink

· ·

*P*ooped by Pepsi? Tired of Tab? Sip a **SOHO NATURAL SODA:** not the first of the boutique soft drinks, but surely the tastiest.

Ten years ago Soho was just a recipe on the kitchen table of Sophia Collier and Connie Best, two young women determined to brave the formidable odds in a market where a billion dollars in sales hardly makes you a serious player. Today they aren't even close to billion-dollar status. But their company, American Natural Products, does have bottling plants in Pennsylvania, Maryland, and California and a growing clientele in 30 states plus Japan.

Soho is made with natural flavorings and colors, fructose sweetener, and carbonated water. No caffeine, no preservatives . . . the whole "no" bit. Soho soda is a bit less sweet than the brand names. That, plus the exclusive use of fructose, means 30 percent fewer calories than Coke or Pepsi. But the real virtue of Soho isn't the health edge—nobody drinks soda to stay young and beautiful. It's the taste.

Soho comes in 10 flavors, ranging from adult black cherry to a slightly tart lemon-lime to pleasantly weird ginseng ginger ale. The nicest is the colorless cream soda, a perfumey vanilla-ish brew that makes you understand why people in Brooklyn used to be addicted to this stuff.

Speedboat

. . . .

Yes, they're symbols of decadence. Yes, they're a danger to life and honest commerce. But, boy, are they fun.

The idea hasn't changed much since Prohibition. Design a long, slender hull to minimize air resistance. Build it from very strong, very light materials (today mostly Kevlar and fiberglass). Attach oversized engines to generate two or three times the horse-power-to-weight ratio of a good sports car. Watch it rip.

In calm water, the bigger, twin-screw boats can easily top 70 miles an hour. That isn't a whole lot compared to specialized off-shore racing boats, which can reach 115 miles per hour. But it's usually enough to outrun the Coast Guard, should you happen to be transporting Bolivia's major agricultural export. And it's always enough to produce a sensation of speed that makes Grand Prix auto racing seem tame.

The basic, knock-your-Topsiders-off speedboat—say, a 21-foot Wellcraft Scarab with a 260-horsepower engine, a smaller version of the boat featured on "Miami Vice"—will cost you about $30,000. From there on, prices quickly get out of hand. For ulti-mate speed and sexy Italian looks, there's the 35-foot Cafe Racer by Cigarette. Figure on spending $200,000, if you want it com-plete with the two 540-horsepower engines handmade by Hawk Marine Power. Those who prefer a more conventional design might opt for a custom-designed model by Apache. The Holly-wood, Florida, company will be happy to load it with as much power as hull technology and common-sense permit. Prices range from $200,000 for a 35-footer to $1,000,000 for a 65-footer.

But for the triple threat of speed, looks, and luxury, there is only one choice: the new Z-series by **DONZI MARINE.** The Z-33, Donzi's 32-foot, needle-nosed, V-hulled top of the line, is only eight feet 10 inches at the beam, and weighs just 6,800 pounds. Machinery is handsome and functional: Kiekhaefer Aeromarine control system, VDO instruments, Venturi windscreen, Aeroquip fuel lines, electrically adjusted helm seat, electric hatch lift, over-sized battery. The Knytex glass-composite hull is finished glossy smooth in light gray, with red, blue, burgundy, or yellow trim. Exposed deck fittings, most of them in light alloy, are a delight to the eye.

Down below, standard equipment includes leather upholstery, refrigerator, enclosed head, Kenwood stereo, plenty of 110-volt

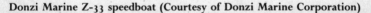

Donzi Marine Z-33 speedboat (Courtesy of Donzi Marine Corporation)

power, and jazzy, mirrored surfaces. The boat can sleep two in compact comfort. Fairly safe to assume, though, that people who can afford a Donzi have better places to bunk.

Equipped with twin 370-horsepower Mercruiser engines—plenty to satisfy your average speed freak—a Z-33 will set you back about $116,000. Those with a passion for anonymity and an intense desire to get there first can plunk down another $28,000 for twin 425-horsepower KAAMA Surface Drives. These fabulous engines can push Z-33 up to 75 miles an hour, yet produce only the most discreet, short-lasting wake.

Donzis are sold by 55 dealers worldwide. For a brochure full of mouthwatering fantasies, write Donzi Marine Corporation, PO Box 987, Tallevast, FL 34270, or phone 813-355-9355.

THE BEST
Sports Car

· ·

S ome people can't imagine why Paul Newman would put his
life on the line in a 400-horsepower race car when he could
just as easily spend his days soaking up rays, sharpening his back-
hand, or improving his salad dressing. But then, some people
never jumped off the high diving board or tried to make out on
the first date. For those who crave the pleasure of the jet roar of
a turbocharger or the squeal of oversized tires, the choices have
never been better.

Start with the sports cars that deliver the thrill for less than the
cost of a Harvard education:

The Toyota MR2 is the refined version of the MGs, Austin-
Healeys, and Fiat two-seaters of yesteryear—lots of dash at an af-
fordable price. The tiny mid-engine roadster is not much to look
at, and can be pushed around a bit in a crosswind, but you won't
find a zippier or better-handling vehicle under $14,000. It has a
great five-speed gearbox, even a comfortable interior with no-
nonsense dash and controls. The only puzzle is why anyone
would shell out equal bucks for a Pontiac Fiero or a Honda CRX.

The Mazda RX-7 Turbo, a silky-smooth, rotary-engined bundle
from Japan's most innovative car company, is also without peer in
its price class (figure $22,000). Power to burn (0–60 in 6.5 sec-
onds); tight, predictable handling; good looks, unmarred by the excessive trim common to expensive Japanese care. Optional
antiskid brakes gild a most admirable lily.

The plain-vanilla Porsche 944 ($25,000) costs more than the
entry-level 924S model, has a lot less vroom than the 944 Turbo or

Chevrolet Corvette (1987) (Courtesy of General Motors)
. . . .

the monster, eight-cylinder 928S4, and lacks the timeless good looks of the 911. But it may just be the most satisfying Porsche to drive. The key is handling—steering and suspension with that solid, German feel, plus plenty of power out of the curves.

Once just another example of Detroit's brute force approach to engineering, the Chevrolet Corvette ($28,000) has graduated from charm school and is well along the road to a degree in world-class performance. The gut-wrenching power is still there (0–60 in 6.0 seconds; top speed: 144). The handling has evolved from adequate to much better. And the Bosch antiskid brakes are marvelously effective.

Okay, fantasy time: The Mets have signed you to a seven-figure, no-cut contract. Better yet, you've been promoted to partner at Goldman Sachs. How to celebrate?

You could do worse than a Lotus Esprit Turbo ($55,000), the mid-engined, bullet-nosed wedge from Britain's serious road car manufacturer. Supercar power (0–60 in 5.7 seconds), bourgeois luxury (wall-to-wall leather), plus a head-turning long-and-lean profile from the design studio of Giugiaro. The only significant shortcomings are mediocre brakes and poor visibility behind the wheel.

If the priority is sex appeal, move up to the 12-cylinder, 380-horsepower Ferrari Testarossa. Inch for shimmering inch, the $105,000 Testarossa is the world's most elegant car. And, as one would expect from the flagship of the Ferrari fleet, it combines explosive power (0–60 in 5.0 seconds; top speed: 176) with race-track handling. Perhaps most remarkable, it verges on practical. The interior offers all the standard luxury-car amenities, including air conditioning that actually works in warm weather. Those who ought to know insist it is the first Ferrari built to stay out of sick bay for months at a time.

Testarossa's only true competitor in the heavy-breathing department is the $120,000 Lamborghini Countach, whose pavement-hugging design would look at home on the set of *Star Wars*. Its 48-valve, 450-horsepower aluminum V-12 will rocket you to 60 miles per hour in just 4.5 seconds. Its ultra-low center of gravity, plus fat, low-profile tires keep it welded to the skid-pad to .87 g's. Darth Vader never had it so good. The only places where the Countach betrays its 15-year age are in the heavy, heavy gearshift and the don't-bother-me-with-details-I'm-Italian interior.

Car buffs salivate interminably over the relative merits of these unmatchable Italian beauties. But sports cars are for driving first, drooling second. And thanks to **PORSCHE,** there's no longer any real argument about which car is best on the road. The German automaker's newly unveiled 959 is a technological triumph, unlikely to be matched for a decade.

The 959's flat-out performance specs are beyond impressive: Its 450-horsepower, fuel-injected straight six employs two sequentially operating turbochargers to ram the 3,200-pound vehicle from 0 to 60 in 3.8 seconds.* Top speed in fifth gear (sixth gear is for cruising) is a stunning 195 miles per hour. But the major magic is in the 21st-century automation of the transmission and suspension.

The driver picks one of four driving condition modes: dry, wet, icy, pure traction (mud or sand). Then the microprocessors take over, instantaneously adjusting the proportion of power fed to each of the four wheels as the car's weight is redistributed in accelerating and turning. The result is an uncanny stability that belies the car's conventionally high center of gravity, a stability that makes it the most forgiving monster since Godzilla. Mistakes that would put a 944 into a spin are computer-corrected before they're noticeable. Braking is, of course, electronically controlled to minimize skidding. Sensors even monitor tire pressure and metal fatigue in the 959's alloy wheels.

Though the 959 was designed primarily for racing, Porsche has not compromised on comfort or style. Leather trim, automatic climate control, and Blaupunkt stereo are standard equipment. The exterior design is a one-of-a-kind; you'll love or hate it on first sight. Soft and sexy, it looks like a 1930s *art moderne* vision of the future.

Interested? The price of admission is $230,000, give or take the play in the dollar-Deutschmark exchange. But tickets are scarce. Porsche plans to build only 200 annually, none of which will be equipped to meet U.S. pollution and safety regulations. Places on Porsche's waiting list have already changed hands for $75,000.

*That's no misprint. From a standing start, a 959 could break the speed limit on the New Jersey Turnpike in roughly the time it took to read this digression.

THE BEST
Stereo Speakers

· ·

The cabinet is a sexy black. The soft-touch controls and LED readouts would fit nicely into the dashboard of a 747. But your stereo doesn't sound much better than the old clock radio in the guest bedroom. Maybe somebody dumped a Bartles and Jaymes on the receiver. Or maybe the cat chewed the wires. More likely, it's the speakers.

Manufacturers know that stereos are usually bought for their electronic bells and whistles, so they put their design and marketing effort into building sleeker boxes with more buttons to push. But the really difficult engineering problems—the most expensive ones to solve—are in the business end of the stereo, where moving parts convert electronic impulses to sound. That's why it makes sense to invest half the price of the system in speakers, and even more if your total stereo budget exceeds $1,000.

Audio magazine's 1987 equipment directory lists roughly 1,500 speaker models, ranging from Quasar's little SW30's, retailing for $50 a pair, to Mavrick Audio's 14-piece, 2½-ton, $110,000 system, featuring low-frequency speakers that measure five feet square. How to choose?

At the cheap end—say less than $300 a pair—the decision is fairly easy because differences in quality can be measured objectively. The basic benchmark is "accuracy," the capacity of the speaker to reproduce sounds across the audible frequencies without significant distortion or deviation in loudness. By this criterion, probably no speaker in the economy class beats the Boston Acoustics A60 Series II ($225 a pair). It faithfully reproduces medium and high frequencies, noticeably missing only in the bass.

At 18 × 11 × 8 inches, A60's fit nicely on a bookshelf. If space is still an issue, though, consider the Wharfdale Diamond ($300 a pair), measuring a tiny 9 × 7 × 8 inches. It is virtually as accurate as the larger Boston Acoustics model; the only significant disadvantage is lack of "efficiency": like virtually all small speakers, the Wharfdale Diamond needs a lot of power to produce loud sounds. An amplifier or receiver rated at 30 watts per channel should do the job.

Neither the Wharfdale nor the Boston Acoustics has enough muscle to fill a large room with music. And neither is really suited to heavy metal or big orchestral pieces, where good bass is crucial. But for an extra $100, you could have a pair of Jamo CBR-70's ($400) which try much harder. These odd-looking Danish speakers are housed in a plastic composite material that reduces the tendency of the box to vibrate when the music gets loud. Jamos can also handle frequencies down to 40 cycles a second, a simply remarkable performance for a small (19 × 10 × 6 inches), moderately priced speaker.

Now the choices are becoming very interesting. In the $600 range, the Boston Acoustics A150 Series II sets the standard for both accuracy and capacity to handle bass. But all conventional, forward-radiating speakers like the A150's seem to generate music from discrete points in the room. Omnidirectional speakers, by contrast, produce a sensation closer to live music, surrounding you with reflected sound. If you're willing to sacrifice some accuracy for this different way to experience music, listen to the dbx Soundfield 1000 ($600 a pair), the cheapest of dbx's floor-standing models.

The sum of $900 will buy a pair of Celestion SL-6S speakers, one of the sweetest-sounding and most accurate small speakers (15 × 8 × 10 inches) made to date. But beware: the SL-6S really slurps up power. An amplifier with a minimum of 60 watts per channel is recommended. Compare the Celestion SL-6S with the same size B & W Matrix I ($1,000). This model offers equally

Infinity Reference Standard, Series III, stereo speakers (Courtesy of Infinity Systems)

. . . .

delightful sound in the middle and high frequencies. And a non-resonating cabinet design gives the Matrix I a slight edge in very loud music.

Up the price again, and the cup runneth over. The aptly named Carver Amazing loudspeaker ($1,500 a pair) employs exotic "ribbon" elements in a flat panel to produce a fabulous room-filling sound. Unlike most other flat panel speakers, the Carver has a very accurate bass. It's a super buy among super-expensive speakers, and a perfect match for a good CD player and a big (100-watts-plus per channel) amplifier or receiver. The one serious drawback is size: Carvers are 66 inches high and 30 inches wide.

In this heady price range, speaker specifications all look great on paper; preferences are entirely subjective. Compare the Carver with two other flat panel speakers which operate on a different engineering principle. The Florida-made Acustat One-Plus-One ($1,600 a pair) is taller (93 inches) but much narrower (11 inches), making it a less obtrusive addition to the living room than the Carver. Some people also like the sharper stereo image created by the narrower sound source. The British-made Quad ESL-63 ($3,600 a pair) offers another variation on electrostatic speaker design, this one with an icy realism that will take your breath away.

Or—if you dare—try it against the Acoustic Research MGC-1 ($3,600 a pair), a stunning alternative to the flat panel approach and surely the most sophisticated omnidirectional speaker system made. The heart of the system is a second set of drivers, producing electronically delayed sounds to reconstruct the ambiance of the concert hall.

One of these models will almost certainly be good enough. But stereo has produced a group of audiophiles who are obsessed with perfect sound reproduction at any price. And where there are more dollars, there is a better way. The audiophiles' favorite speaker system—surely the best system around—is the California-made **INFINITY REFERENCE STANDARD, SERIES III.**

IRS Vs consist of four towers, each 90 inches high. Behind

the brown grill cloth lie 12 low-frequency "woofers" (each with a 12-inch diameter), 24 midrange speakers, and 72 high-frequency "tweeters." Linked to a superb music source with a large supply of power,* it is the closest thing to sitting in the front of the orchestra. Every instrument has a precise location. You can even "hear" the hall in which the music is being played. Is the IRS V worth the $45,000 price tag, and the room you'll have to set aside to use it? Not if you're sane. But, then, think of how much less fun life would be if we all chose our toys from *Consumer Reports*.

---

*Say, a Mark Levinson ML-7A Preamplifier ($5,750) and 200-watt-per-channel ML-3 Amplifier ($6,400), a SOTA Vacuum Star Turntable ($1,600) with an SME Series V Tonearm ($1,750) and Talisman Virtuosi DTi Cartridge ($1,200).

Strategy for Winning the Lottery

. . . .

*T*he lottery—any lottery—is a sucker's game, at best a license
to dream. Right?

Not quite. It's true that drawings are random, making every
number as likely to win as every other. It's also true that the
states generally take a 40-cent cut on every dollar bet. That, by
the way, is more than the racetracks get, and more than the casinos' cut in craps or roulette or keno. More, in fact, than the take
on any legal game of chance except slot machines. But there is
one tiny flaw in the anti-lottery logic. With "pari-mutuel" lotter-
ies, games where winners divide what's left after the state appro-
priates its share, there may still be ways to win at the expense of
other bettors. And Herman Chernoff, a professor of statistics at
Harvard, has discovered just such a strategy.

Chernoff analyzed the Massachusetts lottery for weaknesses and
discovered two.

Some numbers are apparently bet far more frequently than others. Numbers containing nines and zeros are least often bet; those
with ones, twos, threes and fours, most often. Avoiding the low
digits in favor of nine and ten won't make it any more likely that
your number will hit. But if you do win, your share of the pari-
mutuel pool is likely to be much larger.

In the Massachusetts four-digit game, the odds of any number
winning are, of course, one in 9999. The state takes $4,000 out of
every $10,000 in bets, so the average winning return is $6,000.
Now compare that average to the best and worst returns from the
first hundred plays of the Massachusetts game:

Best Returns:			Worst Returns:	
NUMBER	PAYOFF		NUMBER	PAYOFF
9943	$39,170		2147	$1,586
7088	$13,725		5421	$2,015
9702	$13,286		5237	$2,183
5991	$12,661		4716	$2,465
0661	$12,439		8257	$2,476

What a difference avoiding a few digits can make!

All bettors who win with the same number receive equal prizes. But in a system in which different types of bets are permitted, the formula for divvying up the pie may favor some betting strategies over others.

In the Massachusetts game it is possible to bet on three-digit combinations in the four-digit lottery. Those who guess right on three digits share the pot with those who guess right on four digits. A fair division of the pie among three- and four-digit winners would give the three-digiters a prize equal to just 10 percent of the size of a four-digit winner—it is, after all, ten times easier to guess a three-digit number than a four-digit number. In the Massachusetts game, though, the three-digit prize was set at 14 percent of the four-digit prize.

The average return on a bet, you'll remember, is 60 cents on the dollar. However, if everyone else bet on four-digit numbers and you bet randomly on a three-digit number, your average return, Chernoff calculates, would be 84 cents on the dollar.

That isn't good enough to make betting worthwhile. Who, after all, wants to lose, on average, 16 cents for every dollar bet? Besides, everyone else doesn't bet on four-digit numbers. If half the bets are four-digit and half are three-digit, the average return to a three-digit bettor would fall to 70 cents on the dollar.

Suppose, though, you took advantage of both vulnerabilities in the lottery system: the avoidance of nines and zeros, as well as the higher expected return on three-digit bets. Would the lottery be worth playing? That is, would the average return on a dollar bet exceed one dollar?

Armed with computer, high-powered statistical model, and the results from the first few years of the Massachusetts lottery, Chernoff decided to find out. One important discovery was that some unpopular numbers are not always unpopular: In some games a lot of people bet them, in others very few. So he winnowed his list to the following "reliably" unpopular set of numbers:

007	008	020	040	066	068
070	079	080	087	090	300
466	599	655	708	848	859
886	966	970	989	994	

Some of these numbers are, of course, less popular than others, so a coldly calculating bettor might prefer to winnow the list further. But the fewer numbers you bet, the longer the time, on average, between winners. If, for example, you bet on just five numbers a day, you would average just one winner every 200 days. And there would be a reasonable chance of going 300 to 400 days between winners. So, unless you're prepared for very long dry spells, it is better to play more numbers and accept a lower average return. Betting all the numbers on the list, Chernoff estimated, would generate a return of a little more than $1.08 for every dollar bet, or an average profit margin of 8.6 percent.

Is the strategy worth a try? Maybe. If enough people decided to play Chernoff's system, the expected profit margin would fall, perhaps below zero. Then there is the problem of income tax. Under current law, gambling losses can be subtracted from winnings before taxes are figured. But losses can't offset earnings from sources other than gambling. So if you go a whole calendar year without a winner, the gambling deductions are worthless. If you then win big the following January, Uncle Sam gets his full share.

Still, if you really want to win the lottery, it surely makes sense to bet the unpopular numbers. And if you bet in a state with a better payoff for three-digit numbers, it certainly makes sense to avoid the four-digit bets.

THE BEST
Sunglasses

· ·

*P*icking the right sunglasses used to be a snap: What you saw was what you got. If the frames were comfy, the lenses sharp, and the tint dark enough to stop the glare, you'd found the right pair. Big spenders usually opted for metal-rimmed aviators with green or neutral-gray lenses—steel or gold knock-offs of the design issued to pilots during World War II. Peons made do with plastic-framed Foster Grants.

Now science has reared its high-tech head. It's a sunny jungle out there, we are warned, and only the products of modern laboratories can serve as adequate armament. In part, this is advertising hype, an excuse to charge $100 or more for an accessory that used to cost $10. In part, though, it reflects a new understanding of the potential damage to eyes from sunlight, and the availability of clever new technological fixes.

What counts:

Shatter Resistance

Optically accurate hard plastic lenses, made from either the standard CR-39 developed by the PPG company or a newer material called polycarbonate, are more resistant to impact than glass. But the difference isn't very important, since glass lenses must be tempered to meet a tough federal standard.

Ultraviolet Protection

Practically everybody knows that the ultraviolet tanning rays in sunlight cause skin cancer. Only recently, though, has ultraviolet been implicated in the formation of eye cataracts, as well as both short- and long-term destruction of night vision. Glass lenses act as natural UV filters; chemical coatings on plastic lenses can accomplish the same job.

You can't tell by looking whether a lens protects adequately against UV. Some very dark-tinted plastic lenses may actually increase the total amount of UV entering the eye, since they induce the pupils to open wide to emit more visible light. Before you buy, check the label or the package insert. If the manufacturer doesn't claim at least 90 percent reduction of ultraviolet, try another brand.

Glare Protection

Gray-tint lenses with a polarizing filter between the layers of plastic used to be viewed as state-of-the-art. Gray cuts the amount of light entering the eye without messing up natural contrast or distorting colors. The polarizing filter stops much of the background light reflected from water.

Gray is a nice neutral color, and polarized lenses can be a boon to boaters. But neutrality isn't everything. Brown lenses increase contrast by filtering out a lot of blue light, the primary source of glare in bright haze. The Porsche Design American PD model offers a neat solution: interchangeable lenses, one gray, one brown.

No matter what color, the darker the tint, the less the contrast. The most common solution is to create a gradient tint, darker at the top for drivers, or at both the top and bottom for skiers. Bolle offers interchangeable lenses, one screening a modest 65 percent of the light, the other a standard, sunglass-grade 82 percent. Corning offers yet another solution: tints that change with light conditions, running from 74 percent light blockage on a gloomy day to a very dark 92 percent in bright sunlight.

Comfort and Durability

All is in the eye of the beholder. Glass lenses can feel heavy on the nose, particularly large lenses for aviator styles or thick lenses ground for strong prescriptions. On the other hand, glass is much more resistant to scratches than plastic. Wire frames can be more finely adjusted than plastic, but plastic is lighter.

And the best? At about $15, bargain hunters won't go too far wrong with Foster Grant Space Techs. The lenses are neutral-gray and made from an acrylic that resists scratches far better than the plastics used on most cheap sunnies. At the other end of the line, nobody can beat the glitzy, oversized Porsche Design. If you have to ask the price, you can't afford them.

Techno-freaks may be lured by the Nikon Titex, the first sunglasses with a frame made from titanium. The metal doesn't do anything special for you, but it is light, strong, and terribly expensive (about $300). Actually, technology freaks will probably want to own Revo Ventures from Coopervision ($150)—the first sunglasses to employ multiple coatings to filter out both infrared and ultraviolet light with minimal interference to the friendlier parts of the spectrum. The benefits are hard to assess. But Revos do offer a fancy light show from the outside, shimmering like the multicolor reflection from an oil slick.

Our own choice is the SERENGETI DRIVER (about $75), using Corning's photochromatic technology. The frames are black metal. In bright light, the tint is a high-contrast, very sexy copper with a gradient darkening toward the top. Like earlier photochromatic models from Corning, the tint on the Serengeti Driver changes with the light level. But Corning has made the system less dependent on ultraviolet light, so it now works well behind the UV-filtering glass of a car windshield. Dealers can be located by calling Corning at 800-525-4001 or 800-648-4810.

THE BEST
Sunscreen

. . . .

At 20, a good tan looks like a million dollars. By age 50, the interest on the million comes due: wrinkles, skin cancer ... the whole bit. So unless you're sure the Golda Meir look will come into vogue, it pays to stay out of the rays. Or at least to keep exposure to a minimum by using chemical screens against the ultraviolet light from the sun.

Ultraviolet, the sole ingredient of a good (or bad) tan, arrives in two forms. UV-B, which only penetrates the atmosphere in the middle few hours of the day, causes cancer by messing around with the genetic code in skin cells. The longer UV-A rays probably only destroy the skin's elasticity and harden its outer layer.

Next to an umbrella, the most effective screen against both types of UV is zinc oxide ointment, the greasy white stuff people smear on their noses after a really nasty burn. Opaque zinc oxide looks and feels like warpaint—one clever manufacturer is even taking advantage of the resemblance by marketing it in Day-Glo colors. But, while zinc oxide might complement a Mohawk haircut at a New Wave disco, it's nothing you'd care to wear to the company picnic.

The alternatives are lotions containing chemicals that stop the ultraviolet without blocking visible light. Many contain PABA (you guessed it: para-aminobenzoic acid) or its nonstaining cousin, padimate O. PABA is extremely efficient at screening UV-B. Most sunscreen lotions also contain a chemical in the benzophenone family (oxybenzone, methoxybenzone, sulfisobenzone), which works its magic on UV-A.

Assuming the brew contains both UV-A and UV-B screens, the overall efficacy can be read from the "sun protection factor" or SPF number. The higher the SPF, the greater the protection: An SPF of 2 means two hours of exposure will give you one hour's worth of sun, while an SPF of 8 means eight hours to one. You get the idea.

For all but the most fair-skinned, an SPF of 8 should be enough to prevent a burn. But the aging and cancer-producing effects of ultraviolet are believed to be cumulative; so the higher the SPF, the better.

Until recently, the highest SPFs available were 15s. Now it is possible to find brands above 20, though some manufacturers are curiously reluctant to brag about the greater level of protection on the package front. When you're buying, check the fine print for assurance that the product screens both UV-A and UV-B; then look for the SPF. Finally, see whether it claims to resist dilution in water. That's critical for swimmers, of course. But it matters for anybody who is likely to perspire.

Which is the best? Assuming you don't prove to be allergic to the lotion base, any of a dozen brands with an SPF over 15 will do. But the edge goes to TISCREEN, made by Ti-Pharmaceuticals in Moraga, California, and available in many big drugstores. Ti-Screen is water-resistant and runs an SPF of 22. Perhaps most important, it uses a chemical called cinnamate, rather than PABA or its derivatives, to protect against UV-B. PABA, ironically, is now suspected of causing skin cancer. And while the evidence against PABA is far from conclusive, there's no harm to hedging your bets with cinnamate-based protection.

For maximum benefit, apply sunscreen a half hour before exposure. Better still, make it a daily ritual: Your dermatologist will love you. TiScreen can even be used as a base for makeup.

Swim Goggles

. . . .

*L*ap-swimming is a terrific way to burn calories, build pectoral muscles and keep the arteries in tune. It is also murder on the eyeballs. What to do?

The brute-force solution is to use a watertight scuba diving mask, the kind Lloyd Bridges wore to harass great white sharks and capture dangerous criminals underwater. But they are heavy, smell funny, block peripheral vision, and make you look like an idiot swimming your laps at the local Y. Most swimmers use what were once called pearl divers' goggles, the little plastic gadgets with black rubber padding around the rims. They are an enormous improvement over nothing. Wear them loose, though, and they leak. Wear them tight, and they leave raccoon circles around your eyes.

Happily, modern capitalism has built the better mousetrap: the **BARRACUDA GOGGLE.** Manufactured by Skyline Northwest, a nine-year-old, family-owned business in Portland, Oregon, the Barracuda offers several advantages over standard models. It is a bit larger, allowing the rims to follow the line of the bone rather than pressing against the eye socket. It is padded with a generous amount of Ensolite foam that conforms to the shape of the head, creating a tight seal without a lot of pressure. It is attached by a broad double band that distributes the pinch across more of the back of your head. And it comes with a replaceable soft rubber nosebridge that permits much finer adjustment than an ordinary plastic clip.

The result is a light, comfy goggle that rarely leaks and never

Barracuda swim goggles (Courtesy of Skyline Northwest)

leaves a mark. Barracudas come in two shapes: the "standard" and the "racer." The latter sacrifices a bit of comfort and peripheral vision for a more streamlined shape. Both run about $25. For about $100 more, Skyline Northwest will grind the lenses to your prescription.

For information on where to buy Barracudas, or the answer to any other relevant question that pops to mind, call 800-547-8664.

Tennis Racquet

· ·

*F*irst, they made 'em bigger. Then they made 'em smaller. Then they made 'em bigger again. On some racquets, corners replaced rounded edges. Other sprouted "computerized" bumper guards and foam core handles. For a while, very light racquets were in. Then somebody decided that light wasn't always right, so racquet heads put on a few fractions of an ounce.

Oh yes, materials. Wood is straight from the dark ages, valued only by the nostalgia set. Aluminum is downscale. Graphite, prized for its sexy gray looks and high cost, blew away the top end of the market when it was first introduced; now manufacturers often mix the stuff with fiberglass or Kevlar. Titanium and magnesium composites have had a weak start. Boron bombed. The jury is still out on ceramic fiber.

At last count, there were 200 brand-name tennis racquets on the market, with list prices running up to $280. Head sizes range from a "conventional" 70 square inches to an elephantine 137. And cynics might wonder whether any of the endless permutations of size, shape, and ingredients have really mattered.

The answer is a definite maybe. A lot of the changes have been pure hustle, eminently forgettable equivalents of tailfins, opera windows, and pushbutton transmissions. But there have been some bright technical achievements amidst the marketing clutter.

Oversized racquets with wide heads, introduced by Prince in the late 1970s, added power and increased the percentage of the head surface that allowed a clean hit. The switch from wood or aluminum to superstiff graphite immensely increased the power of hard-hitting players without ruining their ball control. Very strong, very light materials, such as graphite and ceramic fiber, made it possible to accommodate the demand for large head size without compromising durability or maneuverability of the racquet. Composites improved shock absorption, permitting the construction of relatively stiff racquets that aren't as likely to give you tennis elbow. Customizable weighting systems, used on the Donnay PC12 and the Tenex Gamma, give the individual a chance to alter the balance as well as the total weight of the racquet.

Now manufacturers are rippling the waters with some new technology that could prove as important as the oversized head. Fischer, the Austrian ski company, has a very stiff model that allows the tension on the six center strings to be fine-tuned within a 10-pound range. The Superform Tuning ($175) could prove popular with accomplished amateurs who would like to vary string tension to match their moods but aren't willing to haul around a half dozen different racquets like the pros. A far more ambitiously designed new racquet, the **BERGELIN LONGSTRING** from MacGregor, is aimed at beginners, older people, and others who don't have the strength or timing to take full advantage of an ultra-stiff racquet.

Invented by Herwig Fischer (a German aeronautical engineer), and named after Lennart Bergelin (Bjorn Borg's former coach), the six-sided, mid-sized, all-graphite LongString incorporates two important technical improvements. As with the Superform, string tension is tuneable by means of a key on the handle. Better than the Superform, the LongString uses a multiple pulley system to adjust the tension on all the strings rather than just those at the center of the racquet; the range of adjustment runs from 80 pounds to no tension at all. Probably the most innovative feature, though, is the stringing system.

According to Fischer, longer strings are more elastic and thus impart more punch without a reduction in control. But ordinary string configurations limit their length to about four feet. So

Fischer devised a diagonal design allowing the use of just two strands, each 26 feet long, for the entire racquet.

One consequence is a big increase in the size of the sweet spot. The other is a stunning improvement in the tradeoff between power and control. Heavy hitters can dial down the tension for maximum control in an aggressive net game. Ninety-pound weaklings and other real people can dial up the tension for the biggest baseline game of their lives.

A number of stores now carry the Bergelin LongString at a list of $225. Should you have trouble finding one, call MacGregor at 800-526-6289.

35-Millimeter Camera

· ·

*T*he choice used to be simple. If you couldn't tell an
f-stop from a G-spot, you bought a pocket camera with no-
hassle film cartridges. There were drawbacks. The way the cartridges were designed virtually guaranteed that the pictures would
be just a bit out of focus. The flash turned everyone into a refu-
gee from a gangster movie. And enlargements made from the tiny
negatives were inevitably grainy. But it was all so easy.

If you did know what an f-stop was (and liked to bore friends
and family with explanations), you bought a 35-millimeter, single-
lens-reflex camera. Lots of dials to set, lenses to change, flash settings to calculate, field depths to measure, accessories to purchase.
Sometimes the pix were great. Other times the film leader
jammed, or you forgot to reset the film speed knob.

Now, thanks to the miracles of microchips and mass merchandising, six-year-olds can produce brilliant photographs with modern versions of the rangefinder, point-and-shoot cameras. And
even the most versatile 35-millimeter SLRs are as easy to use in
automatic mode as a toaster oven.

Good

The Fuji TW-300 (about $175). You want easy? How about easy
and clever? Just drop in a roll of 35-millimeter film and watch
this star do its turn. It automatically threads the film and sets the
light sensitivity (ISO numbers from 50 to 1,600), then winds the
film to the end of the roll. As each frame is exposed, it is auto-

matically wound back into the film cartridge. So even if the Fuji malfunctions mid-roll, or you accidentally open the camera back, the exposed frames are safe.

Now you—or rather it—is ready to shoot. The Fuji automatically focuses on the object in the center of the viewer and alerts you to the depth of the field of the focus. After focusing, you can lock in the setting by holding the shutter button halfway, then recompose the picture. The camera's programmed microprocessor also sets the shutter speed and lens opening. Once turned on, the flash is automatic. Extra-longlife lithium batteries should last through 40 rolls of film. Oh yes: To make life even pleasanter, the Fuji has a built-in "telephoto converter" for close-ups—but you'll have to decide when to use it.

Good-Plus

The Pentax IQZoom (about $250). Imagine a cute little compact like the Fuji with automatic film handling and focusing. Now add a zoom lens that provides a continuous range of focal lengths between moderate wide-angle and closeup. Attach a "smart" viewfinder that shows you what the zoom lens is about to capture and a flash that also adjusts automatically to the lens setting. *Violà!* You've got the simplest, smartest point-and-shoot ever made.

Better

The Olympus OM-77AF (about $300). You're determined to have auto-everything (including pop-up flash) in a small, lightweight package, but still want versatility and picture quality only possible with a single-lens-reflex camera. This compact beauty is almost as easy to use as the autofocus rangefinder cameras, and goes through its paces with far more finesse.

The OM-77AF features a toy chest full of electronic gadgets: an automatic exposure system with different modes for different focal-length lenses; an override feature that permits you to second-guess the program with the press of a button; an infrared beam that allows the autofocus to operate in total darkness; one-touch variable-speed, motorized focusing on manual; and a "static" memory for shooting data while the batteries are being changed.

But the OM-77AF retains the virtues of a modern single-lens-reflex: through-the-lens viewing and light metering; shutter speeds to $\frac{1}{2,000}$ second; optically superior interchangeable lenses. And it offers an option found only on a handful of great cameras: the Olympus F280 Full-Synchro Flash that allows synchronized flash pictures at $\frac{1}{2,000}$ second shutter speed.

Truly Amazing

The Minolta Maxxum 9000 (about $600, with optional motor drive). Minolta marketed the first autofocus, single-lens-reflex camera (the Maxxum 7000), then built a stripped-down, entry-level model (the 5000) and the upscale 9000 version for heavy hitters. No doubt, someone will someday build a better autofocus camera than the Maxxum 9000. But not soon.

Switch off the 9000's autofocus system and you have a rugged, conventional SLR with shutter speeds to $\frac{1}{4,000}$ second, a flash synchronized to $\frac{1}{250}$ second; three auto-exposure modes based on the lens focal length, two light-metering modes, automatic film speed setting, and tons of interchangeable lenses. Impressive accessories, too: a five-frame-per-second motor winder with auto rewind; a Program Back Super 90, which prints everything you might want to remember on the edge of the film and acts as a programming memory for the camera itself; the astounding electronic SVB-90 back that records decent color images for showing on a television screen.

Switch on the autofocus, and watch it prowl. The 9000 continuously focuses on whatever is in the center of the viewer, a process that takes about a third of a second in normal light. That's good enough to catch even the fastest-moving object, as long as you have a chance to pan the scene for a fraction of a second. In

Canon T90 35-millimeter camera (Courtesy of Canon USA)

low-level light, the system is far less efficient. But the model 4000AF flash unit provides a supplementary infrared focusing back-light—enough infrared to focus on objects 23 feet away in total darkness.

Truly Amazing, Part II

The CANON T90 (about $600, with an f/1.4 lens). Let's assume you're no Luddite: You like bells and whistles when they make a camera smarter or more versatile. But you're enough of a purist to want to do your own focusing. The user-friendly Canon T90, the world's most sophisticated SLR, is just what the doctor ordered.

The T90's rounded, hand-contoured shape and rubbery eyepiece make it easy to grip and comfortable to use with eyeglasses. Push-button and wheel controls, plus liquid crystal readout, make it a snap to operate. Three motors, power autoloading, auto rewinding, and a three-speed drive capable of running through 36 frames in just eight seconds. A computer controls seven automatic-exposure programs, three light-metering modes, and a shutter that can open or close in $\frac{1}{4,000}$ second.

Toothbrush

· ·

*E*veryone over 30 knows that if they don't floss regularly, they'll end up doing Polident commercials with Martha Raye. But, then, everyone over 30 also knows they should do 100 sit-ups each morning, stoke up on leafy green vegetables at every opportunity, and avoid Fritos like the plague. The virtuous life, alas, is too boring to practice without strong motivation. And by the time prudence sets in, the chickens are usually well on their way home to roost.

So what's a body to do? We don't have any shortcuts to offer in the exercise or diet departments. But there is one dandy device for taking the drudgery out of dental care.

Kids brush to avoid dental caries. You got it: cavities. A sticky carbohydrate film, or "plaque," immediately forms on tooth surfaces after eating foods rich in starches and sugars. If the plaque isn't removed pronto—by brushing—bacteria colonies blossom. The acid created by the bacteria attacks the hard "enamel" tooth coating, rotting young chompers.

Adults face a more insidious dental menace from plaque: periodontal disease. Left on its own for a day or two, plaque hardens into tartar, which can only be removed by a dental hygienist with one of those murderous-looking steel picks. Tartar left below the gum line is an irritant. Much worse, it serves as a permanent abode for bacteria. Metabolic products formed by these bacteria are toxic, causing the gums to recede eventually weakening the bond that holds tooth to jaw. The treatment for advanced periodontal disease is very painful and very expensive. But once the disease gains a foothold, the only alternatives are false teeth or the Gabby Hayes look.

Regular brushing does remove some of the plaque before it goes to work on the gums. Brushing with Viadent, a brand of toothpaste containing a plaque-fighting substance from the sanguinaria plant, removes a bit more. And Peridex, a new mouthwash currently sold only by prescription, kills some of the bacteria that do the damage. But only regular flossing is likely to break up the plaque in hard-to-reach places before it calcifies.

Or at least that was true until now. A new sort of electric toothbrush, rather grandly named the **INTERPLAK HOME PLAQUE REMOVAL INSTRUMENT,** does the job almost as well.

Interplak is the idea of George Clemens, a full-time professional inventor from Chicago. Disgusted with the inefficiency of the common toothbrush, he set out to build a better plaque trap. The business end of the Interplak contains six long, tapered tufts of bristle that clean between the teeth, and four shorter tufts that polish tooth surfaces. Each of the ten tufts rotates in the opposite direction of the adjacent tuft, and each reverses direction 46 times a second.

This eccentric movement accomplishes a bunch of things. Rotary motion is apparently more effective than up-down or side-to-side brushing in dislodging plaque. Second, opposing motion makes it less likely that the bristles will jam together in tooth crevices and lose their brushing power. Third, Interplak vibrates less than an ordinary electric toothbrush, allowing the bristles to move faster (4,200 rpm) without making the device difficult to steer.

Lest you doubt, consider the evidence provided by Eric Coontz, D.D.S., consultant in periodontics and researcher at Loyola University. Two minutes of conscientious effort with an ordinary toothbrush removes half the plaque. Two minutes with Interplak gets rid of 98 percent.

The only drawback is price. An Interplak, with two interchangeable heads, costs a stiff $100; additional heads cost $12.95.

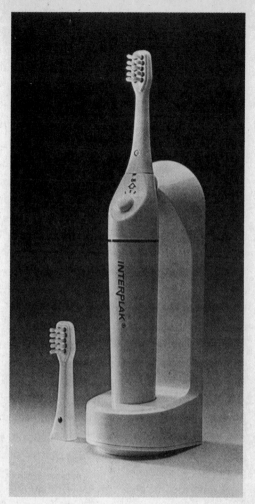

Interplak Home Plaque Removal Instrument (Courtesy of Dental Research Corporation)
. . . .

Still, it's cheaper and a whole lot less unpleasant than gum disease. And it is the only tool going that does a decent tooth-cleaning job for teenagers wearing corrective braces. Some dentists and a few mail-order houses sell the Interplak. It can also be purchased direct from the manufacturer with a credit card. Phone the Dental Research Corporation in Tucker, Georgia, at 800-334-4031.

THE BEST
Umbrella

. . . .

*U*mbrellas, like razors, ballpoint pens, sunglasses, books, flashlights, lighters, watches, and hair dryers, are becoming part of the disposable culture. Hardly anybody pays very much for them or expects them to work for very long. Few tears are shed if they are left behind at the dentist's office.

No, this isn't the opening salvo of a pompous lecture on the corrupting influence of Cheap. On the contrary: Serviceable throwaways should be celebrated as symbols of mass affluence, of factories so efficient that they all but defy natural laws of scarcity. Still, some umbrellas are good for more than keeping the damp off. Like elegant clothing or furniture, fine umbrellas serve art and tradition as well as function.

The prettiest umbrellas in the world are crafted from waterproof paper and lacquered bamboo, in the Japanese city of Gifu. The very best of them are called janome, and come decorated with gorgeous floral patterns in blue or purple or green, inlaid with plum blossom designs. For strength, silk threads are added to the paper and then coated with a derivative of persimmon juice. The finished product is translucent, allowing a soft glow to penetrate even as it drizzles. Rain on the surface creates a muffled patter, like drops on fallen leaves. And once wet, janome produce a pleasant, acrid scent of wood and workshop.

High-quality paper umbrellas are exported in small quantities. But the best selection is to be found in the small craft stores just north of the Gion district of Kyoto, where the Geisha culture once flourished. Visit Tsujikura, a friendly shop on the east side of the

Kawaramachi-dori, where the owner is delighted to explain the nuances of this paper craft. Figure on spending about $125 for the most elaborate janome the place has to offer.

Japanese umbrellas are far more durable than one might imagine. With good care and some caution in the wind, they last indefinitely. But they are relatively bulky and heavy. And even the solid-color versions suitable for men may be a bit flashy for the dash to the executive parking lot. For the ultimate in conservative, western-style umbrellas, consider the remarkable product of the British firm of SWAINE ADENEY BRIGG AND SONS.

By London standards, the firm is barely an infant—it was founded just 45 years ago. But you'll be relieved to know that the Brigg family has been in the walking-stick-and-umbrella trade since 1836. Their 1943 merger with Swaine Adeney, purveyors of riding crops to the Crown, did the umbrella line no harm.

Swaine Adeney Brigg umbrellas come any way you order them—at a store for gentlemen, virtually any eccentricity is tolerated. But the best umbrellas do share common features. The shaft (know as the shank) is made from either maple or ash. Steel shafts simply aren't strong enough to lean on. Moreover, no matter how carefully bonded, they eventually twist loose from their handles.

The best frames, however, *are* made of steel. S. Fox of Sheffield supplies those used by Swaine Adeney Brigg, and just about everybody else who sells high-quality umbrellas. As to fabric, nylon will do but silk is better. The fabric should be hand-sewn to the tip of each rib. The ferrule, the decorative cap at the umbrella tip, should be brass or bone. Bamboo makes for handsome and functional handles. However, if money is not at issue, you might opt for ivory or even mother-of-pearl. A brass or silver collar at the base of the handle allows for engraving.

Your off-the-rack man's umbrella will typically be 35 inches long and have a diameter of 45 inches. But a special pleasure of buying an expensive umbrella is custom fit. Get one that both matches your stride and is long enough to lean on.

A properly built umbie is hard to break and needs little care to survive for decades. The steel joints of the frame are prone to corrosion, though, so it makes sense to allow an umbrella to dry before closing it.

Swaine Adeney Brigg umbrellas can be ordered by mail from a catalogue. Those in silk, with simple handles and minimal adornment, run between $100 and $200. But it is much more fun to browse the old store in London (185 Piccadilly, London W1V 0HA; phone 734-4277) or the new one in San Francisco (434 Post St., San Francisco, CA 94102; phone 415-781-4949).

Undiscovered Hotel
in London

. . . .

*L*ondon is blessed with more than its share of intimate hotels, oases of fine service and good taste. There's the Connaught, of course, the club for country gentry who see no reason to give up 19th-century ambiance for modern convenience. Direct-dial telephones were installed only in 1980. And The Athenaeum, a small establishment built in the 1940s that exudes comfort: huge, fluffy cotton towels, linen sheets, handsome writing desks, maps for joggers ... The Stafford, an elegant converted mansion on a quiet St. James mews with the friendliest, most efficient service in London ... The Basil Street, a lovely Edwardian hotel full of antiques, practically on the doorstep of Harrods ... Forty-seven Park Street, another Edwardian townhouse—this one absolutely bathed in Mayfair luxuries ... Seven Down Street, a weirdly charming place with just six suites and a list of regular customers that includes Ringo Starr ... The Capital Hotel in Knightsbridge, with 56 modern (but fairly cozy) rooms and one of the city's best French restaurants ...

Somehow lost in this crowd, rarely even rating a mention in guidebooks, is a hotel whose name is also its address: **ELEVEN CADOGAN GARDEN.** Converted to a hotel in 1949, Eleven Cadogan consists of four connecting redbrick buildings on a silent street off Sloane Square. The 53 rooms and five suites could pass for guest quarters in someone's aunt's townhouse. A few have working fireplaces; all are comfortably furnished in dowdy Victorian. Lovely English breakfasts in bed. Afternoon tea—the scones are to kill for—is served in a mahogany-panelled drawing room,

amidst a clutter of old copies of *Gamekeeper and Countryside* and
Horse and Hound. There's no liquor license, but the white-jacketed
porters will uncomplainingly run out for Château Léoville Las
Cases. A Rolls is on call for trips to the theater or the airport.

Rates run about $150 a night, triple that for a duplex suite
overlooking the garden. Book months ahead: "undiscovered" is a
relative term. And don't book through a travel agent: The management doesn't cotton to them. Write 11 Cadogan Gardens,
Sloane Square, London SW3. Phone 730-3426. Telex 8813318.

THE BEST
VCR

. . . .

*V*ideo cassette recorders are the triumph of the international
consumer electronics age: fabulous European and American
technology, mass produced to be cheap and reliable in Japan and
Korea. Virtually any model from any manufacturer will do the
basic job of recording "Nightline" or the late-late movie for com-
mercial-zapped playback at a civilized hour. The only tough deci-
sions are figuring the right electronic format and choosing the frills
that are worth the extra bucks to you.

Machines come in three standard formats, and recordings made
on one can't be played on another. Don't even consider the Beta
format, designed by Sony. While Beta delivers excellent sound
and picture quality at a low price, it is becoming increasingly difficult to rent prerecorded tapes. Newer, eight-millimeter VCR are
half the size of other machines and are first-rate technically.
Their compact dimensions make them ideal for home recording
with a hand-held camcorder. But they share the major drawback
of Beta: hardly anybody is selling or renting eight millimeter
recordings.

People willing to buy just one VCR are better off with a VHS-
format machine. The picture quality is a shade inferior to Beta
and eight millimeter, but the popularity of VHS guarantees there
will always be movies to rent and programming to exchange with
your friends.

VHS machines in the $250-350 range generally come equipped
with all you really need: a wireless remote control, a timer to
record at least two programs in a two-week period, a fast-scanning

VCR 261

mode to skip through commercials in seconds, 30 or more pre-set channels for convenient use with cable. Many also come with a memory backup for the clock-timer in case the power is interrupted (nice), automatic rewind after recording (also nice), a tape counter that reads minutes and seconds rather than inches (very convenient), and freeze-frame special effects (a matter of taste).

If price is critical and basic recording and playback are all you really need, buy the cheapest VHS model you can find from Magnavox, Sylvania, Panasonic, GE, Quasar or JC Penney. All are made by Matsushita, the Japanese electronics conglomerate. And according to *Consumer Reports*, all have superior records for reliability.

The frill most people appreciate the most is high-fidelity stereo sound. Every manufacturer offers models with this feature and everybody's technology is basically the same. But be sure to look for the word "hi-fi" — so-called "MTS stereo" alone won't do. Remember, too, that to benefit from the hi-fi feature you will need a TV with a good stereo amplifier and good speakers. Our current hi-fi favorite is the Panasonic Pro-Line series (about $700). Pro-Line model numbers change frequently, but the solid construction, compact design and reputation for reliability don't.

If you watch a lot of sports programming, consider a "digitally enhanced" VHS which can produce sharp slow-motion and freeze-frame effects and has a "picture-in-picture" feature that permits you to watch at least two games at once. The Canon HF-800 (about $800) is perhaps the most advanced VCR in this category and also delivers stereo hi-fi.

Suppose, though, price is no object. The very newest electronic format, ED-Beta from Sony, delivers an incredibly sharp picture. And Sony's top-of-the-line EDV 9000 model (about $1,500), includes every conceivable gadget. But before you buy, remember the serious limitations: no prerecorded software now (or most likely, ever), no compatibility with VHS. Note, too, that you won't get the best possible picture from an ED-Beta machine unless you also shell out $1,000 or so for one of the new monitor-style televisions delivering at least 450 lines of picture resolution and incorporating a special Y/C connector jack.

Last, but hardly least, consider the S-VHS format. These new, very expensive VCRs produce almost as good a picture as ED-Beta when special S-VHS tape is used. But, unlike ED-Beta machines, they can also play ordinary VHS cassettes from the corner video store. There is also reason to believe that S-VHS is the wave of the future. Thus, at some point, prerecorded movies are likely to be available in the new, superior format. Note, before you buy, that S-VHS quality won't be visible unless you hook the machine to an expensive monitor-style TV with high resolution and Y/C jacks.

Probably the slickest S-VHS machine now available is the NEC DS8000U (about $1,200). It incorporates special digital circuitry that raises the quality of four-hour long-play recordings almost to the level of the two-hour, short-play setting.

NEC DS8000U VCR (Courtesy of NEC Home Electronics (U.S.A.) Inc.)

Vegetable Stand

· ·

S ure. You already know this adorable farmer who sells the
freshest, sweetest romaine and arugula from the back of a
'64 Chevy pickup on the road back from the shore. But dollars to
dandelion greens, it isn't in the league with the produce from
CHINO'S, the vegetable stand to the stars hidden in the Rancho
Sante Fe hills outside San Diego.

Chino's is owned by the family of Junzo and Hatsuyo Chino,
who emigrated from Japan some 70 years ago. Most of the state's
successful fruit and vegetable farmers switched long ago to plant
strains that could weather the rigors of mechanical harvesting and
long truck rides to market. *Consumer Reports* once compared the
modern, factory-built tomato to a "tie-dyed baseball." But the
Chino family remains more interested in the taste and texture of
its produce than its ability to survive a nuclear war unbruised.

Chino's most delicate veggies are started in greenhouses, then
transplanted to a 56-acre garden for a few months' pampering in
the sunshine; no chemical fertilizers are used. Among Chino's
triumphs, featured regularly at the roadside stand: 20 variations on
leaf lettuce, each tenderer than the last; at least 15 varieties of
melon; vine-ripened tomatoes in designer red, white, orange,
green, and brown; strains of chili peppers and sweet corn found
nowhere else in the world.

Probably the most dazzling produce from Chino's cornucopia is
the baby veggies—the miniature carrots, eggplant, etc., that provide much of the fun and flash in California Cuisine. In fact, two
citadels of the new food faith, Chez Panisse in Berkeley and Spago

in Los Angeles, have long been regular customers. Check out Chino's tomatoes in the sauce on one of Wolfgang Puck's goat-cheese pizzas at Spago. Better yet, pay a visit. Chino's—formally, The Vegetable Shop—is minutes from Interstate 5, near the town of Rancho Sante Fe. Take the Via de la Valle exit, and drive east about three miles to Calzada del Bosque. Turn right, and the stand is in sight. Chino's is open virtually every day the sun shines.

Video Game

. . . .

You're right. Video games did wear out their welcome a few years ago with one-too-many re-creations of the battle of Stalingrad with stick-figure tanks and monotonous sound effects. But the new, interactive games that run only on higher-powered personal computers are much cleverer and sometimes even a touch kinky. Consider **"LEATHER GODDESSES OF PHOBOS,"** a graphics-enhanced program from Infocom that challenges the player to save the Earth from sexual enslavement by female invaders from another galaxy.

Not exactly the game you'd like to be found playing when your mother-in-law barges into the den? Not to worry. "Leather Goddesses" comes camouflaged in the electronic equivalent of a plain brown wrapper: A single keystroke replaces the action on the screen with a fake spreadsheet.

"Leather Goddesses of Phobos" video game (Courtesy of Infocom)
. . . .

Vinegar

· ·

*I*t can be the simplest of condiments, nothing more than distilled acetic acid diluted with water. Better vinegars are fermented from hard cider, sherry, or wine; the alcohol breaks down,
leaving a mixture of acid and faintly fruity flavorings. Vinegars
from good French and Italian wines reflect the complexity of the
raw material—those, for example, from the Gevrey-Chambertin
commune of Burgundy can be really special.

Once you get the point of balancing the sour of the acid with
other familiar tastes, the vinegar game has no obvious limits. In
their tireless quest for variety and higher markups, food processors
have taken to adding herbs or fruit juice to wine vinegar. Some
combinations have caught on big: For a while there in the early
'80s, every California-style restaurant worthy of its zucchini quiche
and hanging ferns offered at least one sauce flavored with raspberry vinegar. But such tinkering is unlikely to top the success of
one of the oldest and rarest forms, balsamic vinegar from the town
of Modena in northern Italy.

Traditional balsamic vinegar is made from the unfermented juice
of the trebbiano grape, the grape used in many of Italy's white
wines. The fresh juice, or "must," is boiled down to a sweet,
intensely fruity syrup, then put into barrels that contain active residues of the vinegar yeasts.

The young vinegar is set aside to age, picking up flavor from
both the wood of the barrel (chestnut, juniper, occasionally oak)
and the very slow breakdown of chemicals in the fermented must.
As water evaporates, younger vinegar is added to the brew, gradu-

ally concentrating the flavors. The final product is thus a blend of several vintages. Good balsamic vinegars usually have an average age of five or six years. But much older balsamic vinegars can be found: Some families in Modena have century-old casks of the jet-black fluid evaporating away in their attics.

Why the fetish with age? The flavors grow more concentrated, yet more mellow. The acid content remains high—typically 6 percent compared to 5 percent for most wine vinegars—but the bite weakens. Modenians (Modenites? Modeners?) sip very old balsamic vinegar straight, as an after-dinner digestive. You probably won't be tempted to imitate the ritual. But you will find balsamic vinegar to be a remarkably versatile seasoning that, unlike other vinegars, doesn't clash with wine.

Use it to avoid the acid edge in dressings for salads and cold veggies. When substituting balsamic for wine vinegar in standard recipes, cut the proportion of vinegar to oil by roughly one-third.

Dribble it straight on grilled fish or meat, the way you might season with soy sauce. Hard though it is to imagine, balsamic vinegar also works with fruit. A few drops on strawberries or poached pears will make you a believer.

Giuseppe Giusti produces an excellent eight-year-old balsamic that is widely available in food boutiques. But the very best balsamic vinegars come from the FINI family.* Seven-year-old Fini vinegar is comparable to the Giusti brand in both quality and price. Fifteen-year-old Fini is an entirely different brew, shockingly sweet and fruity. For fanatics ready to spend as much as $75 for a half-pint, there is also a 30-year-old Fini. There are worse ways to spend $75. . . .

*The same Fini family runs a superb restaurant in Modena, and retails great sausage and pasta. See "The Best Pasta."

Walking Shoe

. . . .

*R*unning was fun while it—or rather, you—lasted. Got you out of bed early, burned tons of calories, and left a lovely glow that protected the spirit from the sobering influences of 100 percent Bran Flakes and a freeway commute. Unfortunately, it also made a mess of your (a) heels, (b) Achilles' tendons, (c) knees, (d) lower back, or (e) all of the above.

That's probably why you and 10 million other runners have decided that walking isn't just for old fogies after all. And it is certainly why specialized shoes for walking are the best news to hit sports-equipment stores since the invention of Gore-Tex.

There's only one problem: The more you learn about walking shoes, the more they look like a solution in search of a problem. Good running shoes—the ones you already own—are lighter and absorb more shock than good walking shoes. Running shoes also do a better job of distributing shock to the part of the foot that can take the load. So why not stick with the proven product? Your friendly neighborhood walking-shoe salesman is likely to advance three plausible arguments.

Stability

Running shoes are very flexible. That's important for maximum shock absorption, but it inevitably means less support for the arches. Walking shoes, with their thinner, stiffer soles, are a happy compromise.

Durability

Running shoes wear rapidly: Lightweight nylon uppers and soft, synthetic liners stretch and fray; fancy cushioning materials in the soles lose bounce after a few hundred hours of compression and heat. Leather walking shoes, on the other hand, can be made to go the distance.

Looks

Running shoes look weird. Partly, that's intentional: Folks who lay out $70 or $80 for a few ounces of cloth and rubber expect some razzle-dazzle for their cash. Partly, it's functional: Any shoe engineered to cushion four or five times the stress put on a street shoe is bound to look a bit different. Walking shoes, by contrast, can be built to pass for normal.

Is all this reason enough to trade in your Nikes? The durability issue is contrived. Nobody with common sense would sacrifice comfort for the few extra months of wear. Besides, walking shoes are probably a false economy: B-plus-quality running shoes can be had for roughly half the price of comparable walkers. Ditto for stability. Most people like the bounce of a running shoe more than they need the support of a walking shoe.

Appearance is trickier. Reebok and New Balance have become such a common sight on the feet of otherwise well-attired urban commuters that hardly anyone gives them a second thought. The nitty-gritty issue is what happens once you reach the office, where racing stripes and waffle soles are certain to clash with dress-for-success blue.

Women are out of luck. No truly comfortable woman's shoe will blend into the boardroom carpet. However, men may be able to get away with walking shoes that have been disguised as clunky-but-acceptable business shoes.

Two brands fit the description. Rockport DresSports are, to

put it nicely, plain to the eye. But a rubber outer sole, a well-padded lining, and a removable insole make them extremely comfortable. At about $85, they aren't even bad value. DresSports come in brown, wine, and black.

FOOT-JOY DRESS-WALKERS run about $40 more and deliver roughly the same (high) level of comfort as DresSports. Their one important advantage is a prettier face. Dress-Walkers, particularly the wing-tip and lace-up models, really can pass for conservative street shoes. The jauntier slip-on model with a tassel is a better-looking shoe, but thick rubber outer soles telegraph their purpose. Dress-Walkers come in black and burgundy.

Way to Beat the Crowd

*T*here are usually more than enough problems to cope with when you're abroad on business, without the unusual ones," commiserates the full-page ad in the London *Financial Times*. Diners Club, the credit-card company, offers an interesting solution to one of them.

Say you've arrived at West Berlin's Tegel Airport, only to discover that the good hotels have been booked solid for an annual convention of the International Association of Intelligence Operatives. No problem. Plenty of space is always available, and just a few minutes' drive from the Kurfurstendamm.

Enjoy a complimentary drink while your host at the Diners Club Lounge arranges for your room in East Berlin. A chauffeured limo, the ad explains, will then whisk you through The Wall at Checkpoint Charlie—providing, of course, that you aren't persona non grata on the other side.

Way to Make a Billion Dollars

. . . .

Remember when it was hot stuff to be a millionaire? Now every Honda dealer and professional golfer worthy of his or her American Express Gold Card has a net worth in seven figures. To get any respect at, say, The Palace Hotel in St. Moritz or the Connaught Grill in Mayfair, you need at least $100 million. Here are some strategies for getting started on the path to real money.

Steal It

Outright robbery won't do; everything worth a billion is either too heavy to haul away or too difficult to fence. What's needed is a long-term license to pilfer—preferably legally and preferably from a whole country.

As dictator of Zaire, Mobutu Sese Seko Koko Ngbendu was za Banga (translation: the all-powerful warrior who, because of his endurance and inflexible will to win, will go from conquest to conquest leaving fire in his wake) has held the theft concession since 1965. Zaire, with an annual per capita income that wouldn't buy a single dinner at Maxim's, might not seem a promising source of cash. But as absolute ruler, Mobutu has perfected the art of scarfing up everything that isn't nailed down. It's estimated that West Africa's bulwark against communism skims a quarter of his country's $4 billion GNP, enough to amass a personal fortune of $3 billion after expenses. Mobutu has wisely diversified his holdings to include property in Belgium, France, Italy, Senegal, the Ivory Coast—and, of course, Switzerland.

Trade For It

Old wealth has always looked down on those who expose themselves to the rough and tumble of the marketplace. Truth is, though, most of the great fortunes now safely invested in land and stocks were initially won in grubby commerce.

Adnan Khashoggi is the latest and perhaps most successful of the classic traders. The son of a Saudi physician from Mecca, he turned his first deal in high school, selling Egyptian towels to Libya. As a college student in California, he shipped trucks back home to the desert kingdom, then broadened the business to act as agent for Chrysler and Rolls-Royce. Megabucks came in the 1960s, and early 1970s, when foreign arms manufacturers were happy to pay to have a friend in the Saudi royal court. He reportedly cleared $183 million on a single deal for Hawk missiles, and who knows how much on the Iranian hostage connection.

Plowshares may have grown as important to Khashoggi as swords: Triad, the family company based in the Cayman Islands, packs meat in Brazil, lends money in Southern California, develops land in Utah, operates an oil company in the Sudan, and runs a shipping company in Indonesia and a resort in the Seychelles. Khashoggi's net worth, apparently heavily levered with debt, teeters between nothing and as much as $5 billion.

All that hustling has given Khashoggi a thirst for good living worthy of Louis XIV. He owns a 281-foot yacht complete with helicopter, disco, and operating room; three jets, including a DC-8 outfitted as a flying command post; homes in Rome, New York, Paris, Cairo, Marbella, Cannes, Monte Carlo, Riyadh, Jidda, Kenya, and the Canary Islands. His New York pied-à-terre, a duplex in the Eurotrash-laden Olympic Tower, features a swimming pool 400 feet above Fifth Avenue.

Inherit It

With commodity prices in the gutter, inheriting natural resources just isn't what it was once cracked up to be. Consider the sad fate of the children of H. L. Hunt, who have lost enough in oil and silver in the past decade to restage the Napoleonic wars. But Gordon Getty, the fourth son of John Paul Getty and trustee of his estate, had the good luck to quarrel with the management of Getty Oil after his father died. Against the wishes of the other heirs, he sold his family's 31.8 million shares to Texaco for twice their market price—some $4.1 billion. Once the $1.1 billion in capital gains taxes are paid and the remainder is divided with his siblings, he will be left with perhaps $1.1 billion.

The old man was a wildcatter and a Texan, bursting with pride over his capacity to make money and spend it. But how is his son, a musical composer from San Francisco with much simpler tastes, supposed to live with $100,000 a day in interest? Not to worry. Gordon is giving away tens of millions to support the arts, and his wife, Anne, is bent on making an expensive splash as a book publisher.

Go Back to Your Roots

Sam Walton didn't much like selling polyester shirts for J. C. Penney, but it did inspire one great idea: If discount merchandising could thrive in the affluent suburban malls, maybe it could work in less promising territory. Pooling resources with his brother James, he built a chain of off-price stores in towns that were too small or too poor to attract the likes of Sears and K mart. Today he controls a hefty chunk of the stock of Wal-Mart, the discounter with a hammerlock on retailing in the sleepier parts of Middle America.

All that may not seem glamorous, but it does keep the wolf from the door. With about $5 billion in the family investment company, Sam Walton is probably the richest private entrepreneur in the world.

Outsmart the Street

Lots of people have made great fortunes shuffling securities on be-half of others. A few have done extremely well trading for their own accounts. But Warren Buffett is probably the only billionaire who has done it from scratch, purely as an investor.

Buffett studied stock analysis at Columbia University under Benjamin Graham, guru of the fundamentalist, what's-this-company-really-worth? school of investing. Fundamentals must work: Buffett turned $100,000 into $3,000,000 in 14 years, then went big time. In 1965 he bought 45 percent of Berkshire Hatha-way, a creaky old New England textile maker and transformed it into what amounts to a private mutual fund.

B. H. now buys chunks of whatever Buffett values—and the rest of the market doesn't. The strategy has generated an average return of more than 20 percent annually for more than two de-cades. Thanks to the miracles of compound interest, that's been enough to make Buffett's share of B. H. worth more than $1.4 billion. Not that it's gone to his head: Buffett still lives in Omaha and, according to *Forbes* magazine, still prefers burgers and cherry Coke to the sweetmeats of decadent Europe.

Our own favorite route to the top, though, is the very modern strategy chosen by John Kluge:

Borrow It

Just five years ago Kluge was your run-of-the-mill multimillionaire, CEO of a middle-sized entertainment conglomerate called Metro-media. Then in 1984, he and a few investors convinced the other stockholders to exchange their holdings for $1.3 billion in cash borrowed from banks and a mess of junk bonds backed by the reconstituted company. Kluge personally ended up with $115 million in cash for his own stock, plus 75 percent of Metromedia.

With hungry banks and former shareholders to feed, some people thought 75 percent of Metromedia was likely to end up as 75 percent of nothing. Kluge knew better. He quickly sold the company's seven TV stations for $2 billion, its 11 radio stations for $285 million, its outdoors advertising business for $300 million, and its cellular mobile telephone franchises for $1.2 billion. That left Kluge with $2.5 billion for himself—not bad for a guy who started out with less than 10 percent of a business that was struggling to show a profit only four years earlier.

Wine Cooler

· ·

Query: What beverage did Annette Funicello and Frankie Avalon sneak down to the beach to cool their over-heated libidos?

Surely not Schlitz. Dad would have smelled it on her breath when she got home. Besides, beer was for girls who did It, or at least pretended they did.

Not Thunderbird. The price was right, but even Frankie knew the Bird was strictly for winos.

Rum and Coke comes closer. It goes down easy, and Frankie could have filched the bottle of Bacardi gathering dust in the cupboard above Mom's knicknack display. For that matter, he probably could have assembled the ingredients for Seven and Sevens. Still, the mixed drink was a shade too exotic for a couple of teens who had never been east of Barstow.

If Annette had been daring enough to put up her hair and borrow her cousin's ID, she just might have passed for 21 at a roadhouse. The drink of choice would have been a whiskey sour or, better yet, a grasshopper. But we're talking beach drinks here, not full-blown sin.

The true facts, alas, await further work by dedicated historians of the cinema. But we can say for certain what Annette and Frankie would have liked to drink—and what their '80s counterparts now use to get a buzz on between Frisbee games: the wine cooler.

Typically a blend of carbonated fruit juice, flavoring, citric acid, sugar, and inexpensive white wine, coolers have taken the Sun Belt by storm. Wine critics turn up their noses at them because they don't taste like wine. But coolers aren't supposed to; think of them as fizzy fruit drinks with a slight kick. Serve them icy cold and cut the sweet with something decadently salty—say, Fritos or barbecue potato chips.

Those who dismiss wine coolers make little effort to distinguish among the 60 or so brands that crowd supermarket shelves. This is snobbery. Some coolers are orangish; some lemonish. Some have an aftertaste of vanilla flavoring. Some come in bottles; some, in cute little cans. Some evoke small-town America; some the Caribbean. At least one is made with red wine rather than white—definitely a mistake.

According to the trade press, the cooler biz is overdue for a shakeout. The survivors will be the heavyweight conglomerates with the most creative ad agencies and the savvyest television time buyers. That's okay by us, since the best, **CALIFORNIA COOLER,** has found a home with the Brown-Forman Corporation, the folks who bring you Jack Daniel's, Southern Comfort, and Lenox china. Try the citrus flavor, a tart-sweet blend enlivened by a cloud of fruit pulp and a hit of almond extract.

CONTENTS

. . . .

PRODUCT INDEX

● ●

Dalmane, 216
Dark Passage, 85
Darvon, 145
Data General computers, 157
Datril, 144
David's Cookies, 46–47
dbx Soundfield 1000, 230
De Cecco, 151
Deerfield Academy, 160–61
Delta Queen, 66
Del Verde, 151
Demerol, 145
Demonstrator Boron, 214
Detour, 85
Devil Dogs, 154
Dewars, 202
Diadora Impact 3000, 198
Diamond Seafood, 44
"Dick Van Dyke Show, The," 209
"Diff'rent Strokes," 209
Dilaudid, 145
Dilaudid-HP, 146
DOA, 84
Dolophine, 145
Domaine Chandon, 7
Dom Ruinart champagne, 36
Dom Ruinart rosé, 184
Donnay PC12, 246
Donzi Marine Z-33, 223–24
Dorchester, 107, 174
Dortmunder Kronen Classic, 10
Double Indemnity, 85–86
Duke University, Fuqua School at, 28

Egri Cabernet Sauvignon, 123
Egyptair, 2
Ehret method, 178–79
Eldridge Pope Brewery, 11
Eleuthera, Bahamas, beaches at, 141
Eleven Cadogan Garden, 259–60
Empirin No. 2, 145n
Envader, 166n
Episcopal High School, 160–61
Epson computers, 157
Eugénie Les Bains, 98
Europa, 139
Evergreen Fund, 135
Evian, 24, 99
Exeter, 162–63

Fairmont, 108
Federal Redemption Center, 137
Felix Frères silver, 68
Ferrari Testarossa, 34, 227
Ferre, 175
Fidelity Magellan Fund, 131, 135
Fieldston, 160
Fini pasta, 151
Fini Vinegar, 270
Fiocci di Neve, 111
Fit and Trim, 77
Folgers, 70
Foot-Joy Dress-Walkers, 273
Force of Evil, 84–85
Ford Falcon, 57
Ford Mustang, 57–58
Ford Taurus, 30–31
Formentera, Spain, beaches of, 139
Forty-seven Park Street, 259
Foster Grant Space Techs, 240
Fountain Valley, 160
Four Seasons, 182
Four Seasons-Clift, 108
Frusen Glädjé, 112
Fuji TW-300, 248–49

Gannett, 127
GA pig, 190
"General Hospital," 218
General Housewares pans, 60
Georgetown Prep, 160
Gerber cutlery, 119
Gevrey-Chamberlin vinegars, 269
Gillum rods, 89
Giusti vinegar, 270
Glendronach, 202
Glenfarclas, 203
Glenfiddich, 203
Glenlivet, 203
Glenmorangie, 203
Globe, 138
Gloria Ferrer Brut, 7
Golden Door, 102–103
Gold Wing motorcycles, 131–32
Goodwood Park, 109
Grand Canyon Airways, 94
Grand Canyon Dories, 96–97
Granite Bay, Australia, beach of, 141

Grant's Celtic Ale, 125–26
Granville Market Letter, The, 115n
Greenhouse, 102–103
Grid Systems computers, 157
Gritti Palace, 108
Groton School, 160–62
Growth Stock Outlook, The, 115
Guinness Extra Stout Draught, 11

Häagen-Dazs, 82n, 112
Hag, 70n
Hagafen Cellars kosher wine, 122
Halcion, 178, 216
Haleakala National Park, 140
Hangover Square, 85
Hanna helmets, 18
Hanns Kornell Sehr Trocken, 6n
Harrods, 259
Harvard pans, 59
Harvard University, 27–29, 40, 106, 234
Hassler, 108
Hawk Marine Power engines, 222
Heileman's Light, 125
Heineken, 10, 125
Henckels cutlery, 119
Hersey Hi-Top and DPS II, 199
Hewlett-Packard computers, 157
Hills Brothers, 70
Hill School, 160–61
Hilton, 108
Honda Accord, 200
Honda Acura Legend, 31
Honda CRX, 225
Honda motorcycles, 131–32
"Honeymooners, The," 209
Hong Kong Regent, 108
Hotchkiss School, 161
House of Martelli, 151
Howard Johnson's ice cream, 111
Howard Rusk Institute for Rehabilitation Medicine, 105
Howells rods, 89
HSF, 180
Hublot, 175
Hulbert Financial Digest, 114–15
Hunan, 44–45
Hutschenreuther china, 68
Hvar, Yugoslavia, beaches of, 140
Hylarious Bird Feeder, 19–20

Hyundai, 127
Hyundai Excel, 30

IBM, 128
IBM computers, 157–59
"I Love Lucy," 209
Imperial, 108
In a Lonely Place, 85
Inderal, 143
Infinity Reference Standard, Series V, 232–33
Ink Spots, 195
Interplak Home Plaque Removal Instrument, 254–55
Ios, Greece, beaches of, 140
Isomeride, 74

Jack Daniel's, 281
Jaguar XJ6, 32
Jamin/Robuchon, 189
Jamo CBR-70, 230
J & B, 202
Janus Fund, 135
Japan Air Lines, 3
Jif peanut butter, 154
John Burroughs, 160
Johnnie Walker Black, 202
Johnnie Walker Red, 202
Johns Hopkins Hospital, 106
Joslin Clinic, 105
Joy Division, 196
Judge Pulsar, 166n

K2 VO Unlimited, 213
KAAMA Surface Drives, 224
Kalalau Beach, 140
Kangaroos Omnicoil, 200
Kata Beach, 141
Kaypro computers, 157
Kent School, 161
Key Largo, 85
Kiss Me Deadly, 85
Klein, 15
KLM, 2–3
Knock on Any Door, 85
Korbel Brut, 6–7
Korean airlines, 2
Kryptonite locks, 50
Kun Lun, 66

SUBJECT INDEX